# Save Me

## M.K.AWAN

*For the dreamers, keep your head in the clouds. It's nicer up there.*

# Contents

Preface                                    1

1.  Bloody Lips                             3

2.  A Little Excitement                    12

3.  Clouded Outings                        23

4.  Dysfunctional Allies                   32

5.  Moody Interrogations                   39

6.  Close Calls                            48

7.  Makeshift Family                       59

8.  Late Night Parties                     66

9.  Enemy Territory                        76

10.  Breathless                            87

11.  Baby Steps                           100

12.  Just a Glimpse                       112

13.  Civilized Battles                    118

14.  Bloody Reunion                       129

| 15. | Midnight Rescues | 137 |
|---|---|---|
| 16. | Runaways | 144 |
| 17. | Cars and Girls | 150 |
| 18. | Changes | 162 |
| 19. | Drug Runs | 177 |
| 20. | Saving the Bad Boy | 184 |
| 21. | Reunion | 196 |
| 22. | Checkmate | 209 |
| 23. | Bittersweet Endings | 221 |
| 24. | Goodbyes Suck | 231 |
| 25. | Late Night Breakdowns | 241 |
| 26. | Hello Stranger | 244 |
| 27. | Closure is Overrated | 253 |
| 28. | Fuck It | 263 |
| 29. | One Last Fight | 270 |
| 30. | Unstable Happily Ever Afters | 281 |

# Preface

"One last ride," Roman muttered.

Roman reached into his pocket and pulled out a gun. Malaika froze as Roman handed her the weapon. It was cold and heavy. Its black metal grip glinted in the moonlight. As Malaika's fingers wrapped around the butt of the gun, her heart drummed against her chest. Fear crept through her veins at the thought of what would soon unfold.

"Don't do anything crazy." Roman kissed Malaika's forehead. "Wait for me."

Malaika nodded. Her eyes filled with tears as Roman made his way toward the battlefield. "Be careful, Roman," she called.

Roman stopped, turned to her, and smiled. Then he disappeared into the night.

Something hard struck the side of Malaika's head, and spots invaded her vision. Darkness threatened to overtake her. She raised the gun and tried to aim it at her assailant but missed. The sound of the gun firing echoed through the night, a desperate cry for help. Another hit to her head, and she was drowning under waves of unconsciousness.

*Come on, bad boy. Come and save me.*

# CHAPTER ONE

## *Bloody Lips*

MALAIKA RAN THROUGH THE school's deserted halls, the echo of her footsteps intensifying her paranoia. Not even a quick glance behind her, confirming that she was alone, could re-assure her. Why did a rational conversation with her parents have to turn into a screaming match? Malaika had barely dodged her mother's stream of attacks. She quivered, terrified that at any moment, her mother would arrive and deal out another kick to her ribs.

Malaika knew her fear was irrational. She was at school; her mother couldn't abuse her here. Yet, her nerves refused to settle and her burning lungs made it hard to breathe. Malaika opened the door to her class and toppled inside. Heads turned up at her noisy arrival. Her teacher, Ms. Williams, rushed toward her with her black eyebrows furrowed and her lips pulled down into a frown.

"Malaika, why are you late for class?"

With shaking hands, Malaika wiped her copper locks away from her face. She tried to speak, but her dry mouth only allowed for quick breaths and unintelligible whispers. Heat rushed to Malaika's cheeks as the kids in her class stared at her with gaping mouths. Malaika didn't blame them for staring. Had she been in their shoes, she would have done the same. It's not every day the model student is late, let alone drenched in sweat from head to toe. Ms. Williams shot a warning look at the class before gesturing for Malaika to take her seat. She gave her shoulder a tight squeeze as she passed by.

Malaika fell into her seat and closed her eyes. Her hands quaked as the exhaustion caught up to her. She clenched her trembling hands into fists and counted to ten. *One. Breathe in. Two. Breathe out. Three. Breathe in. Four. Breathe out.* When she reached ten, she exhaled and found that her pounding heart slowed, her shaking limbs stilled, and her erratic breathing softened to a low hum. She opened her eyes. Everything was right again. She was just another face in the crowd, and it was just another mundane day at school.

Ms. Williams stood at the front of the class. Her hands waved around a homemade board game. She wore a broad grin as she held up her work for the class to see. Malaika smiled. Her teacher's happiness brought Malaika a sense of normalcy. Unfortunately, as usual, her teacher's enthusiasm died down as her gaze flicked around the room.

Malaika looked around the classroom at her peers. Some were blank-faced, while others were a source of entertainment. The boy next to her was busy picking his nose. The boy across from her was having a full course meal, and it looked like the girl in the corner is stuffing her bra with toilet paper. To her right, another student was fast asleep, a stream of drool sliding down his chin. Two seats down from her, a pair of grey glazed eyes shone with mischief.

*Probably high.*

The owner of the grey eyes tossed and turned in his seat. His gaze met Malaika's. Her heart jumped, and she turned away to hide her burning cheeks. She turned back to Ms. Williams. Malaika's mouth fell open as she saw her teacher's scowl and clenched jaw. Normally, she would just give up and focus on those students who actually paid attention, but today there was a blazing fire radiating off her Malaika had not seen before.

"Seeing as most of you are not paying attention, how about I raise the stakes? I'd say, given your uncaring attitude, most of you are confident in your ability to graduate. Why not test that theory? From this day on, every project I assign, you will work on in pairs. To top it off, each grade will count as a test grade."

Ms. Williams' proclamation stunned Malaika. She stared at her teacher. Her glasses slipped off her nose as she leaned forward in her seat. The rest of the class, it seemed, did not share her horror; instead they jumped up with peps in their steps. A few classmates glanced at her. No doubt they were considering her as a candidate to freeload off.

"Not so fast. I will assign the partners and there will be no switching," Ms. Williams said. A triumphant grin spread across her lips as the students groaned and stomped their feet in protest. She ignored the whining and fussing and called out the student's names, lastly assigning Roman and Malaika to be partners.

Malaika regarded the grey-eyed boy. Underneath his hood rested his signature raven tresses. Baggy clothes enveloped his sculpted body and hid the many tattoos that adorned his russet skin. Roman Rodriguez was cloaked in mystery and citations.

The school's resident bad boy, Roman, was known for four things. One: drinking himself into oblivion. Two: smoking until his lungs burned out. Three: partying until dawn. Four: fighting anyone who looked at him the wrong way. Girls drooled over his good looks and mysterious persona. Guys envied his street credit and reputation. In short, every girl wanted him, and every guy wanted to be him.

Malaika realized she was ogling and instead studied the agenda her teacher gave her. Ms. Williams gave the last paper to Roman. In a low voice, she asked him to sit beside Malaika. Roman grunted in response and rested the back of his head against the chair.

Malaika *tsked* and turned her attention back to the agenda. Once she finished reading it, she looked back at Roman. He was fast asleep! Malaika stomped to his desk, determined to have him contribute, but her bravery disappeared as she took in the size of his biceps.

She cleared her throat. He did not move. She cleared her throat once more. Again, there was no movement. She changed tactics and reached out to tap him. Roman turned his head just as her finger made contact. Instead of touching his arm, her finger accidentally went up his left nostril.

Roman's eyes shot open. He jerked back in surprise and glared at Malaika. "What do you want?" he asked in a rough, menacing voice.

Malaika took a step back. Her throat went dry. She held her paper for him to see.

Roman scoffed. "Listen, Munequita, this is how it's going to go down. You do all the work and put both of our names on the paper. Oh, and don't mess up." Despite there being a good thirty minutes left of the class, he got up and walked out of the room.

Ms. Williams called out for him. She huffed and pressed the security button, a frown on her face. Clearly, she hadn't expected this.

Malaika sat down, her head a jumbled mess. Slowly, an idea brewed in her mind. With a renewed sense of hope, Malaika began planning Roman's demise.

*Two can play at this game.*

Malaika waved at her friends across the lunchroom.

"Yo, Malaika!" Justin called out.

The sunlight hit his head, casting a yellow glow over his blond locks. She smiled at him as he got up and met her halfway.

"How did it go?" he asked.

"How did what go?"

"You know," he said. He lowered his voice and leaned toward her. "This morning with your parents. How did it go?"

"Oh, that." Malaika's shoulders sagged.

Justin pulled her into a warm embrace. Malaika wrapped her arms around him. "We'll get through this somehow, Malaika, I promise," he said, then kissed the top of her head.

Malaika dropped her arms and put on a fake smile that sold her lies to everyone but him. Justin returned her emotions and offered her a cupcake.

Trying her best to smile, she thanked him and took the cupcake. The two made their way to the lunch table where their friends were waiting.

"You have some frosting on your nose," Carina said, tying her caramel locks into a ponytail.

With a finger, Malaika transferred the frosting to her mouth, not wanting it to go to waste. "Did you guys hear what Ms. Williams is doing?"

Arriving and settling down next to Carina, Akira let out a monotone laugh. "Who hasn't?" he asked, shoving a handful of fries into his mouth. He muttered to himself in Japanese while wrenching open ketchup packets.

"What did she do?" Susan asked as she secured her messy bun with a pencil.

Akira's hands balled into tight fists. "She has decided that from now until the end of the year, all projects are to be worked on in pairs. To make matters worse, she's assigning the partners."

Susan, a usually soft-spoken and gentle soul, exploded. "You mean to tell me I have to put my 4.0 GPA at risk because some hormonal middle-aged woman finds amusement in our suffering?"

Someone cleared their throat.

"Oh my God," Susan whispered. Ms. Williams's lean face was peering down at her. "I- I'm so sorry, ma'am," Susan stuttered, her face turning a dark shade of red.

Ms. Williams shook her head, a small smile painted on her angular features. As soon as the woman walked out of view, Malaika broke into a fit of laughter, accidentally hacking out her cupcake on Akira's face. Akira closed his eyes, his lips tightening into a thin white line.

"S-sorry Akira," Malaika said.

Carina passed Akira a napkin. Akira sat still, though the muscle in his jaw was twitching.

Malaika took off through the double doors before Akira could pounce. She sprinted across the grassy field, spared a swift glance behind her, and slammed into someone. She bounced off his chest, falling to the ground.

"Watch it, Munequita," Roman said.

Loud laughter echoed around her. Malaika kept her head down, too humiliated to respond. She got to her feet, rubbing her sore butt. Turning to walk away, she was stopped by a sudden comment.

"Make sure you don't jack our project up," Roman said.

Malaika's eyebrows knitted together. As far as she knew, Roman never cared about his schoolwork. *So why now?* She looked him over, finally taking notice of the plastic bottles lying under the tree shade. She doubted the clear liquid inside was water.

A shiver ran down Malaika's spine. She turned away to see Akira marching towards her. With a sense of relief, she could see by the wariness in his body that he was no longer trying to get even with her.

"Come on," Akira said, taking Malaika by the arm. She hurried to catch up with his pace, not sparing a glance at the wasted boys behind her.

The shrill ringing of the bell summoned Malaika to her last class. She and Susan walked down the crowded halls, fighting to stay upright.

"Heard you nearly tackled Roman to the floor," Susan said, grinning.

Malaika snorted. "That boy is as hard as a wall. There's no way I can take him down."

Justin popped up, throwing an arm over Malaika's shoulders. "One: that's what she said and two: you sound like you're planning on fighting him."

Malaika laughed humorlessly as she entered the classroom. Her gaze landed on Roman, who was lounging against the back wall. His stony gaze swept over her. She looked away, heat rushing to her cheeks.

As the class dragged by and the teacher droned on, Malaika found herself on the edge of unconsciousness. His monotone voice was putting her to sleep. She was not the only one. Snores began echoing across the classroom. It was dumb luck that a thunderous roar broke out, snapping everyone out of their sleepy trances.

"Roman!"

Already sensing what was coming, Malaika and her peers moved their desks away as an unfamiliar student stormed into the classroom with his fists raised.

"This ought to be good," Justin said, motioning his head towards the teacher.

The poor old man was a trembling mess. His lip was shaking and his eyes were popping out of his sockets as he took in the intruder's size. He pushed the security button. Malaika turned to look at Roman.

Roman's uninterested demeanor melted off him. He stood up, his loose limbs tensing, his muscles coiling as the intruder shoved his way through the crowd. Roman's towering frame stormed over to meet his opponent halfway. The stranger landed a fist on Roman's face. Roman retaliated, with a blow to the chin and one to the boy's belly.

Malaika struggled to maintain her footing as the spectators grew rowdy at the show unfolding in front of them. Students shoved each other, as most were desperate to capture the fight on film. Her heart jumped as the crowd pushed forward. She was too close to the fight. She needed to get back. Panic swelled inside of Malaika as the stranger's punches grew sloppy. Roman slammed his fist into the student's face, drawing blood.

With his hood blocking his vision, the instigator threw his arms around. The back of his hand slammed into Malaika's face. Red hot pain spread across her face. It felt as if a brick had struck her. She fell to the floor. She could hear the crowd gasp.

Dark spots danced in her vision. Malaika held her face and felt something wet dripping down her chin. Over the sound of blood rushing through her ears, Malaika could hear a loud thump, followed by a student's shriek. A warm hand grabbed her arm and pulled her up. She opened her eyes. Roman was guiding her away from the fight. He stared down at her with an unreadable expression on his face. Tears pooled in her eyes. Her lip quivered as she struggled to keep her composure.

A pair of security officers ran into the room. One cuffed Roman and the other knelt by the fallen boy. He was unconscious, bleeding from the nose and ear. Malaika's stomach lurched at the gruesome sight. A third adult hurried in, one of the vice principals. After a quick survey, he barked an order to the students to leave quietly and reassemble in the cafeteria.

His gaze landed on Malaika's bloody lip. His thick brows shot up.

"You attacked a young woman?" he asked Roman, his voice booming around them.

"No sir! Malaika was struck by the other student. It was an accident, I saw it with my own eyes," the teacher said, finally regaining his composure.

The vice principal shoved Roman out the door, yelling behind him. Before disappearing from view, Roman turned to look at her one last time. His silver eyes were swimming with guilt. Malaika looked down and blinked away the tears.

Justin ran over to her and cradled her face. "Let's get you to the nurse."

He carried her to the infirmary. Malaika hid her face in Justin's chest, not wanting to see the stares of the curious onlookers. Luckily for Malaika, she would not need stitches. After disinfecting the area, the nurse applied a liquid bandage, assuring her the wound would heal within the week. Malaika sighed. The heavy weight in her gut disappeared.

The last thing she needed was a scar. If she looked anything less than perfect, her mother would have a stroke. She wouldn't be the only one, though. There were others who cared about Malaika's appearance. Under no circumstances did Malaika want to disappoint *them.*

Her stomach wound into a knot at the thought of having to see them tonight. After today's traumas, she did not feel ready to face them just yet. As Malaika headed towards her car, she caught sight of a piece of paper stuck under the wipers. She removed the scrap of paper and examined it. In a sloppy scrawl, a single word sat in front of her eyes.

*Sorry. – R*

# CHAPTER TWO

# A Little Excitement

"TURN AROUND."

The hairs on the back of Malaika's neck rose as her mother's cold, calculating gaze swept over her. She fought back the urge to curl into a ball. Malaika turned slowly so her mother could inspect her appearance. She could feel the judgment seeping through her bones. Her mother had made it very clear that she expected nothing less than *perfection*. After ensuring that every pin was in place, her dress smooth and teeth sparkling, her mother nodded in approval.

As soon as Malaika heard the click of the door, she collapsed. Her breathing became ragged, her limbs trembled, and her heart thundered violently. Malaika clawed at her chest as she fought with herself to regain control of her mind and body.

She screwed her eyes shut and wrapped her shaking arms around herself, taking deep breaths until she calmed down. Eventually, the spinning lessened, her racing heart slowed, and her quaking limbs stilled. All was well with the world. Malaika opened her eyes and stared at her reflection in the mirror.

Amber irises filled with despair and angst stared back at her. Pale, sickly skin enveloped her small frame. She sat upright, smoothed her dress, and patted her wet lashes with a tissue. Malaika hated what she had become. Then she would remind herself that no one would remain sane had they been in her shoes.

The doorbell caught her attention. It was time. *They were here*. As Malaika made her way to the foyer, she prayed this night would go by without incident. The knots in her stomach should have been warning enough that things would never go as she wished.

A stinging pain spread across Malaika's face. She winced and struggled to keep the tears at bay as they threatened to spill over. Another hard slap connected with her cheek. Malaika's lip quivered as her head jerked to the side.

"How dare you dance with a man like that?"

Malaika did not dare open her mouth to tell the woman it was not her fault. The man who forced himself on her was drunk beyond belief and much too strong for her to push away. She knew if she opened her mouth to defend herself, the woman would abuse her again. Malaika was quick to realize that she could never win. Not against *them*.

"Leave, and if I ever see you do something like that again, I will not spare you."

Malaika did not need to be told twice. With her heart in her throat, she left the suffocating atmosphere, shying away from the intrusive stares of the partygoers. As she stepped through the double doors, cold air washed over her. Goosebumps rose across her bare arms as she circled the parking lot. It seemed as if her parents had already left, leaving her to find her own way home.

Knowing there was nothing she could do, Malaika kicked off her heels and began walking. She would have called a cab, but her parents had cut off her internet and messaging services. She had no means of contacting anyone other than those listed in her contacts.

Malaika doubted her parents were in any condition to drive. By this time of night, the alcohol would have taken over. She could have called her friends, but the situation was already delicate as it was. She did not want to risk involving anyone else.

Malaika was grateful that stars graced the night sky. They kept her company as she followed the moonlit path towards home. Not long after she had left, Malaika arrived at the beach. She smiled as she took in the vast ocean before her.

The indigo waves danced along the shore, their hypnotizing motions tempting Malaika to join them. A pang of guilt shot through her as she walked towards the entrancing waves. She forced herself to stop and turned back around, heading back to reality.

When the moon was at its brightest, Malaika arrived home. With her breath held, she entered the house and tip-toed up the stairs. Raucous laughter echoed through the empty halls. Golden light spilled through her parents' open bedroom. Malaika peeked her head through the doorway. She found her parents drunk to the point of no return and laughing as they counted the money that lay at their feet. Malaika scoffed and trudged into her bedroom.

She stripped out of her dress and crawled into bed, thankful that tomorrow was Friday. Sleep claimed her easily, her dreams swirling around in a jumbled mess. Amongst the curious happenings, she saw Roman's charcoal grey eyes. Unblinking, he seemed to stare straight into her soul.

Malaika woke up the next morning with a smile on her face. It was finally Friday. "Good morning," she begrudgingly greeted her mother as she headed down the stairs.

"Morning." Her mother gazed at her, the muscle in her jaw twitching.

"What?" Malaika asked, challenging her mother.

Her mother's hand flexed, instantly causing Malaika to give in. She shrunk back, lowered her gaze and made her way to the kitchen. Malaika was not a coward, but there were certain people in the world who were not to be crossed, and her mother was one of them. She ate a small breakfast, wanting to get out of the house.

Halfway through her breakfast, Malaika's parents entered the kitchen. She struggled to breathe as both her mother and father watched her with laser-like focus. With trembling fingers, she grabbed her car keys and backpack and ran out the door, suffocating silently.

It was not until she reached her car that she was able to catch her breath. Blinking away the spots that blocked her vision, she slid in and grabbed onto the wheel for support. Finally coming to her senses, Malaika turned the key and backed out of the driveway. She drove at a leisurely pace. The early morning fog and radio tunes kept her company as she headed to school. Malaika allowed the music to wipe away her worries for a moment. Though it was short-lived, she could finally breathe.

"Hey Carina," Malaika said as she pulled into the parking lot.

"Hi." Carina's smile was bright with amusement. "How's your face?"

Malaika grinned and shook her head as the events of yesterday afternoon played in her mind. Her heart skipped a beat as she thought of the note Roman left her. "Honestly, I was hoping for a concussion. That way I would've at least gotten a three-day weekend."

Carina laughed, her chestnut eyes crinkling.

"All right, I'll see you later. I have to record my song," Malaika said.

Carina waved goodbye and headed towards the field for cheer practice.

"Good morning, Mr. Dibb," Malaika said as she entered the choir room.

"Good morning, Malaika, your booth is ready. You can go in and record." He gave her a smile.

Malaika nodded and went inside the booth to adjust the mic. She took out her lyric sheet and sang. She was very proud of her composition. This piece was the product of a summer's worth of pain. It was something she held very dear to her heart. Knowing her teacher was on the other side listening to her bare her soul frightened Malaika. *What would he think?*

Singing her song was a bittersweet affair. It was the first time she was proud of something she had written. Unfortunately, it would be the last time Malaika could sing. *They* had made their instructions very clear.

Frustrated tears sprung to Malaika's eyes as *they* invaded her mind. Their rules, regulations, and restrictions were choking Malaika. Her will to fight was wavering. She could feel herself losing control again. Malaika did not like to use the word *hate* so loosely, but there was no other way to describe the way she felt about them.

Malaika loathed them. Just thinking about them made her chest tighten. With her fists shaking and blood pounding, she came to a finish. Mr. Dibb turned the recording light off, signaling she could come out. She exhaled sharply and exited the booth with her composition gripped in her hands. Out of the corner of her eye, Malaika saw a shadow peeking through the cracks of the classroom door. As the last note of the piano echoed through the room, the shadow disappeared.

"Good job, Malaika. I could hear the pain in your voice. It was beautiful," Mr. Dibb said. He gave her a proud smile.

"Thank you."

"Would you like to talk about it?"

Malaika shook her head, her face blazing.

Not missing a beat, Mr. Dibb changed the topic. "Are you sure you don't want to pursue a career in music? You really are talented, and I'm not just saying that."

Despite herself, Malaika smiled, though it quickly fell when she remembered the rules imposed on her. "You're too kind, Mr. Dibb, but I can't—I need to stop dreaming and come back down to earth," she whispered, more to herself, then turned on her heel and left.

The bell rang, signaling the start of the day. Malaika made her way to her history class, fighting through the crowded halls, ignoring the 'over the top' couples, secret drug deals, and petty fights.

Malaika slipped into her classroom, took a seat, and worked on her project. She took out two sheets of paper and composed a list of specific instructions for Roman to follow so he could do his part for the project. She got up and slid the first copy under his sleeping frame and put the second copy in his pocket. Malaika felt as if she were being watched and looked up. Her heart jumped and her body burned as Ms. Williams threw her a wink, a cheeky grin on her lips. Malaika gave her a shaky smile and went back to her seat.

She knew Roman would not contribute to the project, but just in case a miracle took place, she had slipped him the instructions. Of course, she was going to do his part as a precaution. As his snores filled the quiet room, Malaika knew Roman had probably forgotten all about her and their assignment.

Lunch was a quiet affair. With Justin absent, Akira did not have anyone to bicker with. While he was busy sulking, the girls discussed the winter dance, an event they all thought was useless, mainly because they had never had a date to any of the previous dances.

The conversation about the dance reminded Malaika of last night's fiasco. Her cheeks burned as she thought of the beating she had received from *her*. Malaika's heart clenched. A lump formed in her throat as she relived the horrors from the previous night.

Abruptly, she stood up and went to the trash can, using these few seconds to gather herself. So absorbed in her own world, Malaika did not realize she had bumped into someone. She looked up, her eyes met the dangerous ones of Roman. Her insides flipped as she met his silver eyes. "S- Sorry," she said. His gaze was intimidating. She could not look at him for long. Malaika stepped around him, dumped her trash, and hurried to her next class.

Malaika was grateful when the weekend rolled around. She had finished her project Friday night so she could go out on the weekend with her friends, but it seemed her parents had other plans.

*They* were coming to dinner Saturday night, so that meant she, along with the housekeeper, had to spend all day inside cleaning the already spotless house and making herself look impeccable. *How was she to accomplish that when she looked like she was on the verge of death?*

Once night fell, Malaika's mother barged into her room. She barked out orders while Malaika whimpered. "I don't want a single hair out of place. Wear the pearls Mr. O'Neal bought you. Make sure you thank him for them. Most importantly, don't speak unless spoken to, and don't you dare embarrass me."

Nodding mutely, Malaika obeyed her mother's every command. She sprayed one last spritz of perfume and observed herself in the mirror. Her skin was sinking in again, her hair, though curled and smooth, was losing its shine. *She was fading away.*

Malaika took a deep breath and balled her fists as they shook. She could not do this. She had to escape. *I need someone. Anyone.* Malaika threw her door open and ran out, only to crash into something.

Malaika gasped. Her breath left her as she fell forward and landed on something hard. She felt the firm planes of someone's chest underneath her dainty figure. Malaika looked up. She stared into a pair of green eyes. Though unfamiliar, she found them welcoming.

"Sorry," the mystery man said.

The man's arms wrapped around Malaika's waist. In one swift movement, he had lifted both Malaika and himself upright. Malaika's feet dangled in the air as the man's arms still clung to her. He placed her down and straightened up his appearance.

"Hiya, sweetheart," he said, running a hand through his ginger locks.

"Hi, I-I'm Malaika."

"Nice name. I'm Connor O'Neal. Let's go downstairs. My folks will be here in a bit, and I know they're going to want to find another reason to give you a hard time." Connor chuckled as he took in Malaika's bewildered face. "Yes, I hate them as well," he revealed.

"How are you related to them?"

"My father. Through him, I play the role of cousin and nephew. I'm staying with them for the weekend. A little *family reunion*." He rolled his eyes as they made it to the front door.

"I see. What are you doing here before them?"

Connor grinned mischievously. "I'm here to start a fire."

Malaika gaped at him in awe as she understood what he was implying. "So, what's the plan?" Malaika asked, throwing away her fears. For once, she wanted a little excitement in her life.

"Well, some of my old friends are meeting up tonight. Do you want to ditch this joint and hit them up?"

"Yes. Yes, I would." Malaika smiled.

Connor beamed at her. "All right then, it's settled."

The doorbell rang. In an instant, chills erupted on Malaika's skin and her hands turned clammy. *Do not make any mistakes!* Her father opened the door as her mother stood at his side.

"Welcome," Malaika's father greeted, holding the door open.

As usual, Malaika plastered an artificial smile on her face and moved forward to greet the guests. The dark-eyed girl, Amara, smiled back, though Malaika could feel the judgment her cold eyes held. The young man, Liam, simply grunted at her.

Malaika stuck out her tongue behind their backs, but froze when Liam turned back to look at her. *Uh-oh.* She watched, transfixed, as he made his way towards her. His pale hand rose and reached out for her face. She stood still, not wanting to make any sudden movements. It was as if she were the prey and he were the predator. Malaika kept a careful watch on his hand. She was afraid that he, like his mother, would hurt her. His stiff fingers reached her cheek and wiped off a black fleck.

"Mascara," he mumbled, then straightened up and walked away.

Malaika took a moment to steady herself, then made her way over to the living room where her mother was busy entertaining the guests.

"Malaika, go get the drinks," her father said.

"Y-Yes, F-Father."

His jaw clenched and nostrils flared as she stuttered. *She had upset him.* Connor, probably noticing the dark glare her father threw at her, stood up to help Malaika.

"Oh no, Connor, why don't you sit down? Liam, go help Malaika with the drinks instead," his aunt, Mrs. O'Neal, said.

Malaika stopped herself from panicking. She drew a breath and focused on the task at hand. She went to the kitchen and grabbed the cider from the fridge. Stretching on her toes, she reached to grab the glasses from the cupboard, but her short limbs would not allow it. She looked around for her step stool. It was nowhere in sight.

"Here, I got it," Liam said from behind her.

Malaika froze when she felt his breath near her ear. Gulping, she slid to the side to get away from him. "Thank you." Malaika prepared the drinks and placed them on a tray, then took them out to the living room where everyone was waiting expectantly.

"What took you two so long?" Amara asked, wiggling her eyebrows suggestively.

Malaika's cheeks burned. Her hands shook as anger coursed through her. She wanted to defend herself but was afraid of Mrs. O'Neal, who she saw was glaring daggers at her.

"Watch your mouth, Amara." Connor ordered in a dark tone that stunned everyone into silence.

Malaika's mother was the first to break the awkward atmosphere. Laughing uncomfortably, she engaged Mrs. O'Neal in useless small talk. Malaika composed herself and handed out the drinks. After a few minutes of superficial conversation, everyone made their way to the dining room. Malaika, feeling uneasy, took a seat next to Connor.

Dinner was a rather edgy affair. Every time Connor made Malaika laugh, Mrs. O'Neal threw an icy glare her way. By the time dessert rolled around, Malaika was a mess. Her hands were clammy, her heart was racing, and a sheen of sweat ran down her back. As soon as Malaika's father took center stage, she excused herself and ran up to her bedroom. Connor joined her a few moments later.

"Ready?" he asked with a wide grin.

Malaika slowly, brewing with excitement, smiled in response. "Yes." She was practically teetering.

"All right, let's go."

He slid her window open. Malaika watched with bated breath as Connor made his way down the side of the house, using the floral vines and branches to balance himself. "All right, I'm going to check if my friend is here. Stay there."

"Okay."

She heard muffled voices in the distance. The sun had long set, though the moon helped illuminate the darkened silhouettes walking towards the house.

"Malaika, I'm going to bring the car around. My friend is waiting below. You can jump, he'll catch you."

"O-Okay," Malaika squeaked out, terror laced in her voice. Her legs quaked as she straddled the windowsill. *Here goes nothing.* She closed her eyes, crossed her arms over her chest and jumped out the window, praying she would not die.

The air whooshed around her for a few seconds before she landed on something hard. The sudden impact knocked her breath away. She felt a pair of arms tighten around her. Faint hints of cedar and citrus trailed up her nose, captivating her. She opened her eyes and stared straight into the hypnotizing gaze of none other than Roman Rodriguez.

# CHAPTER THREE

## Clouded Outings

PANIC BUBBLED IN THE pit of Malaika's stomach as striking grey eyes peered down at her. Her blood ran cold as she realized she had fallen into the arms of the most dangerous boy in school. "R- Roman," she yelped.

He raised an eyebrow at her and placed her down. Malaika's legs quaked as she took in Roman's towering frame. She prayed she wouldn't fall.

"Do I know you?" he asked.

Malaika's mind blanked. *Why did he not recognize her?* A small part of her was offended that he had forgotten her so easily, though she could not blame him. Roman Rodriguez was popular, always surrounded by people. He would not remember someone as insignificant as her. She trailed her eyes over him and finally took notice of Roman's slightly red eyes, glazed expression, and trembling limbs. He was wasted.

"Oh, thank God!" Malaika's sudden exclamation made Roman jump, but she was too busy celebrating to care. "Whew, that was a close one. I almost died." Malaika continued talking to herself as Roman stood there with a bewildered expression plastered on his face.

"I'm leaving," Roman said.

Malaika wiped the sweat off her forehead and hurried after Roman, struggling to keep up with his long strides. Connor pulled up and stopped the truck. Roman slid in first, Malaika hopped in after him.

Amara's voice echoed through the empty street as Connor took off. "THEY'RE LEAVING!"

Both Malaika and Connor shared a secret smile. Connor drove, refusing to allow Roman near the wheel, as he was under the influence. *Heavily under the influence*, Malaika noted as the smell of weed invaded her nostrils.

"I'm surprised you didn't crash the car on your way here," Connor said to Roman, disapproval coating his voice.

"Shut up, man," Roman said, punching Connor in the shoulder.

It wasn't a light hit either, Malaika thought, as Connor lost control of the wheel for a split second. The truck swerved to the side of the road, tires squealing, and brakes screaming as he struggled to regain his hold. Malaika shrieked while Connor cursed up a storm.

"Goddamnit, Roman, I'm driving! I want to live, get married, and have kids! What if my balls tore off in the accident or something, huh?" he screamed in a high-pitched voice.

A moment of silence followed Connor's sudden outburst. Roman was the first to break out into a fit of laughter. Malaika joined him after muttering comments about using God and balls in the same sentence.

"Y-Y-You screamed like a girl," she said through her laughter.

"Damn, bro, relax," Roman said, settling back into his seat. "With a face like that, you'd be doing the world a favor by not reproducing," he added with a grin.

Connor, despite himself, chuckled at Roman's jab. The three were silent, enjoying the soft hum of the radio. Malaika's eyes widened in excitement when Connor pulled up to the bowling alley. Connor parked and got out. Roman followed suit. Malaika blushed as Connor opened her door and helped her out of the truck.

"Thank you," Malaika said.

A few of Roman's and Connor's friends joined them. Malaika was glad no one took notice of her. As the group moved towards the bowling alley, catcalls and whistles emerged from a trio of guys standing in the parking lot. Malaika felt like curling into a ball when their dark gazes landed on her.

A rough hand shoved Malaika to the middle of the group. She looked back and saw that it was Roman who had pushed her away from view. Malaika's heart fluttered at his unconventional way of protecting her.

*Guess the bad boy isn't all that he puts out to be.* A small smile graced her lips, though it quickly fell when Roman punched one of Connor's friends for exhaling his cigarette in his face.

Connor chuckled. "Roman, you ain't ever going to change, huh?"

Roman shook his head and playfully tugged Connor's facial hair.

Connor slapped his hand away. "Stop it! You're going to pluck the hairs out. My beard is finally connected, don't touch it," he said with a pout and inspected the hairs on his cheek.

Roman laughed. "Don't worry, I'm sure Eva won't notice if a few hairs are missing from those goat chops." He poked Connor's sideburns. Connor grabbed Roman in a headlock as the group entered the bowling alley and made their way to the counter to pay for the game.

"Malaika!"

Malaika looked for the source of the sound. She smiled when she saw her friends were here as well. "Hey Susan,

Carina." She gave them a quick hug. An arm fell across her shoulders. "Hi Akira." Malaika smiled up at him.

"'Sup, Malaika. Who are these guys?" he asked, nodding towards Connor and his friends.

"This is my friend Connor and some of his buddies," Malaika said.

"What's up? I'm Akira." He held his hand out for Connor.

"Hey man, I'm Connor. Nice to meet you," Connor said, grinning as he shook Akira's hand.

With a rather large group, they got two lanes next to each other.

"So, what's with Roman?" Susan asked Malaika in a low voice, as he made his way up to the center.

"He's Connor's friend," Malaika said, sneaking a look at him.

He concentrated on the lane in front of him. He threw the ball forward. Everyone watched in amazement as it went smoothly down the lane and knocked over all the pins. Despite being totally trashed, Roman stayed focused.

The rest of the night flew by in a blur of unanswered phone calls, pins falling, and Malaika and Roman competing in an unspoken match. Malaika smiled to herself as she saw the scoreboard. She had beat Roman by one point.

"Good game, kid," Roman said and slapped her shoulder so hard she fell to her knees.

Malaika winced as her knees collided with the waxed floor. Her shoulder stung from Roman's slap. Connor chuckled and pulled her up as she rubbed her now sore shoulder.

"Oh!" Carina's sudden exclamation caused Malaika to jump. "I understand Roman's behavior now. He's high," she whispered.

Malaika laughed, nodding in confirmation.

"Fascinating." Susan scanned Roman from head to toe. "It's my first time seeing someone under the influence this close."

Akira scoffed. "Oh please. I come to school high all the time," he lied.

Carina smacked him upside the head.

"You're lacking brain cells as it is. The last thing you should do is indulge in recreational drugs," Susan said with a stern look.

Akira mumbled unintelligible words under his breath.

"Come on, let's get you home," Connor said, and led Malaika out to the truck.

She waved goodbye to her friends and walked in between Connor and Roman. Sparing a glance at the two, she hid her smile. All it took was a little excitement to wash away her worries. *Who would have thought the bad boy would come through?* Malaika arrived home and climbed up to her window with Connor's help.

"Good luck!" he whispered from below. "Sorry in advance if I get you killed."

Malaika grinned at him. Even though he was kidding, she knew that their little game would cost them. Malaika was in and out of sleep. Her thoughts swam around in her mind, leaving her to toss and turn all night. She woke up the next morning with a pounding headache. Her paranoia began bubbling in her chest as the first rays of the sun touched her skin. It was a new day, but knowing her parents, nothing good would happen.

Not wanting to put it off any longer, she washed up and got dressed for the day. When she tried to leave her room, she found her door locked from the outside. Shock coursed through her. Her parents had locked her in as punishment. Malaika scoffed.

A wave of anger washed over her. She threw her leg forward and kicked the door. The door shook with her effort. Malaika threw her foot forward repeatedly. An aching pain spread through her toes, but her frustration pushed her forward. Once her foot had gone numb, she stopped. She took a deep breath and wiped away the sweaty tendrils of hair away from her face. The door sat unscathed. She could feel its white panels mocking her. Muttering curses under her breath, Malaika turned to face the window, hatching up a plan.

Usually, she would have stayed in her room and starved, but after last night's events, she found herself just a tad bit braver this morning. She slipped on her shoes and slid open the window. She took a deep breath, grabbed onto the nearest branch, and made her way down slowly, knowing if she tried to act cool like Connor, she would break a bone. Finally, she made it down. With a skip in her step, she made a run for the taxi parked at the end of the street.

"Good morning," she said as she slid in.

"Hey there, sunshine," said a familiar voice.

Malaika looked up, her eyes widening in shock when she realized who it was. "Connor?"

He laughed and hit the accelerator. "The one and only! IHOP?"

Malaika nodded. "I don't mean to pry, but why are you driving a taxi?" she asked, as her curiosity got the best of her.

"It's not real," he said with a chuckle. "My boys and I are into racing. I painted my ride and designed it to look like a taxi, so if the cops ever show, they'll just pass me up."

"That's brilliant."

Connor grinned at her reaction. "Want to come watch me race one day?"

"I'd love to."

"So how much trouble did you get in?"

"I'm not exactly sure. I didn't have to face my parents yet, they locked me in my room."

"Get ready, sweetheart. This is just the beginning. Your parents are not exactly people you want to piss off," he warned.

His words of warning were unnecessary. Malaika was well aware of the measures her parents could take. Her stomach lurched as the memory of her mother kicking her ribs flashed in her mind. Malaika's breath quivered as her body relived the attack.

"Here we are." Connor announced, breaking her out of her depressive thoughts.

The two slid into a booth and skimmed through the menu, engaging in easy chatter. Midway through their meal, Malaika noticed Connor sneaking glances at her. She put her fork down and gave him her undivided attention. His sudden blush matched his blazing locks.

"I'm sorry if I'm being nosy, but I need to ask. Do your friends know?" he questioned, shifting around uncomfortably.

"Know what?"

"You know..." He looked around to see if anyone was paying attention, then leaned forward. "The deal."

Malaika shook her head. "No. Only one does. Justin."

Connor grabbed her hand. "I'd be lying if I said it'll be all right, but that's all I've got right now."

Malaika squeezed his hand in response. Connor's eyes were blazing with strength and reassurance. Malaika knew that no matter what, he would be there for her. A friendship had been forged, hopefully, one that would last a lifetime.

After breakfast, Connor dropped Malaika back home. She snuck back into her room with his help and waved goodbye. Her parents' car was not in the driveway. She wondered where they could be. Malaika decided to take advantage of their absence. She took out her hidden compositions and began working on her songs. Her pain held one positive note. She could write beautiful songs.

It was after four in the afternoon when her parents came back home.

"Malaika," her mother greeted as she entered her room.

Her father, Malaika noticed, stood outside the door. Hints of his shadow peeked through the space between the door and floor. Malaika looked up. Her mother's face was pale and sweaty. *Had she been crying?* The powerful scent of alcohol invaded her nostrils. *No, she was just drunk.*

"Malaika, what you did last night was out of line," she said, sitting herself down on the edge of the bed.

"What you did last year was out of line," Malaika fired back.

"Watch your tone young lady."

"And if I don't?" Malaika challenged. "What are you going to do? Starve me? Beat me? You need to come up with something more original. Your punishments are becoming mundane!" Malaika's chest heaved following her tirade.

"How dare you speak to me like that?"

Without warning, her mother sprang. Grabbing Malaika's hair, she threw her to the side, knocking her head into the wooden desk. A sharp pain spread across Malaika's skull. Malaika tucked her head between her knees, shielding herself from the attacks that followed. Luckily for Malaika, her mother was tipsy, so her movements were sloppy. When she finished her attack, she stormed out of the room, locking Malaika in once again.

Malaika's tense muscles loosened as soon as she heard the click of the door. She collapsed to the ground, fighting back tears. Her aching limbs shook with every breath she took. A throbbing pain spread through her cranium and trailed down to her neck. With a groan, she got up and made her way to the bathroom. She stripped down and filled the tub with cold water. Breathing shakily, she stepped into the tub, finding peace in the numbness the icy water provided. She closed her eyes and prayed that a miracle would come forth.

*Little did she know her miracle was praying for one as well.*

The next day in history class, Malaika waited for Ms. Williams to see the note she had left her. Roman did not do his part of the project. She turned in their—scratch that—*her* project and saw Roman throw her a dark look.

"We better not fail, Munequita, or else." He left his threat unspoken.

She didn't need him to say anything to know what he was capable of. Shaking her head, she realized he did not remember the events of Saturday night. When the bell rang, signaling the end of class, Malaika stood outside the door and eavesdropped on the conversation between Roman and Ms. Williams. She'd instructed Roman to stay after class. Ms. Williams probably saw the note Malaika taped to the back of the project.

"Roman, did you contribute to this project at all?" Ms. Williams asked. Malaika could hear the disappointment in her voice.

"Yeah," he replied.

"Are you sure about that?"

"Yeah."

"Well then, why don't you tell me how I should interpret this note? *Despite leaving Roman two sets of instructions, he failed to contribute to this project. I and I alone am responsible for this project in its entirety.*"

Roman said nothing, but the lack of response was satisfying. Knowing she'd been able to stun the notorious bad boy into silence had Malaika jumping in excitement.

"Detention for not doing your work and detention for lying to me." Ms. Williams said.

Malaika heard Roman's footsteps approaching. She ran away and did not dare look back as the door flew open.

"Munequita!"

# CHAPTER FOUR

# Dysfunctional Allies

MALAIKA RAN AS FAST as she could. She could not believe her own boldness! *Oh well, Roman had it coming.* She grinned as the excitement and adrenaline pushed her forward. Malaika looked back and saw Roman had disappeared into the crowd. Thank God. She wiped the sweat off her forehead.

Malaika turned the corner, slumped against the wall, and closed her eyes, fighting to control her racing heart. The sound of heavy breathing just inches away from her face alerted her to the fact that someone stood in front of her. Malaika opened her eyes and bit back a scream as she saw what lay before her. Roman's enormous frame towered over her, a murderous glare plastered on his chiseled face.

"Munequita, what you did back there wasn't very nice."

Malaika's stomach dropped. Not having the courage to face him, she took off without a backwards glance.

"Munequita!"

Malaika did not look back. Instead, she ran, putting even more distance between the two. *Maybe it wasn't worth it after all.*

"Malaikaaa," Susan sang, waving a hand in front of her face at lunch.

"Huh?" Malaika snapped back to reality.

"You were spacing out again," Carina said, her thin brows knitted together.

"Is everything okay?" Justin asked.

Malaika nodded and stuffed her mouth with food to avoid what was sure to be an uncomfortable conversation. The past week had been hell for her. Her parents were on her case 24/7, and to make matters worse, *they* were advancing all of their plans forward, giving her very little time to figure out a solution. With her worries plaguing her mind, Malaika did not notice the days as they passed her by.

"Do it," Susan said, jabbing Justin in the chest.

"No, I can't! You do it," he said, turning paler by the minute.

"No, you're older, you should do it."

"I'll do it," Malaika said, and grabbed the disposable lancet to prick their fingers. Today's lesson was blood typing. An activity Malaika had not been looking forward to. Inflicting pain onto herself willingly had her curling her lip in disgust. Malaika pricked Susan's finger. Crimson blood oozed out of the tip of her finger.

Malaika grabbed another lancet and pricked Justin's finger. Muttering a weak thanks, he turned to place a few droplets of blood on his card. Malaika picked up another lancet, ready to prick her own finger, but she found herself rooted to the spot in fear. She took a deep breath and quietly cheered herself on.

"I can do it, I can do it, I can do it." Despite the mini motivation session, Malaika stood unmoving. "I can do it, I can do it, I can—ow!" Someone had pricked her finger for her.

"What the hell?" She looked up to glare at the culprit. Malaika was ready to go off, but her voice died down to a whisper when she saw who stood by her, a bloody lancet in hand.

"You talk too much," Roman said, turning back to his own work.

Though annoyed, Malaika was secretly thankful. It did not matter how long she cheered for herself, she would not have been able to prick her own finger. Not knowing what to say, she mumbled a small thanks. Roman, a mysterious man of a few words, simply grunted in response.

*Haha. He sounds like a monkey.* Roman turned towards her, eyebrow raised. Malaika noticed him staring and looked away. *Crap, can he read minds?*

"Munequita."

"Y-Yeah?"

"You're saying all of that out loud."

Malaika's body went rigid. "S- Sorry." She snuck a peek up at him, only to find he had already left. The bell rang, signaling the end of the day. Malaika thought back to forensics. That was the first time Roman had spoken to her since her little play on him on Monday. She was pleasantly surprised that he had gotten over the project incident so fast. "Crap," she whispered when she saw who was waiting by her car. *Amara!*

Malaika froze in panic, too afraid to face the girl. *What was she doing here?* The squealing of tires caught everyone's attention. Heads turned from all sides to watch the unfamiliar electric blue sports car screech to a stop in the student parking lot.

"Amara!" Connor yelled, stepping out of the car. He was still in his dress shirt and slacks. It was obvious he came straight from work.

Excited chatter broke out at the sight of the enraged boy.

"What do you want, Connor?" Amara asked, irritation etched into her beautiful features. Her dark eyes were seeping with hatred, and her stiletto nails dug into the hood of Malaika's car.

"What the hell are you doing here?" Connor strode forward and yanked Amara away from Malaika's car. Amara's crimson nails left a ragged trail behind.

"I wanted to talk to Malaika myself." She struggled to remove the vise tight grip he had on her arm.

"Stay away from her."

Malaika watched, entranced, as Roman raced over to Conner and pulled him away from Amara.

"Chill out, man." He kept one hand on Connor's shoulder as a precaution.

"Roman, get the doll out of here and head to the pit," Connor said.

Malaika, not knowing what to do, turned around and ran. She sprinted through the empty halls, heading towards the bathroom to hide. In the time she had known Amara, Malaika realized she was a psychopath. The thought of Amara confronting her had Malaika wheezing. Her breath left her lungs. A cold chill wrapped around her body, seizing her limbs. Stars clogged her vision. She ran down the halls with blinded eyes. Malaika yelped as she tripped and toppled to the ground. Holding her head in her hands, Malaika choked as a heavy weight settled over her chest.

Rough hands grabbed Malaika's arms, bringing her to her knees. Malaika looked up, her eyes widening in shock when she took in Roman's stormy gaze. "Breathe," he said.

Malaika gasped, trying to take in some air.

"Breathe."

Roman inhaled deeply. Malaika mimicked his movements. She took in slow deep breaths, counting the amount of times Roman's hypnotic eyes closed. Slowly, the spinning stopped, the stars cleared, and the knots in her stomach loosened. Finally, Malaika regained control of herself. "Th-thank you, Roman," she said, feeling both grateful and embarrassed. Her skin blazed under his touch.

Roman's eyes flashed with an unknown emotion as he stared Malaika down. Malaika gulped at the intensity of his stare.

"Come on, Munequita." He cleared his throat. "Conner needs me to get you out of here."

"Why are you helping me?" Malaika asked as Roman pulled her to her feet.

"I'm not helping you, I'm doing a favor for a friend."

Malaika stayed silent and followed him back to her car.

"Keys, Munequita."

Malaika handed them over without a word. She slid into the car and held on for dear life as he sped out of the parking lot. Malaika did not say a word during the drive, nor did Roman. The silence, though thick, was not uncomfortable. She was grateful when they finally arrived at their destination, she did not think her transmission could handle another second of Roman's aggressive driving.

She looked out the window, taking in the scenery. Before her sat an old brick building covered from top to bottom in elaborate graffiti. Neon colors rested against the aged bricks. The building sat in front of a grassy field. Its rough exterior stood out against the gentle background. The contrast of the hard brick against the soft landscape captivated Malaika. "Beautiful," she whispered.

Roman stood silently by the entrance as Malaika admired the building from afar. Her eyes lingered on the cars lined up in the open garage as she made her way towards Roman.

Her hand twitched as the urge to get behind the wheel shot through her.

"Malaika!" Conner exclaimed when she and Roman made their way into the building.

"Hey Conner."

He threw an arm around her shoulders and led her down to the basement of the building. "Malaika, welcome to the pit," Conner said with a grin.

"Woah." Malaika's jaw dropped as she took in the room. A dark blue glow engulfed the room. Neon paint and signs lined the walls. The north wall consisted of nothing but mirrors, a ballet barre resting in front of it.

"Roman, we need to talk." He motioned for Roman to follow him down the hall. "Feel free to look around while I talk to Roman," he called out.

The two disappeared into an empty room. Malaika used that opportunity to explore the pit. This place was incredible. Through her thorough exploration, she realized the building, while obviously a spot for entertainment, served as a home as well. She saw multiple unmade beds on the second floor, backpacks thrown around, and unfinished assignments sat on night tables. The owners of the untouched homework were probably still at school.

"Come on, Malaika, I'll take you home," Connor said as he came out of the room.

Roman followed suit and grabbed a set of keys from the peg on the wall. The drive home was quiet, both Malaika and Connor lost in their own thoughts. Roman followed closely behind them in the second car.

"Malaika, I'm sorry about the decision they made," Connor said, wrapping his hand around hers.

"It's all right. I'll figure something out, eventually."

"Er, about that...I already did."

"What do you mean?"

"I have thought of a plan to help get you out of this situation." Connor pulled up to her house and killed the engine.

"And what's that?" she asked as she got out of the car.

"Roman."

"Roman?"

"He hates Liam's family, for personal reasons. He's willing to go to great lengths if it means he'll be able to take them down. If you teamed up with him as well, that would pose a great threat to my family," Connor explained, tossing Malaika her keys.

"It sounds as if his vendetta runs deep. Why would he want to team up with me on such a delicate matter?" *Why on earth would the bad boy want anything to do with someone like her? She was weak, an emotional wreck, and, above all, useless.*

"He's not aware of it yet, but you've caught his attention and that's an accomplishment in and of itself."

Malaika looked at Connor indecisively. *She needed help, that was true, but could she really trust Roman? And would the two be able to work together in harmony?*

"Oh, one more thing. Roman knows nothing about your situation," Connor said, then gave her a quick hug as Roman pulled into the driveway.

Malaika waved goodbye as the car disappeared from view. Lost in her thoughts, she stood outside until the sun set, making way for the moon to come forward. *Who would have thought that the bad boy would become her partner in crime?*

# CHAPTER FIVE

## Moody Interrogations

"Rise and shine, sweetheart. Your parents aren't home. It's time to get to work." Connor's familiar voice rang in Malaika's ears.

She grumbled in response and pulled the covers over her head. "Go away!"

Fingers danced on Malaika's exposed foot. She curled her toes and kicked his hand away. It seemed Connor was unfazed as his icy fingers reached for her foot once again. Malaika groaned and pulled her feet under the safety of her covers.

"Wake up, wake up, wake up," Connor said as he jumped on her bed.

"Leave me alone."

Finally, Connor gave up, hopped off the bed, and left Malaika's bedroom. Malaika sighed in content as she heard the click of her door. She was just about to slip back into the peaceful world she had created for herself in her dreams when suddenly; the covers were pulled off her. The bitter cold air attacked her body. Letting out a ferocious roar, she opened her eyes, shot up, grabbed one of her pillows, and viciously attacked Connor.

"Connor!" she screeched as she slapped the pillow repeatedly in his face. Malaika froze when she realized that the man she was attacking was not Connor. It was Roman. Her body froze and her blood ran cold as she saw the irritation etched into his frown.

Roman's eyes were brewing as he stared at Malaika. "Munequita." He took a step forward. His gaze trailed down from her eyes to her locked limbs. He froze mid-step, averted his gaze, and cleared his throat. "Breakfast is ready, get dressed, we got work to do," he said, locking her door from the inside then left her room.

Malaika stared open-mouthed at his retreating figure. Though confused at his odd behavior, she followed orders and headed to the bathroom to get ready for the day. She stripped out of her pajama shorts and took a quick shower. Too lazy to dry her hair, she left her wet locks to fall down her back. She slipped on a grey sweater and some old jeans, then headed downstairs for breakfast.

"Good morning, sunshine." Connor threw her a wink.

Malaika shot him a glare in return.

"Ooh, someone's in a bad mood." He chuckled.

"Shut up."

The doorbell rang, catching Malaika's attention.

"Miss Evans, your friend Justin is here," the housekeeper, Candace said, and led Justin into the kitchen.

Malaika nodded in thanks and got up to greet him. "Hey Justin."

"'Sup, Malaika," he said and gave Malaika a quick hug. "Where are your parents?"

"They're at breakfast with the O'Neals."

"Ugh, ew." Justin rolled his eyes. "How have you been?"

"I'm good."

Justin gave her a stern look. Malaika realized he could see straight through her façade.

"I'll be all right. I have a plan," she said.

"And what exactly is your plan?"

Malaika nodded her head towards Roman, who was making his way down the stairs.

"Roman?" Justin said, his eyes going wide. "What the hell is he doing here?"

"He's kind of my partner."

"What's going on, Malaika?"

"Come on, I'll explain." She dragged him into the study. "All right." Malaika began her little tale, making sure the door was locked. "The red-haired guy is Connor. He's the O'Neals' cousin. He doesn't like them very much and turns out neither does Roman. Roman has got a personal beef with them, so we're teaming up to take them down. Roman is in it so he can get revenge, and well, you can guess why I'm doing this."

Justin looked into Malaika's eyes. His fiery gaze never wavered. After searching Malaika's honey eyes for what seemed like an eternity, he nodded, silently letting Malaika know he approved and would be there to help.

"Are you sure you can trust him?" Justin asked, peeping through the doorway at Roman.

Malaika shrugged in response. "I don't know if I can trust him, but he's all I have right now."

"Does he know about your situation?"

Malaika shook her head, her eyes going wide. "No! Of course not. Besides, he has no reason to know."

"All right, so what's the plan?"

"I don't know yet. Let's go find out." Malaika stepped out of the room.

"Hey man," Justin called out to Connor.

Connor turned around with half of his waffle sticking out of his mouth. "What's up?" Connor slurped up the rest of his waffle.

"My name's Justin, I'm a good friend of Malaika's. It's nice to meet you, man." Justin held out his hand.

Connor swallowed his food and grinned at Justin. "I'm Connor, it's good to meet you too." He shook Justin's hand. "All right, gather around, everyone," Connor said, and led everyone to the study, a briefcase in hand. The dysfunctional group took a seat at the round mahogany table as Connor placed various folders and files down, distributing one to each person.

"Okay, here we go. Despite popular opinion, money can buy happiness. In this case, it will buy us revenge. Now Malaika, while you and I were lucky enough to be born with silver spoons in our mouths, our wealth is nowhere near that of my cousin's. The only way to take these people down is to take away their source of power, which is a lot of Ben Franklins."

"I know a guy who's good at hacking. Give him some time, and he'll be able to take control of their bank accounts," Justin said.

Malaika nodded in agreement. While Akira may have an unassuming persona, he was particularly gifted in coding, hacking, and creating algorithms. If anyone could gain access to the O'Neals' bank accounts, it would be Akira.

"I wish it were that simple. My family places their money in private bank accounts and *charities*. We won't be able to get a hold of their money that easily, but what we can take control of is their shares in the company. If we can get both Liam and his father to transfer their shares to me, I'll have enough money to take them down and you all will have the satisfaction of watching your enemies reduced to nothing."

Malaika raised her hand, trying to control her shaking fingers. As everyone's gazes shifted to her, she struggled not to shrink back, overwhelmed by all the attention. Connor smiled at her.

"Yes, Malaika?"

"Will they be absolutely penniless? It seems wrong to leave them with nothing." Guilt was flowing through her veins at the thought of leaving the O'Neals with nothing.

Connor laughed, though nothing about it was warm. "Don't worry, Malaika, they have multiple houses, yachts, and cars they can sell."

Malaika nodded, feeling the knots in her stomach loosen.

"What's the first step?" Roman asked, giving Malaika a curious once over. Malaika pretended she didn't notice his staring, though she was sure her burning ears were giving her away.

"In order to bring them down, we have to destroy them from the inside. We start by bringing you two into the company," Connor said, pointing at both Malaika and Roman.

"You two will work with me after school as both secretary and assistant. Your primary goal, though, is to befriend anyone who is close to Liam and my uncle. Once you do that, begin filling their heads with unappealing images of the two. You must get their friends to turn on them. This way they won't have anyone in power on their side."

"That's risky. We can get caught!" Malaika protested.

"And if we do, what'll you be losing?" Connor countered. *He was right. Malaika truly had nothing to lose.* She nodded in agreement.

"Okay, that's all for today. Roman, take Malaika down to the pit and have your ID badges made."

Roman stood up and made his way out. Malaika reluctantly followed. Her hands turned clammy at the thought of being alone with the dark-haired mystery. She snuck a glance at him and saw him staring back at her with a blank expression.

"I didn't drive here," he said, looking up at the sky. The golden sun illuminated his russet skin.

"W-We can take my car," Malaika said, momentarily dazed by his eyes. The sun shone against his grey irises. *A beautiful thundercloud waiting to explode.*

The two made their way to the garage. Malaika entered the passcode, grimacing when the door slid up, revealing all of her father's unnecessary sports cars. He was spoiled beyond belief. Malaika grabbed the keys to her Jeep and unlocked the door, hopping into the driver's seat before Roman could. She didn't want Roman driving her car again. She doubted her transmission could handle Roman's aggressive driving. About halfway to the pit, she got lost.

"I don't remember how to get there," she said.

"Turn right."

Malaika nodded and turned right, sparing a glance at him.

"Eyes on the road, Munequita," he said. His gaze darted to her seatbelt. "Get on the highway and take the third exit."

"Okay, thanks."

The two were quiet during the drive. Malaika wanted to strike up a conversation, but every time her gaze landed on him, her heart took off, leaving her breathless. She could feel the awkwardness building in the atmosphere. Roman finally broke it by asking Malaika the one question she wished he wouldn't. "What'd they do to you?"

"Huh?" she questioned, hoping Roman would let it go.

"What did their family do to you to get you to hate them so much?"

"It's complicated," Malaika replied, her voice faint. "My parents made a business deal with the O'Neal family that went bad and now they want me to fix it."

Roman nodded and, thankfully for Malaika, he asked no more questions. "Pull in here," he said as the pit came into view. Malaika parked the car and got out.

"Roman!" A very high-pitched voice rang out across the empty lot.

Malaika winced in response to the sudden sound. The duo turned around, searching for the source. Malaika wrinkled her nose in disgust as a young woman's overly sweet perfume invaded her nostrils. Brushing past Malaika roughly, the beautiful stranger ran to Roman. "Oh, my God. I haven't seen you in so long. Where have you been, babe? And why haven't you called me back?" she asked, clinging onto his arm.

Malaika saw Roman's free hand clench into a tight fist. "Because I didn't want to talk to you," he replied.

The girl let out an awkward laugh, fanning her red cheeks. Malaika headed inside, not wanting to be a third wheel. Roman finally made his way inside, fixing his ruffled clothing, an annoyed look plastered on his usually stony face. "This way," he said, leading Malaika up the stairs.

Malaika's eyes went wide when Roman led her to an open room. Inside were various computers and printing machines. What she assumed were fake licenses and IDs lay inside the room. This was the first glimpse she was getting into the life the *bad boy* lived outside of school. Roman handed her a pair of thick-lensed glasses and a silky black wig. Malaika, though confused, slipped on the wig and switched her glasses. She observed herself in the mirror, surprised to find that despite the change in eyewear, her vision remained the same. The thick lens magnified her eyes. They helped reveal the specks of forest green hidden in the depths of her amber eyes.

"How did you know my prescription numbers?" she asked.

"I stole them from the nurse's office."

Malaika went rigid. Her stomach flipped at his words. "Y-You could've just asked me what my prescription was."

Roman dropped the plastic card he was holding. The tops of his ears turned a bright shade of pink. Malaika hid a smile at his idiocy. Regaining his composure, Roman pointed to the plastic chair in front of the white backdrop. She sat down as Roman set the camera in place. Without warning, the camera flashed. Malaika blinked, at a loss for words. Roman stepped away from the camera, motioning for Malaika to take over.

"I wasn't ready," she protested.

Roman made no sign that he heard her. Chanting curses in her head, Malaika made her way to the camera, slipping off her disguise.

"Ready?" Malaika asked.

Roman nodded in response and stared blank-faced at the camera.

"Are you not going to smile?" she asked.

"No."

"O-Okay," Malaika counted to three and snapped the photo.

Roman stood up, removed his chestnut wig and chocolate contacts, and motioned for Malaika to follow. He took out his phone as he received a text message. Malaika sped up, not wanting to invade his privacy. She made way to walk in front of him but stopped when he tapped her on the shoulder.

"I need to pick up my car," he said.

Malaika nodded, making her way to the parking lot. She got into her car and waited for Roman to get in, who was busy glaring daggers at some guy with oversized biceps and colorful tattoos. Surprised at her own boldness, Malaika honked at the two young men. She cursed under her breath when Roman's fiery gaze landed on her. She looked away from his thunderous glare.

*Oh man, he's going to kill me.*

Roman stormed over to the car and got in, slamming the door behind him. Malaika winced but kept her mouth shut, not wanting to upset him even more.

"Go to the school," he said.

Malaika nodded and took off. After five minutes of silence, he broke it once again. "Think hard about this, Munequita. Once you're in, you can't back down."

Malaika froze at his words. She stole a quick look at him and saw that he was staring at her once again, an intense look in his eyes.

"I-I really don't have much to lose. Either way, I'll end up dead," she mumbled, then groaned internally. *Dammit! Why did she say that?*

"What did you just say?"

Malaika shook her head. "Nothing, I didn't mean it literally."

"Oh really? Then why're your hands shaking?"

Malaika gritted her teeth and ignored him, hoping he would drop it. Roman scoffed and turned back to face the front.

"Where to now?" she asked as they approached the school.

"Just pull in here. My ride is in the back."

Malaika nodded and pulled into the parking lot. "Er—bye!" she called out as Roman stepped out of the car.

Roman grunted in response. Malaika smiled as she watched him walk away, though it fell as she saw him swerve past the corner in a police cruiser. The windows were rolled down and rap music was pumping through the speakers. An overweight, red-faced cop with crumbs on his face chased after him.

"Hey! Come back here!" the officer yelled. "I need backup!" he called out into his walkie-talkie.

With her heart beating a million miles a minute, Malaika sped away, not wanting to get arrested. *Roman was going to be the death of her.*

# CHAPTER SIX

## Close Calls

MALAIKA WOKE UP TO loud scuffling outside her bedroom. She rubbed the sleep from her eyes and made her way to the hall to see what was going on. "Oh." Her shoulders sagged in dejection when she saw Candace taking her parents' suitcases down the stairs. "Another trip?" Malaika asked.

Candace nodded and gave her a small smile. Malaika sighed as she slid back into the warmth of her room. Her parents were going on another getaway. It seemed as if the already silent home would become even quieter, a little more lifeless, and a lot lonelier. With a yawn, she made her way to the bathroom, took a shower, and freshened up for the day.

"Good morning, Malaika," Chef Ron greeted as she entered the kitchen.

"Morning."

Malaika wanted to invite her friends to come live with her while her parents were away, but they had too many responsibilities on their shoulders. She ate her breakfast in silence, then headed out, waving once to her parents, who were too busy looking over their flight tickets to notice.

Malaika walked down the driveway to her jeep, getting ready to sit inside when a faded black motorcycle pulled up. The stranger got off and removed their helmet. It was Roman. Malaika stared open-mouthed as he made his way up the driveway.

"Here." He held out some sort of card to her.

"What is this?"

"Your new ID badge," Roman said, his grey eyes lingering on Malaika's slightly swollen cheek. Malaika, uncomfortable by his heated gaze, turned away, and thanked him for the ID badge. She got into her car and watched Roman speed away.

Slipping the ID badge into her backpack, she turned the key in the ignition and took off. Her eyes kept glancing at the class drop out form that lay on the passenger seat. She could feel her neck getting warm as the events of last night ran through her head.

*Malaika's parents had received a phone call from Mr. Dibb. He had called to inform them about how phenomenal her recent composition was. Her parents thanked him, lying through their teeth. It was close to midnight when Malaika's mother barreled into her room, her breath reeking of alcohol.*

*"I just got off the phone with your teacher," she said, gazing at Malaika through narrowed eyes.*

*Malaika stayed silent and monitored her mother's twitching hand.*

*"Your teacher praised your songwriting abilities," she began, her hand flexing. "What I do not understand is how he is praising you when you told us you had dropped out of all of your music classes."*

*Malaika looked up and met her mother's gaze. For a moment, Malaika allowed her mother to see the rage in her eyes. Though the display of emotion was short, her mother took it as a challenge and sprang, releasing her fury.*

*Her mother threw a hard punch. Malaika did not dodge quickly enough. Red hot pain spread across her face. Her head snapped back as she fell to the floor. While she lay there, stunned, her mother wrought havoc in her bedroom.*

*She rummaged through Malaika's desk and took out all of her songs, compositions, lyrics, and poems. Malaika watched frozen as her mother shredded all her work with trembling hands and tossed them into the wastebasket.*

*Her mother reached into her pocket and pulled out a lighter. She pushed down the wheel. A small orange flame danced in the darkened room, casting an eerie glow on her mother's sunken face. The sight of her hollowed cheeks and dark circles caused goosebumps to erupt over Malaika's arms. The light that used to shine from her eyes had gone out, leaving behind soulless, dead eyes. Malaika noticed for the first time how terrifying she truly looked. Her mother dropped the lighter into the wastebasket, burning Malaika's heart and soul to ash.*

*"You will drop out of your music classes tomorrow. If not, the consequences will be severe," she whispered, her voice trembling with unspoken anger.*

*Malaika, too afraid to speak, nodded mutely. She had lost this round. Once her mother left the room, Malaika broke. Silent sobs spilled from her lips. Her body shook as pain and despair flowed through her veins. For once in her life, she wanted someone to hold her as she lost her mind, but as always, she was left alone to patch up her wounds.*

Malaika pulled into the parking lot, grabbed the papers, and headed to Mr. Dibb's classroom.

"Good morning, Malaika," he said and gave her a smile.

"Good morning, Mr. Dibb. Th- These are for you." She handed him the documents.

Mr. Dibb read over the papers. Slowly, his smile turned to a disappointed frown. "Why?"

Malaika shrugged. "It's complicated."

Mr. Dibb studied her face closely. Malaika turned away before he could see the swelling.

"Is there anything I can do to help?"

Malaika smiled, but shook her head. "Thank you for every-thing you've done for me, Mr. Dibb. Goodbye." She waved once, then left the room before he could break her. As she left the room, a pair of broad shoulders turned the corner and vanished from view.

Malaika walked through the halls, trying to clear her mind before the bell rang, signaling another dull day at school. She was confused and lost. She had no clue what to do. *Without her dreams, what was there for her to cling to?*

Malaika jumped and broke out of her depressive thoughts as the shrill ringing of the bell echoed through the school. She raced down the empty halls. From the corner of her eye, she saw a hand reach out. The rough hand covered her mouth and pulled her backwards. Malaika threw her legs around as a newfound fear claimed her. She clawed at the hand, her breathing edging towards hyperventilation as a million violent thoughts swam around in her mind. Malaika forced her mouth open and bit down. Her teeth dug into her kidnapper's flesh. The metallic taste of blood seeped onto her tongue.

"Relax," a gruff voice said. Malaika's body relaxed as she recognized the voice. He dragged her into the locker room, which was nearest. Her kidnapper shoved her into a shower stall and finally released his hold. Malaika whirled around and watched as he pulled the shower curtain.

"Roman," Malaika panted. Her chest heaved in and out as she fought to catch her breath.

Roman turned around, meeting her confused gaze head on. "She's here."

"What?"

"That Amara chick. I don't know her deal with you, but Connor told me to keep her away from you."

"Oh," Malaika said, trying to absorb Roman's words. "OH!" she exclaimed when her brain finally registered what he was saying. "Why is she here?"

Roman shrugged in response. "Munequita, since I saved you—twice—I think it's only fair that you give me an answer."

Malaika looked up to meet his eyes and yelped in surprise when she did so. Roman was dangerously close. She could see the indigo specks in his grey eyes.

"What do you want to know?" she asked, tearing her gaze away. She had a hard time maintaining eye contact when his grey eyes smoldered darkly.

"What's your beef with them?"

Malaika groaned internally. Anything but that. "I can't tell you."

"You don't have a choice." Ice dripped from his voice as he took a step forward.

Malaika moved back in fear. Roman took another step forward, Malaika stepped back again, her head hitting the wall. She shrieked when bitter cold water burst through the showerhead, soaking both her and Roman. Malaika looked up at Roman, who reached behind her and slammed the button she had bumped into, stopping the water flow.

He exhaled sharply and ran a hand through his wet hair. His gaze met Malaika's. She froze, not being able to look away. Roman narrowed his eyes at her, but quickly looked away when he lowered his gaze.

Confused, Malaika looked down and saw that her soaked shirt clung to her body. Her bare skin and bra peeked through the wet fabric. Heat rushed to her cheeks, and she covered herself with shaking hands. Roman left the shower. A second later, his hoodie landed on her head.

"Thank you," she whispered.

Roman grunted in response and made his way out of the locker room. Malaika slipped the black hoodie over her head and followed him out into the deserted hallway.

"Get out now," he said.

"Why?"

Without glancing back at her, he yanked the fire alarm lever. Malaika ran outside as the alarm went off. The shrill bell echoed throughout the building. Soon enough, students and staff members poured out of the building. The students wore broad grins, obviously excited that they were missing class. The teachers had varying degrees of confusion plastered on their faces.

Malaika looked around for Roman. She found him sitting with his crew on the steps of the school. Drenched from head to toe, his raven tresses clung to his cheeks and neck. The white tank top he wore was soaked, revealing his chiseled body. Naturally, the female population circled around him like ravenous lionesses. Moments later, jealous boyfriends made their way towards Roman. Already smelling a fight brewing, Malaika ran towards the steps. Without thinking, she jumped in front of Roman, her back to him as he and another student began sizing each other up.

"Are you really about to fight someone who's done nothing to you?" she asked, turning to look at the jealous boy. Malaika felt Roman's warm hand grasp her upper arm. She did not back down.

"Stay out of this, little girl," the instigator ordered.

Malaika was unfazed. "The fact that your girlfriend can't keep her eyes to herself has nothing to do with Roman. If anything, you should talk to her, instead of trying to fight someone who hasn't wronged you." Malaika was nervous, but her voice did not waver. For the first time in her life, she was proud of herself.

Before anything could happen, security made their way to the steps and broke up the crowd. Roman placed a hand on Malaika's shoulder, guiding her through the throng of students. Her skin burned under his hold. Malaika noticed his unblinking stare, but she did not look up at him. She was too embarrassed. She hoped Roman didn't take her involvement in the wrong way.

"See you later, Munequita." Roman nodded at her, then headed towards his motorcycle.

Malaika waved at his retreating figure. The school had closed early, an investigation was pending to see who had pulled the fire alarm. Malaika knew Roman wasn't worried, for it was common knowledge the security cameras were just for show. She slid into her car and drove off, her mind filled with thoughts of charcoal eyes and cold water.

"I'm home," she said, entering the empty house.

"Finally," echoed a voice from behind her.

Malaika froze as she was locking the door. She turned around and dropped her keys at the sight before her.

"We're going to be your new housemates," Amara said, with Liam smirking next to her.

In her panic, Malaika almost turned around and ran back out the door. "Oh, uh, welcome." Malaika plastered a fake smile on her lips.

"Where were you today?" Amara made her way over to Malaika.

"What do you mean?" Malaika hurried towards the kitchen where Chef Ron was, not wanting to be alone with these two for even a moment.

"You weren't in class today," Amara pressed.

Malaika's heart dropped. "I felt a little sick, so I was at the nurse's office. What were you doing at my school?"

"Oh, has no one told you? I've transferred to your school." Amara smiled dangerously.

Malaika gulped. They had infiltrated her only safe space.

"Brunch will be ready in about half an hour. Would you care for a snack in the meantime?" Candace asked, stepping in between Amara and Malaika.

Malaika shook her head, grateful that Candace picked up on the tense atmosphere. "Make yourselves at home. I'll be back in a bit," she said, then ran upstairs. She slid into the nearest bathroom and slammed the door shut. Malaika stripped out of her wet clothes and hopped into the shower, wanting to warm herself after getting soaked with freezing cold water. Malaika sighed as the water thawed her cold limbs. Dread filled her heart when she realized that Amara and Liam would stay with her for a month. Malaika groaned when she realized she forgot to bring a change of clothes. Grabbing the towel off the shelf, she wrapped it around her body. She stepped out of the bathroom and tiptoed into the hall, heading for her bedroom.

"Woah," Amara's familiar voice rang out.

Malaika turned around, her hand flying to her chest.

"Damn girl, with a body like that, you could have any guy you want. Why keep it hidden?" Amara asked, tugging at Malaika's towel.

Malaika yanked herself out of her grip. "Don't touch me," she spat, her temper flaring.

"Excuse me?"

"You heard her," a low voice said from behind the two.

Malaika turned around. Connor was standing behind her, with a mysterious blue-eyed beauty at his side.

"Stop being a pervert," the mysterious goddess said, her slim hands balling into tight fists.

"Eva, please take Malaika to her room," Connor said, ushering Malaika behind him.

Malaika spared a look behind her and saw that Amara was fuming. Gulping, she made her way to Eva. She put a hand on Malaika's shoulder protectively.

"Are you all right?" Eva asked, when they had made it safely into Malaika's room.

Malaika nodded in response. "Thank you."

Eva smiled. "No problem. Besides, a friend of Connor's is a friend of mine." She stuck out her hand. "I'm Eva."

Holding her towel firmly in one hand, Malaika took Eva's warm hand and shook it. "I'm Malaika, it's a pleasure to meet you. I'm assuming you're Connor's girlfriend."

Eva nodded. She jumped when the bathroom door flung open and in walked Roman with nothing but a towel covering his lower body. He shook out his wet hair while Eva and Malaika looked at his sculpted body, entranced. His bronze body was chiseled to perfection, an intricately detailed tattoo sat on his arm, trailing to his chest.

"Roman!" Eva screeched, snapping Malaika out of her trance.

Roman looked up and cursed under his breath. He grabbed the folded clothes that sat on Malaika's bed, then left the room, keeping his gaze down. "S-sorry," he said, then shut the door behind him. A warm blush spread across Malaika's cheeks.

"All right, let's get you dressed before Liam sees you like this too." Eva chuckled.

"Why is Roman at my house?"

"Connor found out about Amara and Liam's stay, so he told Roman to meet him here. I don't know what plan he's concocting, but be prepared. Knowing my boyfriend's love for theatrics, it can't be anything good."

Malaika nodded. She slipped on a pair of leggings, and an oversized sweater, then blew dry her hair, not wanting to catch a cold. Unfortunately, the downside of this was that she was left looking like a cat's hairball. Knowing she couldn't tame her tresses, she tied her hair into a bun, not bothering to fight the frizz.

"Shall we head down then?" Eva asked as Malaika came out of the bathroom. Malaika nodded, slipping on her house shoes. The two made their way to the dining room.

"Brunch is served," Chef Ron said as everyone sat down at the table. Malaika thanked him, smiling. He made her favorites, probably knowing that she needed a little something to brighten her day.

"So, Connor," Liam began, popping a shrimp into his mouth. "What are you doing here?" He gazed at Connor with a stony expression.

Connor, unfazed by Liam's frosty attitude, responded, "I heard Malaika's parents would be gone for a while, so I figured I would stop by whenever I get the chance."

"Mom and Dad didn't tell me you would stay here too," Amara said.

"That's because they didn't know."

"Well, why didn't you tell them?"

Malaika could tell by Connor's ticking jaw, Amara irritated him. "Sorry." Sarcasm laced his words. "I didn't realize they were my parents too." He rolled his eyes.

Amara sucked her teeth, clearly struggling to control her temper. "Who are you?" Amara moved onto her next target. She eyed Roman up and down, in both distaste and interest. Roman raised an eyebrow at her. He wiped his mouth and met her gaze. Just as he opened his mouth to reply, Connor cut him off.

"He's Malaika's boyfriend!"

Malaika gasped and choked on her food, holding her throat as she struggled to breathe. Candace rushed over and hit Malaika's back repeatedly. While she was having a near death experience, Roman was unaffected, simply finishing his food.

"What?" Amara screeched.

"Sorry, if I had known you were into me, I would've never agreed to go out with him," Malaika wheezed out. Her eyes widened at her own comment. *Did she really just say that?* The red spreading across Amara's enraged face confirmed she did. Roman turned his head and met Malaika's wide eyes. He raised his glass of water at her and gave her a shadow of a smile.

# CHAPTER SEVEN

# Makeshift Family

"WHAT DID YOU JUST say to me?" Amara asked. The veins in her forehead looked like they were about to burst.

Saving Malaika from a painful death, Connor came to her rescue by breaking the tense atmosphere with his horrendous laugh. Eva shook her head at her boyfriend's embarrassing behavior. Malaika breathed a sigh of relief as Connor's screeching laughter distracted everyone.

"All right, Connor, I gotta go," Roman said, getting up.

Malaika walked him to the front door.

"Hey," Connor called out.

Roman and Malaika turned around to face him.

"What's wrong?" Malaika asked, as she took in the worried lines on Connor's forehead.

"Roman, you have to come over more often now since I said you were Malaika's boyfriend." Connor shifted from foot to foot.

Roman glanced at Malaika for a fleeting moment, then turned back to Connor. "My ma is working overtime, you know that."

"Bring your mom and siblings over, then. Besides, who's going to watch the baby while your mom is at work? You've already used up most of your absences to take care of her," Connor said.

Malaika looked up at Roman in question. *What was going on?* Roman stared at Connor with an unreadable expression, but a single whine from Connor sent him out the door.

"What's going on?" Malaika asked.

"In order for Roman to come over more often, he would need someone to watch his little siblings, as his mother works overtime. The best solution is for Roman and his siblings to stay here for the duration of the month. This way, you two can act out your lie and Roman's siblings will have a caretaker. Besides, I'm not about to leave you here with Liam and Amara unprotected." Connor cracked his knuckles as he turned around to stare at Liam, who stood by the entrance of the foyer, watching the two with laser-like focus. "It'd be safer if Roman was to stay rather than me."

"And why's that?"

Connor grinned sheepishly. "This may come as a surprise, but once upon a time, Roman was the one who would hold me back, rather than the other way around."

Malaika looked Connor up and down. He did not strike her as the type of person to throw a punch. He was too safe, too tame. Roman, on the other hand, was a mysterious man, cloaked in chaos and cologne. He struck her as the type to throw both the first and last punch.

"Would Roman be okay with this?" Malaika asked.

Connor shook his head. "He's not exactly happy about the situation, but there's no other way. This is the best solution for him right now."

Malaika nodded. "I'll go prepare their rooms." She headed off in search of Candace. "Oh wait. How many siblings does he have?"

"Three. His brother is thirteen years old, his sister is six, and the youngest is a newborn," Connor said, then made his way into the kitchen where Amara's bird-like screeches and Eva's sharp tongue were colliding.

Malaika caught up to Candace and informed her of the new living arrangements. Along with Liam and Amara, Roman and his family were moving in temporarily as well. The two women worked together to dust and tidy up the spare bedrooms for Roman and his family. The doorbell rang, catching Malaika's attention. She put down the feather duster and raced down the steps to open the door. A genuine smile erupted across her face when she saw an adorable little girl standing in the doorway. Chubby cheeks, dark curly locks, bright eyes, and dimples stood before her.

"Hello," Malaika said.

The nervousness that was plastered on the little girl's face melted away. She smiled back brightly.

"My name's Malaika, it's nice to meet you."

"My name's Meredith."

Malaika ushered Meredith inside the house. She caught sight of Amara making her way to them. The hairs on the back of Malaika's neck rose at the dark look in Amara's eyes. She pulled Meredith's tiny frame behind her, taking a protective stance.

"Who's this?" Amara asked, eyeing Meredith in distaste.

Malaika narrowed her eyes at her. "She's my friend and will stay here."

Amara glowered at Malaika, clearly not liking her sudden confidence boost.

"Careful now, might pop a blood vessel," a boy's voice said.

Malaika turned and saw a miniature version of Roman standing in the doorway. Raven tresses pulled back into a bun and round grey eyes like Roman's. While Roman's were clouded with mystery, the young boy before her had eyes that twinkled with mischief. She hid a smile at his comment. He stepped in and made his way to Meredith, wrapping his hand around hers.

"Is she bothering you?" he asked Malaika, pointing a finger towards Amara.

"It's nothing I can't handle." Malaika smiled at him.

He grinned back. "Roman, bring your girl around more often. She's more fun than those other skanks you hang out with."

Malaika's mouth fell open. She was at a loss for words. "L-Language."

He chuckled and shook his head. "The name's Jet." He stuck out his hand. Malaika shook it, smiling like an idiot.

"I'm Malaika."

Malaika walked the children up to their rooms. Bright smiles broke out across their faces when they saw the rooms they would stay in. Malaika had a gaming console delivered as well as a life size dollhouse for Meredith. The gratitude on their faces was enough to bring Malaika to tears. The usually tense household seemed lively despite the two sour-faced enemies that lurked in the corner. Even Chef Ron went an extra mile and whipped up desserts in a matter of minutes.

Malaika made her way to Roman's room and knocked. The door opened up, revealing Roman, who was rocking a baby in his arms.

"Connor wants you to meet him at the pit," she said.

He nodded, handing the baby to Malaika. "Watch her." His hands hovered over the baby for a moment, almost as if he was afraid to leave her.

Malaika took the child into her arms. She gazed into her emerald eyes, fascinated by their magnificent color. "What's her name?"

"Angel," Roman said as made his way out of the room.

Malaika peered down at Angel. She had the same russet skin as Roman, although her eyes were a different story. While

Roman's irises were as dark as a thundercloud, Angels were as bright as jade gemstones.

Cradling Angel close to her nonexistent chest, Malaika headed to Jet's room. Despite the age difference, Malaika got lost in the company of Roman's siblings. Meredith was shy and soft-spoken, but when irked by her brother, she turned into Roman. A thunderous explosion on a calm night. Jet was an amplified version of Roman. His insults could rival his older brother's. She entered his room as his fingers tapped away on his game controller. Furious curses and creative comebacks flew out of his mouth, shutting down his middle-aged opponents. By the end of his tirade, Malaika was a wheezing mess. She couldn't tell if her tears were from laughing too hard or a remnant of her constant pleas to get Jet to stop cursing.

A knock on the door caught their attention. "Dinner is ready," Candace said.

Malaika nodded in thanks and got up, making her way downstairs with the kids in tow. Dinner was a rather edgy affair. Liam glowered at Malaika all throughout their meal, while Amara and Jet argued back and forth. Jet didn't hold back. He cursed at Amara for staring at his little sister for too long. Though she didn't speak, Malaika could tell Amara was judging the state of their clothing. Malaika didn't bother scolding Jet. She enjoyed the stupefied look on Amara's face.

"Shut your raggedy ass up and stop looking at my sister from head to toe. Do you really think that Chanel you have on is helping you? You're a whole ass rat with and without the name brand. Don't you dare think you're better than us."

Amara opened her mouth to retaliate, but Malaika was quicker. "Don't bother fighting back Amara. He already buried you six feet under. There's no coming back from that. Do yourself a favor and keep your mouth shut." She turned to Liam. "Unless you have something to say to me, lower your gaze."

Liam averted his gaze, but a small smile played on his lips at her outburst. Just like that, it disappeared, as if it had never been there.

Once the kids finished their meal, Malaika led the kids back to their room. She tucked Meredith into bed while Jet stood at the door, watching.

"Good night, Meredith." Malaika gave the young girl a quick hug, then left the room with Jet in tow.

"You know what, Malaika?"

"Hmm?"

"You're pretty cool for a white girl."

Malaika laughed. "Thank you, but I'm not white. I'm mixed."

Jet went to his room and waved goodbye. Malaika cradled Angel to her chest and headed down to the study. She took a seat and stared out at the setting sun, falling asleep with Angel in her arms.

Malaika woke up to the sound of heavy breathing. She opened her eyes and had to refrain from jerking back in surprise. Liam stood in front of her, his forest eyes examining her and Angel intently.

"Do you think it was a good idea to let them live here?" he asked.

"Hm?" Malaika responded, still dazed.

"The children."

Malaika nodded, looking down at Angel's sleeping form. "Yes, we have the facilities to take care of them." Malaika met his hard gaze.

He stared at Malaika, unblinking. "Roman, huh? You'll end up being a breeder just like his mother." His eyes narrowed in disgust.

Malaika's eyes widened in response. "What did you just say?" She jumped up as her anger took over. She had to look up to meet his face.

"You heard me."

"If you know what's best for you, you'll walk away now," she said in an icy tone, furious at his words.

"If you know what's best for you, then you would stay away from Connor," he said, grabbing her arm.

Malaika winced as his grip tightened. "What's your problem?"

Liam hardly spoke to her, and now he was being abusive and hurtful. Before Liam could answer, an arm shot out, shoving him backwards. His long limbs tripped over the ottoman, sending him toppling to the floor. A warm hand wrapped around Malaika's arm, pulling her back. Malaika looked up to see Roman standing in front of her protectively.

"Back off," he said in a dangerously low voice. His eyes were glittering with malice. The muscle in his jaw was twitching and his hands closed into fists, revealing the criss-crossing of his veins.

Though the unspoken threat was not directed at her, Malaika also shivered in fear. Liam took the hint and walked away. Roman turned to Malaika. "Are you all right, Munequita?"

Malaika nodded, lying. Her arm was hurting, she was sure Liam left her a bruise. Angel's movement caught their attention. The two looked down to see her yawning.

"It's time to feed her," Roman said and carefully took her from Malaika's arms.

Roman's hand brushed against Malaika's. She had to look away from his intense gaze, not liking the way her heart rate increased every time he looked at her. He walked away with Angel in his arms.

"Yo, Munequita."

Malaika turned around to face him.

"We start tomorrow."

Malaika nodded. *It was time to get revenge.*

# CHAPTER EIGHT

## Late Night Parties

As the clock struck ten, Malaika's demise began. Panic swelled in her chest. A cold sweat broke out across her forehead as teenagers barrelled through the front doors. Drinks in hand and excited gleams in their eyes, Malaika knew that tonight would end in complete chaos. Roman ran down the steps as music blasted through the speakers. It hadn't even been fifteen minutes and already the sound of breaking glass reached Malaika's ears.

"What's going on?" Roman asked and looked down at Malaika, his grey eyes guarded.

"A-Amara threw a party. I tried to stop her, but she wouldn't listen." Malaika gasped and toppled forward as a hard force knocked into her. Roman caught her and placed a hand on the small of her back to steady her. Malaika mumbled a small thanks as she slid her glasses up. Her body burned up at his touch.

"Get lost, you drunk piece of shit." Roman shoved the boy who had bumped into Malaika.

The boy's eyes narrowed into thin slits, his fists balling up. "Yeah? I'd like to see you try—"

What he was going to say was anyone's guess. Roman punched him in the face, knocking him out cold. The boy's mouth fell open and his eyes rolled back. Malaika looked away as the whites of his eyes met hers. Roman caught the unconscious boy before he could hit the floor and dragged him out the front door.

"Oh, yeah! Girls!"

Malaika looked up as Jet's familiar voice echoed through the foyer. He stood on the stairs, peering down at the partygoers with a wild gleam in his eyes. Roman cleared his throat, catching Jet's attention. Wielding a flip-flop in one hand, Roman gave Jet a meaningful stare. Malaika, despite herself, laughed at Jet's dejected shoulders as he trudged back to his room. Roman caught her eye and gave her an amused grin.

Loud screaming caught their attention. Malaika and Roman shoved their way through the crowd. She shivered in disgust as their sweaty bodies and hot breaths stuck to her skin. Roman's rough hand grabbed Malaika's wrist and pulled her forward to escape the mob of partygoers.

"You have got to be kidding me." Malaika stared wide-eyed at the scene in front of her. The sliding glass door that led to the pool had shattered. Beyond that, she saw an inky black truck parked in the middle of her mother's boxwoods. Malaika's stomach rolled as she saw the crowd throw their hands in the air, their bodies moving up and down. Their excited cheers and hoots vibrated through the ground. Malaika caught sight of Candace and Chef Ron trying to drive the partygoers away. Their pleas fell on deaf ears.

Malaika could feel Roman looking at her. Her breath trembled as his silver eyes caught hers.

"What do you want to do?" he asked.

Malaika scanned the crowd, her gaze landing on Amara's wicked grin. "This is a challenge." Malaika motioned towards Amara.

Roman followed her line of vision. Amara threw him a cheeky wink. Roman's eyes narrowed, his full lips pulled back into a disgusted sneer. Malaika hid a grin as Amara shrunk back into the crowd, a frown on her face.

"Amara knows I can't call the cops, so I need to play her little game." Malaika knew that calling the cops on an O'Neal was futile. They had enough money in their bank accounts to tempt an entire precinct to turn a blind eye.

Roman whistled as he took in the multiplying crowd. "It's one hell of a game, Munequita. You think you can handle it alone?"

"Nope, but I'm going to fake it until I make it."

Liam snaked his way forward, his eyes on Roman. "For a couple, you two sure keep your distance from each other."

Without a word, Roman grabbed Malaika into a bridal hold. Malaika gasped as the floor disappeared from under her. Her hand splayed against Roman's chest. His racing heart hummed through her fingers.

"This good enough for you?" Roman asked, standing toe to toe with Liam. His eyes were blank, but his posture was challenging. Roman's fists balled, the veins prominent under his russet skin. His muscles were coiling, eager for a fight. Liam didn't falter. He stared at Roman, his emerald eyes hard. Malaika could feel the hostility between the two. It wrapped around her body like a snake, keeping her entrapped in its chilling hold. The crowd, it seemed, caught on too.

"Fight, fight, fight—"

Malaika's chest bubbled with panic, her hands turned clammy as the crowd screamed for bloodshed. Cackling laughter diverted the crowd's attention. Malaika rested her head on Roman's chest and sighed, the tension leaving her shoulders as Connor caught the crowd's eyes. A handful of college students flanked him.

"The king has arrived, now let's party!" He ripped his shirt off, claiming the partygoers' attention. The crowd cheered and ran to Connor and his friends, eager to grab a cup of whatever he was handing out.

Eva touched Malaika's elbow as Roman placed her down. "Come with me."

She led the duo to the safety of the basement. Entering the passcode, Malaika entered the dimly lit room, locking it behind her.

"What's going on?" Malaika asked, taking a seat next to Eva.

"Amara knows that this party is out of your comfort zone. She plans on publicly embarrassing you, which will lead you to being bullied at school."

Malaika scoffed. "That's so childish."

Eva shrugged. "That's Amara. In order to win this round, you have to play her game and win."

Roman yawned. "I'm going to bed."

Eva raised a sharp brow at him. The sudden fire in her gaze took Malaika by surprise. "I don't think so. Whether you like it or not, you and Malaika are dating. This is an act you have to keep up."

Malaika's neck burned at Eva's words. She could see Roman staring at her from the corner of her eye. He sighed, running a hand through his hair. "What do we have to do?"

"Play the game and bring home a win."

Malaika, though nervous, nodded. She knew Amara would place her in uncomfortable situations tonight, but she had to win. The trio made their way back to the party. Eva pulled Roman back and whispered something in his ear. Malaika walked on and winced as the pumping bass vibrated through her body. Another crash echoed through the house. Malaika groaned, holding her head in her hands. Roman's familiar, calloused fingers wrapped around her shoulder.

"Don't worry, we'll fix everything tomorrow," he said.

Amara shoved a cup in Malaika's face. "Have a drink."

The overly sweet scent invaded her nostrils. Malaika took a step back, her breath catching in her throat. *Alcohol.* Amara's eyes brightened at the disgust on Malaika's face. Malaika could smell a victory going Amara's way as onlookers noticed she turned the alcohol down.

Roman snatched the cup from Amara, downing the contents in seconds. The onlookers cheered as he threw the cup to the side. "That stuff's weak as hell. What else have you got?"

Amara shrunk back into her shell when the onlookers laughed at her. The music changed to a fast beat song. The crowd screamed out the lyrics, their limbs entangling. Malaika wrapped her arms around herself as she was pushed through the crowd.

Sweaty hands grabbed her from behind. Someone yanked her into their hold. She yelped, surprised by the invading hands. Someone's hot breath trailed down her neck, their body brushing against her back. Malaika's eyes widened. Panic bubbled in her chest as the hands trailed down to her thighs. She was rooted to the spot in fear. She couldn't bring herself to move. Her mind was screaming at her to fight back, but her body would not obey. Instead, it stayed where it was, limbs locked, as her harasser did what they pleased.

She choked as someone else pulled her forward. Her body was pulled flush against someone's chest. Malaika recognized the intoxicating scent. Musk and subtle hints of savoury wood. *Roman.* She breathed a sigh of relief, melting into his hold. Roman's warm hands circled around her. She looked up at him. His eyes were shining dangerously. He glared at the harasser.

"If you ever touch her again, I'll break your hands in eight different ways," Roman said.

The harasser turned tail and ran out the door, escaping Roman's fiery stare. Those that watched the drama unfold ap-

plauded Roman. Roman didn't let go of Malaika. He held her
close as the songs continued; the crowd getting more rowdy.
Malaika's heart pounded as Roman's hands rested against her
body. Her skin was tingling as his chin sat on her head. Malaika
felt like her body was on fire. Every vein sizzled at the smallest
of Romans touches.

As the hands of the clock turned to eleven, Amara's voice
bounced off the walls. "All right guys, time to play truth or
dare. Malaika, why don't you take the players down to the
basement?"

Malaika's face burned when everyone turned to look at
her. Roman released her, but kept a hand on her shoulder
as she led a handful of teenagers down to the basement. She
could tell by their slurred words and sloppy movements that
they were wasted. A few more drinks and they would fade
into oblivion. She hoped the partiers didn't turn into abusive
drunks like her mother.

The group entered the basement and sat down in a large
circle. Malaika's heart was in her throat, she knew by the
malicious glint in Amara's eyes; she was planning something
horrendous. Eva and Connor came toppling down the steps.
They squeezed themselves beside Malaika and Roman. Liam
trailed after them, his gaze freezing on Malaika. Amara spun
the empty glass bottle to start the game. It landed on a straw-
berry-haired girl. Malaika recognized her from her history
class. Amara's lips pursed.

"Truth or dare?"

The girl bit her lip. Malaika knew by her wringing hands
that she was afraid.

"Truth," she said.

Amara sneered. "Is it true that you've never had a
boyfriend?"

The girl winced, her eyes brimming with tears. Connor
threw an arm over her shoulders. With a cheeky grin, he said,
"Before Eva, this was my girl." He landed a kiss on her cheek.

The girl blushed tomato red. Malaika exhaled, grateful that Connor stepped up. The girl spun the bottle. It landed on Amara.

"Truth or dare?" she asked.

"Dare," Amara said.

Connor whispered something in the girl's ears. Her eyes went wide at his words.

"Are you sure?"

Connor nodded, a wide grin on his lips.

Eva groaned under her breath. "I hope it's nothing too bad."

The girl faced Amara. "I dare you to shave off your eyebrow."

Amara rolled her eyes. She licked her finger and ran it across her eyebrow. The brown color faded away, revealing sparse hairs. Connor groaned and slammed his fist against the ground with a pout. Amara ignored him and spun the bottle once more. It landed on Malaika. Malaika's heart jumped when Amara looked up at her.

"Truth or dare?"

"Tr-dare." Malaika was going to say *truth*, but Roman tapped her leg, stopping her.

Amara's mouth fell open. Judging by the disbelief on her face, Malaika realized Amara was expecting Malaika to chicken out. Amara's dark eyes trailed over Malaika, then they moved over to Roman. A grin spread across her face. Malaika's hands turned clammy at the vicious spark in her gaze.

"I dare you to play seven minutes in heaven with Roman."

Malaika's heart lurched. Butterflies erupted in her stomach, fluttering violently. She looked up at Roman. He stared back at her, his grey eyes for a moment flashed dangerously, then they went blank. He took her hand and led her to the closet. Malaika's hand tingled as his rough fingers intertwined with hers. Cheers and hoots erupted as Roman locked the closet door. Malaika looked down, staring at her untied shoelace.

The closet was dimly lit, illuminated by an aged bulb that hovered above them.

Roman faced her. His gigantic frame took up most of the closet. Malaika took a deep breath. His addicting scent hypnotized her. The tension was thick in the air. Malaika could feel sparks of electricity brushing against her skin. She was too aware of Roman. Malaika didn't doubt that he probably knew this, too. She looked up and gasped when she realized just how close he was. His charcoal eyes stared down at her. His nose and lips were only inches away. Malaika's gaze trailed over his face. Her neck burned as Roman's eyes darkened.

"Are you all right?" he asked, his voice barely a whisper.

Malaika nodded mutely, not trusting herself to speak. She looked away when Roman's eyes locked with hers once again. Her heart took off, beating a million miles a minute. The minutes ticked by. Roman's body heat was seeping into her. His scent was entrapping her in its captivating hold. Malaika became more and more drunk by the second.

"One more minute!" Amara's voice screeched through the crack in the door.

Malaika looked up as Roman inhaled. "You can win this game, you know?"

"How?" she asked.

Roman stayed silent. His penetrating gaze trailed over her. "Do you trust me?"

Malaika hesitated. She didn't trust him completely, though she didn't not trust him either. She nodded, not meeting his eyes.

"Good. I'm sorry but I have to do this."

"Do what?" Malaika stepped back, her head knocking into the wall, when Roman began taking his shirt off. "Wh-what are you doing?" Her heart skipped a beat as the layer of dark green cotton slipped off his body.

"Winning."

Roman stuffed his tee shirt into his back pocket. Malaika gulped, her body flaming as Roman's bare chest danced in front of her eyes. An intricately detailed tattoo sat on his muscular arm, trailing to his chest. His russet skin was beautiful under the dim light. His calloused hands reached for her.

"May I?"

Malaika nodded, her eyes flying back to her untied shoe. Roman's warm hands pulled Malaika close. He picked her up, guiding her legs. He wrapped her legs around his waist. Malaika felt his body tense under her. She grabbed his broad shoulders to steady herself. His body was unnaturally warm. His fingers traced her jaw. Malaika's heart skipped a beat at his touch. It was as if every nerve in her body was a live wire, reacting to the smallest of his touches. He tucked her head under his chin, burying her face against his chest. His hands cupped the back of her thighs. Malaika gasped. Roman cursed and apologized.

"Bear with me, Munequita, it'll be over soon."

Malaika, though terrified, nodded. She hid her face from view when the closet door opened. She screwed her eyes shut, terrified to see what emotions the partygoers' eyes would hold at the scene before them. Excited cheers erupted when Roman made his way out of the closet. His hold on Malaika tightened.

"Party's over, go home," he ordered.

Malaika could hear his heartbeat. It was racing. She felt Roman making his way up the steps. She didn't dare open her eyes. Slowly, the sound of pumping music and exuberant cheering faded away. The click of the door alerted her she was safe. She opened her eyes and was met with darkness. Roman placed a hand on her back and placed her down, laying her on a bed. His eyes trailed over her face. "Are you all right?"

Malaika nodded. "I'm sorry you had to do that for me."

"It's fine." Suddenly, his eyes were guarded. The wall was back up. "People may talk about this, Munequita. Don't let it get to you."

She nodded. Malaika knew her classmates would spread news about this party. She prayed that the part about her and Roman stayed under wraps. "Th-thank you for everything. Good night." She got up, heading to the door.

Roman's hand shot out, stopping her. "If you leave now, Amara and Liam will know it's all a lie."

Malaika stopped, the blood drained from her face. Roman was right. If she left the room now, Amara and Liam would realize their relationship was just a façade. An act. A lie. Her eyes darted to the bed. Roman grabbed the duvet off of it and headed to the chaise.

"Goodnight, Munequita."

Malaika crawled into the bed, a multitude of emotions swimming through her. Fear, nervousness, and anxiety. She knew Roman would never hurt her, but the idea of spending the night with him terrified her. "G-Good night, Roman."

The moon's beams shone through the blinds, casting a white glow on Roman's raven tresses. Malaika did not understand him. He was contradicting—a paradox. One minute he would speak to her as if he's known her his whole life and others he would stay silent, granting her an occasional grunt. He was short-tempered and yet patient. Ruthless, yet kind. He was a raging thundercloud and, at times, the calm after the storm. He was the school's bad boy. But after all he did for her tonight, Malaika had a hard time believing that.

# CHAPTER NINE

## Enemy Territory

MALAIKA SAT ON THE bed, covered in darkness. The sun had yet to rise, and she was already having a panic attack. With her eyes screwed shut, she wrapped her arms around her small frame and whispered to herself. "B-Breathe."

She kneeled forward as her chest heaved. Familiar grey eyes flashed behind her closed lids. She took a deep breath, held it for ten seconds, then released it, feeling her heart slow as the last of her stress left her body.

"Breathe," said another voice.

She obeyed and took in a lungful of air then released it slowly. Her trembling limbs stilled. Malaika unwrapped her arms and opened her eyes. She gasped, fighting down the cry of surprise that was tempted to escape her lips. The grey eyes which invaded her thoughts were now staring right at her. She gulped as Roman's gaze met hers.

"Roman," she whispered.

"Munequita."

He rolled over on the chaise. The blanket slipped off his built frame, revealing his bare back. Malaika couldn't look away. His broad shoulders, bulging deltoids, and chiseled shoulder blades crowded her vision. Her gaze flew down his copper skin, lingering on the scars that sat there. Faded and feather light, these scars pulled at her heartstrings. She tore her gaze away, her heart pounding. *Who was Roman, really? What was his story?*

As Roman's snores filled the room, she snuck out of the bedroom and tiptoed down the hall, past Liam's room. Malaika could see his shadow peeking through the door. As she passed by, his door flung open. Malaika jumped back and stumbled into the wall. His fierce gaze burned a hole through her head. Malaika fidgeted under his heated gaze.

"Good morning," he finally said, breaking the tense atmosphere.

"M-Morning."

"Did you have an enjoyable night?"

Malaika's eyes narrowed at the hostility hidden in Liam's words. "That's none of your concern," she seethed, then stormed away, shoving thoughts of Liam to the back of her mind. The world was waiting for her. It was time to greet it. Freshening up, she made her way out of the house. She couldn't take it anymore. The anxiety was building up again. She got into her jeep and took off.

It was the first day of her mission. She and Roman were to work with Connor after school and on Saturdays. Even though she did not need to show until nine a.m. today, her fried nerves wouldn't allow her to sleep, so instead she headed to the office early to familiarize herself with the enemy's lair.

Malaika pulled into the parking lot and followed the janitors to the main doors. She watched as they inserted their ID badges into the scanner. When the red light turned green, the gate opened. Malaika struggled to keep a straight face as she inserted her fake ID. The seconds ticked by. Her heart beat wildly in her chest. *What if it didn't work? What if she was caught?* Her hands turned clammy as the machine was taking a little too long to read her card. Finally, the scanner turned green, allowing her to pass through. Malaika exhaled, grateful that Roman's illegal activities were paying off.

She made her way up the elevators, being sure to keep her head down, not wanting to attract any unnecessary attention to herself. She got off on the fifteenth floor and headed down the hall towards Connor's suite.

A large glass window greeted her as she walked into the suite. A magnificent view of the city sat below her. Minimal in furniture, the room consisted of a small seating area, along with two large desks facing each other, one on either side of the room. Malaika assumed the desk with the giant cutout of her face belonged to her. She smiled as she took in Roman's cutout. As usual, his stony face gave away nothing. Malaika's face, on the other hand, was tomato red with wide eyes and a goofy grin. A second door next to Roman's desk led to Connor's personal office.

She breathed a sigh of relief at having made it this far. Malaika sat down at her desk and skimmed through the training binder Connor had left her. Using the time to her advantage, she memorized her duties and began color coordinating all of her tasks. She hoped that in the future she could put this job down on her resume, though the fake identity part she thought might cause a bit of a fuss.

She sat in silence, working to the ticking of the clock. When the shrill ringing of the telephone went off, she shrieked and jumped, slamming her knee on the desk. Mumbling curses under her breath, she reached for the phone with shaking fingers.

"H-Hello?"

"Hello, who is this?" a deep voice asked from the other side.

"My name is Mal-Madeleine. I'm Connor's new secretary," she lied.

"I see, well, Madeleine, will you let Connor know that there is a board meeting at noon today?"

"Yes, sir." She jotted it down. "May I please have your name?"

"Mr. Charles."

She wrote it down, thanked him, and then hung up.

"Hey, Malaika," Connor greeted as he opened the door.

"Hi Connor."

"You're here early."

"Nerves wouldn't let me sleep."

"Don't worry, you'll be fine," he said, patting her head.

Connor took a seat on the leather couch and flipped mindlessly through his phone.

"Oh, I almost forgot. You have a board meeting at noon today," Malaika said.

"Who called it?" he asked, not taking his eyes off of his phone.

"Mr. Charles."

Connor dropped his phone. "Charles called?"

"Y-Yeah." Malaika grew concerned by his reaction.

Connor nodded, making his way to the windows. "Roman will be here soon. When he arrives, you two have some tasks to complete. If you run into anyone, remember to use your fake names."

Connor froze at his own words. His eyes bulged as he stared at Malaika. "Damn it! I forgot to bring your disguises." He ran a hand through his hair, exhaling sharply.

Malaika's heart dropped. *She and Roman were exposed.*

"Okay, don't panic." Connor paced the room. "Liam and my uncle don't show until twelve on weekends. Eva should be awake soon, so I'll have her drop off the disguises before Liam and my uncle get here. We should be fine. We'll be fine."

Malaika was unsure. Her stomach was in knots. It was risky, really risky, but what were the odds that they'd be found out the one time they forgot their disguises? Connor was right. They would be fine. Her clammy hands should have warned her otherwise.

Malaika nodded, watching as Connor locked himself in his private office. She answered a handful of emails and took a few calls while she waited for Roman to arrive. A few minutes later, the door to Connor's suite was thrown open. Roman stormed in with a furious look on his face.

"R-Roman, are you all right?"

He grunted in response. Roman stormed over to Connor's office and pounded on the door.

"Come in!" Connor said.

Malaika opened the search engine on her computer, wanting to know if there was a male equivalent of menstrual cycles. That would help explain Connor's and Roman's sudden mood shifts. Roman came out after a few minutes, dressed in a crisp white shirt and black slacks with a tie hung awkwardly at his neck.

"Screw it," he said, throwing the tie aside. "Come on, Munequita, we got work to do."

Malaika grabbed the spare folders and scurried after him. She stopped when she saw Roman had frozen in his spot. His eyes were blank and glazed over, giving nothing away. Malaika followed his line of vision and saw that he was staring at the cut-out of his face. With his jaw ticking, he strode forward, grabbed the cut-out and threw it into Connor's office. A muffled crash, followed by Connor's creative cursing, echoed through the room.

"Let's go," Roman said.

He held the door open for Malaika. The two walked down the hall and entered the elevator, trying to avoid eye contact with the man inside.

"Which floor?" he asked.

"Second please, thank you," Malaika said.

"Are you two working for Connor?"

Roman nodded.

"My name's Wyatt. I'm Connor's intern." He stuck out his hand.

Roman shook it once. "Rome."

"What's your name?" Wyatt asked Malaika.

She looked up, meeting his aqua eyes. They reminded her of the ocean. Usually, she found the blue waves enchanting and wanted to join them, but looking into Wyatt's eyes had her coiling away from the thoughts of submerging in the ocean's cold waves. "Madeleine." She took the hand he held out.

"Nice name."

Malaika shook his hand and tried to pull back, but Wyatt did not let go. She looked up at him in question. Wyatt smiled in return. Roman grabbed Malaika's arm, easily pulling her away. Wyatt narrowed his eyes at Romans retreating figure.

"Nice meeting you guys. I look forward to working with you," he said as the doors shut.

Malaika turned back to look at him. He winked, a little smirk painted on his lips. Malaika turned away and suppressed the shiver that threatened to run down her spine. Putting him out of her mind, Malaika and Roman got to work. If they wanted their plan to succeed, they needed to stay focused. They could not afford any distractions.

The two made their way back to the office. Malaika took a seat at her desk while Roman went into Connor's suite. His eyes were unusually focused. She heard Connor's questioning concern as Roman stood in the doorway.

"That Wyatt guy—" Roman began as he shut the door behind him.

Malaika wondered what was on Roman's mind. A low beep caught her attention. Wyatt walked into the office with a stack of papers in his arms. He smiled at Malaika and placed the papers on her desk.

"Since Rome already claimed that desk, you and I can share this one. We'd be a pretty good fit, don't you think?"

"There isn't any room here. I'll have a desk brought up for you. I don't think you'll fit."

"It'll be tight, I can tell, but I'll fit."

Malaika stared at Wyatt, wondering why he was smirking at her. She played his sentence in her mind a few times. The blood drained from her face when she realized what he was implying. Before she could find her voice to fight back, Roman had already thrown Wyatt to the ground. He towered over Wyatt's sprawled body.

"You're fired. Get lost."

Wyatt choked. He looked at Connor, who stood in front of his suite doors with a nonchalant expression on his face.

"C-Connor?" Wyatt whimpered.

Connor shrugged. "I only have three rules. You already broke the first one. This was just the icing on the cake. Now get out before my friend here drags you out."

Wyatt stared at Roman, his fists balling. Roman took a step forward. Wyatt instantly put his arms up in surrender.

"All right, all right, I'm leaving." He grabbed his backpack and ran out the door, sparing a glance back at Malaika.

Malaika squirmed in her chair, not liking his dark gaze. Roman moved to block her from view, shielding her from Wyatt's disgusting gaze.

"You good, darling?" Connor asked.

Malaika nodded. Connor smiled at the two, then went back to his office.

Roman took a seat at his desk. He and Malaika sat in silence, lost in their own thoughts. Malaika's heart skipped a beat at Roman's thoughtful actions. Though violent, there was kindness in them. She looked up at him and blushed when she found him staring at her. She tore her gaze away and fiddled with her fingers. A knock on the door caught their attention. Malaika got up and answered it.

"Oh, you must be Mrs. Warren," Malaika said, letting her in. "Nice to meet you."

Mrs. Warren gave her a polite smile.

"Connor will be out in just a moment," Malaika said, leading her to the couch. "Would you like anything to drink in the meantime? Coffee, tea?"

Mrs. Warren shook her head. "Oh no, I'm fine, dear."

Malaika nodded and headed back to her desk. Suddenly, the door flew open. Surprised, Malaika tripped over her chair and fell to the ground, her glasses flying off.

"Mom!" an obnoxious voice ran out.

Malaika got on all fours and squinted her eyes, trying to find her glasses.

"Yes, dear?" Mrs. Warren asked, as calm as ever.

"You promised me a new Balenciaga purse for my birthday," the voice whined.

Malaika had her hands against the woolen carpet, trying to find her glasses, for without them she was blind. Warm hands slid her glasses back onto her face. Malaika looked up, squinting as her blurred vision cleared. Her eyes focused on Roman's intense gaze.

"Th-Thank you," Malaika whispered.

Her heart skipped a beat at his proximity. Roman held out his hand for her. Malaika's heart hummed at his thoughtful actions. She took his hand and fought back a smile as a pulse of electricity shot through her body at his touch. Roman pulled her up, then shoved his hands into his pockets.

"Your birthday party isn't until tonight. I couldn't give you your gift before the party, now could I?" Mrs. Warren said, breaking Malaika out of her trance.

"But Mom!"

"Shut up," Roman said.

"Excuse me?" The girl sneered at Roman.

"I said shut up, *mujer*," Roman said, not taking his eyes off Malaika.

"Do you have any idea who you're talking to?" Her voice raised an octave.

"Yeah, I do." His eyes moved across Malaika's facial features. His gaze flew from her thick eyebrows to her amber eyes, down to her rosy lips. Malaika stood frozen, not understanding why he was watching her so closely.

"You're the girl who cheated on my boy," he said, finally turning around to look at her.

Malaika cursed in her head. *Roman! You're going to get us killed!*

Shocking Malaika, Mrs. Warren started laughing. "Britney, don't pick a fight against someone you can't beat."

Connor emerged from his office. He skipped to Mrs. Warren, a smile on his face.

"Ah, Connor, good to see you. By the way, I love the new assistant. He's quite the man," Mrs. Warren praised, making Roman turn tomato red.

"That he is." Connor threw him a friendly wink.

Malaika ducked her head, hiding her amused grin.

"Come on in," he ushered the pair of women into his office.

"Did she really cheat on your friend?" Malaika asked.

"That's Connor's ex," Roman said, heading to the coffee machine. "They were engaged."

Malaika choked on her spit, whipping her head to the side so fast she was surprised she did not get whiplash. "What? Why would Connor want to marry her?" Malaika asked. She spared a quick glance at the door to ensure it was still shut. "She seems vile."

"That she is," Roman agreed, then took a sip of his coffee. "He proposed to her out of guilt. They had been together since high school and he felt pressured to marry her, but when Connor caught her with another guy in his bed, he had enough reason to call it off."

"And he's been with Eva since?" Malaika asked, her curiosity peaking.

"Not exactly, no. For a short while, his family arranged him into an engagement. Purely business."

"What do you mean?"

"Connor was supposed to marry another girl but wasn't interested in the business deal, so he turned it down."

"Who was he supposed to marry?" Malaika's mind became more and more jumbled by the minute.

"You," a smooth voice said from behind the whispering duo.

Malaika whirled around. Her heart stopped beating at the man's words. Roman's coffee mug slipped and fell to the floor. The porcelain shards echoed through the deathly quiet room.

"Kidding." The newcomer chuckled. He straightened up and smoothed down his sharp coal grey suit. Connor's office door opened up. With a fake smile plastered on his lips, Connor walked the women to the door, bidding them goodbye.

The mysterious man ran a hand through the top of his jet black hair. Though his back was to Connor, Malaika was positive he was aware of the effect he had on Connor. Connor's enraged face matched his bright orange locks. His body was taut with nervousness, his eyes bulging in anger. Roman, Malaika noticed, stood a little straighter as he took in Connor's appearance. Malaika realized that the man standing before them was an enemy.

"Charles." Connor composed himself, smoothing down his flaming tresses. "What are you doing here?" He moved forward to stand in front of Mr. Charles, blocking Malaika from his line of vision.

"Just came to visit my new co-workers," Mr. Charles replied.

"Sure you are."

Mr. Charles clenched his jaw, momentarily breaking his cool façade. "I wanted to remind you we both have to attend Britney's party tonight."

"I can't make it. My secretary and assistant are going in my place. Since two people are already attending, you won't have to go either."

"I'll take Malaika instead. It'll be rude if no one from the family attends," Charles said, looking at his watch.

Malaika's heart dropped when Mr. Charles spoke her name. He knew who she was. Connor's fists balled, the veins in his hands bulged dangerously. *Now that Mr. Charles knew who she was, what would he do?*

"Never mind then, I'll take her," Connor said.

"I'll pick you up at eight o'clock," Mr. Charles said, ignoring Connor.

Malaika stared open-mouthed at the scene in front of her. Mr. Charles turned on his heel and left the room. She had to grit her teeth to keep from screaming out in frustration. *She was not an object!*

"Who the hell was that?" she asked, losing her temper.

"That was Mr. Charles," Connor said. With his lips at Malaika's ear he whispered, "He wants to marry you."

# CHAPTER TEN

## Breathless

NIGHT HAD FALLEN. MALAIKA stared out at the glass ceiling and took in the indigo sky before her. Infinite stars shined down on her, the moon a guiding white orb in the inky darkness.

"Come on, time to get you dolled up." Malaika broke out of her trance as Eva's calming voice danced around her. "Are you ready for tonight?" she asked, handing Malaika a bathrobe.

Malaika took it and slipped it on as she stepped out of the bubble bath. "As ready as I'll ever be." Malaika sighed.

"That's the spirit!" Eva cheered, leading Malaika out of the bathroom. "Here, put your dress on, then I'll do your hair and makeup." She handed Malaika a two piece beaded black dress.

"I thought I was going to wear the red dress?" Malaika asked.

"Yeah, but Meredith saw this and insisted you wear it." Eva shrugged. "Speaking of Meredith, I'll go get her before Amara can sink her claws into her."

Malaika slipped the dress on, admiring the beautiful chiffon fabric. It was soft to the touch. The pleated skirt flowed down her body. The beaded halter top shone under the light, sparkling like a thousand stars in the sky. A knock on the door caught her attention. "Come in."

Jet's head peeped through the door. He grinned at Malaika and stepped inside. "Dude, you won't believe what I just did." He laughed.

Malaika looked at him, a cold sweat breaking out across her forehead. Seeing as he was Roman's brother, it couldn't have been anything good. "What did you do?"

"I put itching powder in Amara's underwear," he said, his eyes gleaming with excitement.

Malaika shot up in panic. "You what?"

He guffawed. "It's going to be so epic. Her date is coming over tonight. I'll record the whole thing for you," he said.

Despite her nervousness, Malaika laughed. "Sounds good, but if we get caught, it's all on you."

Jet nodded. "Don't worry, I got this."

"All right, it's glam time," Eva said, setting Meredith on the bed.

"Where's Angel?" Malaika asked, as she popped on her contact lenses.

"Roman's watching over her until his mother comes home. Have you met her yet?" Eva asked, brushing through Malaika's tangled locks.

Malaika shook her head. It had been two days since Roman and his siblings moved in. Their mother, who she had yet to meet, would come by in the early hours of the morning. She only slept for about four hours, then went back to work.

"You'll get to meet her tonight. She gets off early," Eva said, as she took a section of Malaika's hair and twirled it around the curling iron.

Eva worked in silence, allowing Malaika to mull over her thoughts. Mr. Charles' greedy little eyes swam in Malaika's mind. His serpent smile and predatory stance danced behind her closed lids. Malaika was afraid of him, and rightfully so. Just a few short hours ago, Connor revealed to her Mr.

Charles' true intent. He wished to marry her for her inheritance.

Upon his death, Malaika's grandfather had passed his wealth onto her. Unfortunately, this wealth could only be accessed once Malaika was married. Now, along with the O'Neals, there was another money hungry monster Malaika had to add to her list of enemies. Malaika felt a headache growing as she thought of the root of this nightmare. *Money.*

The O'Neals and Mr. Charles had struck a business deal with her parents. Unfortunately, her parents' venture failed. In order to protect themselves from being sued, her parents offered Malaika's inheritance. The O'Neals, being devious and slick in nature, left off a few zeroes when informing Mr. Charles just how much money Malaika had. Not interested in her measly sum, Mr. Charles turned the offer down, instead striking a deal to be paid back in increments.

Now that Mr. Charles knew the extent of Malaika's wealth, he wanted her. Malaika knew he would take any means necessary to have her, or rather, her money.

Malaika rolled her eyes at the thought of Mr. Charles. He would go to any lengths to get his hands on more money. *He was already swimming in it! What would a few more blue faces do for him?*

"All right, you're all done," Eva said, waking Malaika from her trance.

Malaika looked in the mirror. Her heart soared as her reflection stared back at her. Her copper locks were curled and pinned to the side, crimson red painted her lips, natural smoky tones sat on her eyelids, and her once lifeless eyes seemed to have recovered some of their previous spark. Malaika pulled Eva into a hug, grateful tears springing into her eyes. She felt beautiful and confident.

"Thank you, Eva," she said.

"Oh, you're more than welcome, darling. Have fun tonight."

"Holy shit!" Jet exclaimed in awe. "Yo, Malaika, want to go out?"

Malaika laughed, a goofy grin erupting across her face. Malaika thanked her once more, then made her way out of the room as Jet continued his shower of compliments.

"Mm mm mm, Roman is one lucky guy," he said, running a hand through his hair. "Hit me up in ten years," he said as the door shut.

Malaika shook her head, laughing to herself. She froze at the top of the staircase as she caught sight of Roman emerging from the library. A fitted black suit enveloped his tall frame. The dark fabric accentuated his sculpted body. His jet black hair was slicked back into a bun, strands of raven locks framed his face. *He was beautiful.* Malaika tore her gaze away. Heat crept up her spine and settled onto her cheeks.

"Hello."

Malaika looked up, searching for the source of the sound. A stunning woman with warm brown eyes and honey skin smiled at her.

"Hello," Malaika greeted, shaking her hand. "You must be Roman's mother. It's nice to meet you."

She smiled at Malaika. Kindness radiated off of her, warming Malaika's heart and soul.

"Please call me Carmen. It's good to meet you as well. I wanted to thank you for allowing my kids to stay here," she said.

"It's no problem at all," Malaika assured, her ears burning.

"Thank you, Malaika." Carmen gave her a quick embrace. "I'll let you go now. I don't want you to be late."

Malaika smiled and made her way down the staircase. The doorbell rang. Roman answered it. Malaika froze mid-step when she recognized the man at the door. Mr. Charles was here.

"Connor!" Roman said. "Your friend is here."

Connor ran down the stairs, coming to an abrupt stop when he saw Mr. Charles standing in the foyer. "What are you doing here?" he asked, storming towards the cool, collected man.

Mr. Charles did not answer. Instead, he stared up at Malaika. She met his gaze and felt a chill go down her spine. He smirked in response, his eyes gleaming with power. Malaika was sure he was aware of the effect he had on her.

"I'm here to pick up my date," Mr. Charles said.

Roman tore his gaze away from Mr. Charles, finally taking notice of Malaika. His jaw dropped as he took her in. Malaika grew nervous as he continuously gaped at her. *Did she really look that bad?*

"Munequita," he mouthed.

Roman seemed to snap out of his trance as Mr. Charles charged up the stairs, stopping in front of Malaika.

"May I?" He held his arm out.

Malaika hesitated, not knowing what to do. Mr. Charles forcefully took her hand. Malaika tried to break free but there was no need, seeing as Roman shoved Mr. Charles away. Mr. Charles fell down the marble steps and slid across the foyer. His back slammed into the open door.

"Don't touch my girl," Roman seethed, pulling Malaika behind him.

Malaika's heart did somersaults as Roman referred to her as *my girl.*

"I already told you that Roman and Malaika would go to the party. There's no need for you to be here," Connor said, not bothering to hide his amused grin.

Mr. Charles stood up, his back rigid and posture tight. He smoothed down his suit. His enraged eyes met Roman's. "I'll be seeing you all soon. Good evening," Mr. Charles said, his snake-like eyes flashing dangerously.

"Let's go, Munequita." Roman motioned for her to follow. Malaika nodded and trailed after him to the garage. Candace tossed him the keys to the sleek black sports car. The two got into the car and took off.

"You good?" Roman asked, breaking the tense silence.

Malaika nodded in response. "Thank you, Roman." She was grateful that he kept her away from Mr. Charles' slimy hands.

"No problem."

"That was impressive."

A grin broke out across his usually stony face. "That was nothing." His eyes shined with excitement.

Malaika rolled her eyes, amused at his childlike side. She liked this side of Roman. The easy-going teddy bear who'd knock you out without a second thought. They made their way to the party in silence. Unlike before, Malaika did not find the silence suffocating.

"Here we are," Roman said, pulling up to the massive estate.

The two were greeted by fire breathers. Bright orange flames spilled from their mouths as they ushered the two out onto the lawn. Malaika's eyes widened in awe. Britney really knew how to throw a party. Men dressed in sleek suits and women draped in elegant gowns lined the doors, wanting to be let in. Fireworks cracked in the night sky, casting colorful glows on their faces. The two made their way up the stone steps. Malaika hooked her arm through Roman's out of habit. She felt Roman tense at the sudden contact.

"S-Sorry," she said.

She made way to remove her arm, but he placed a hand over hers, silently assuring her it was all right. Malaika's skin tingled as Roman's calloused palm brushed against the back of her hand. Hoping her cheeks weren't blazing red, Malaika watched luxury cars pull up. One by one, guests dressed in designer clothing and jewelry stepped out, arrogant smirks painted on their lips. She rolled her eyes. *Rich bastards. But then again, she was one as well.*

"Invitation?" the butler asked, holding out a gloved hand.

Roman handed him the intricately detailed gold card. The butler examined the card for a moment then handed it back to the duo, a fake smile on his lips. "Welcome. Do enjoy yourselves."

The two headed inside the mansion, suddenly over-whelmed by the amount of guests. What was more suffocating was the scent of pride and entitlement that swam in the air.

"Champagne?" offered the server.

"Er, no thank you." Malaika politely declined.

Roman, she noticed, put back the champagne flute he had grabbed, a pink blush spreading across his cheeks. Clearing his throat, he nodded his head towards the birthday girl. Malaika pulled out an envelope from her clutch.

"Good evening," Malaika said, as they approached Britney. "The O'Neal family wishes you a happy birthday. Connor unfortunately could not be here tonight, though he sends his best." Malaika handed Britney the envelope.

Britney took the envelope, trembling with excitement. Her eyes widened when she saw what lay inside. "Thanks!" She smiled, her brown eyes sparkling. For a moment, Malaika could see why Connor fell in love with her. The warmth radiating in the depths of her eyes was enchanting enough to make anyone fall for her.

"Excuse us," Roman said and, with a featherlight touch on her elbow, guided Malaika away.

As Malaika and Roman headed towards the tables, two men stopped them. Malaika looked up, taking in their crisp suits and sharp ties. *Board members.*

"Good evening. Our apologies if we seem too straightfor-ward, but did you say you came in place of the O'Neals?"

Malaika hesitated. She was thankful when Roman took over.

"The O'Neals find it hard to control their liquor. It was in their best interest to avoid an event like this where temptation is everywhere."

Malaika winced, her cheeks burning up as the memory of a drunk Mrs. O'Neal played in her mind. Roman was spot on. The O'Neals were lightweights.

"I see. That is understandable. I heard at a previous gathering, Mrs. O'Neal lost her temper and attacked one of the guests." The board members gossiped amongst themselves.

Malaika's face blazed as the humiliating beating she had received from Mrs. O'Neal flashed in her head. She blinked away the tears that surfaced. Her cheeks stung, reminding her she was nothing more than a game piece.

Roman tugged Malaika along. He led her to an empty table. The two took a seat, feeling out of place, as the sea of unfamiliar faces doubled. A server placed two plates of food in front of them. Malaika, too nervous to speak to Roman, picked at her food.

"You really aren't going to eat anymore?" Roman asked Malaika, eyeing her barely touched plate of food.

Malaika nodded. "I'm not hungry." She was in unfamiliar territory. In order to feel safe, she needed to do something that made her feel as if she were in control. Though the world was spiralling around her, at least she could still control what she ate. She was sure Roman was unconvinced, though he stayed silent.

The pop music suddenly shifted, transforming into a gentle tune. A slow, romantic melody echoed throughout the room. The lights dimmed. The golden glow from the table candles illuminated Roman's flawless complexion. Malaika looked up and met his gaze. Neither of the two spoke a word as they stared each other down. The energy between the two was confusing. On one hand, she felt sparks of electricity sizzling between the two, and on the other, she felt a line being drawn. She didn't want to cross it, but she didn't want to stay where she was, either. Malaika gulped as Roman's gaze flew to her lips for a split second. She met his eyes once more, but like before, his gaze changed. His eyes were no longer welcoming. Instead, they were guarded. His walls were back up.

"I'll be right back," Malaika said, wanting to escape the tense atmosphere. Being so close to Roman under that soft atmosphere was unsettling. She had never felt her heart race that fast before. *Was she sick?*

Malaika balled her trembling hands, trying to regain control. Closing her eyes, she took three deep breaths, ordering her body to calm down. Eventually, her hammering heart slowed down. Her racing thoughts came to a stop and her trembling limbs fell still. Back in control, Malaika made her way to Roman.

"May I have this dance?" a deep voice asked from behind her.

Malaika turned around. In front of her stood a muscular man, maybe in his early twenties. Before she could respond, Roman's familiar hand took a hold of hers. "Keep that filthy gaze to yourself," he said, then dragged Malaika to the middle of the dance floor. Without a word, he placed his hands on Malaika's waist and pulled her close. Her skin burned under his scorching touch. Her body tingled as his warm hands guided her over the dance floor.

Malaika looked at her feet as the next song began. The two danced in silence. Not a word spoken, nor a breath taken. Malaika was lost in her thoughts, confused, but content as she entered unfamiliar territory.

Without warning, Roman stopped. Malaika looked up as his hand travelled up to her arm. His fingers traced the bruise on her bare skin. Four thin violet bruises wrapped around her upper arm. *Liam had left his mark.* With a featherlight touch, Roman's warm fingers touched the bruises. He let out a shaky breath.

"Are you all right?" he asked.

Malaika nodded. "It doesn't hurt." It was true. Malaika was used to being abused. This was nothing for her. She didn't want Roman to worry for no reason.

He dropped his hand and placed it on her waist again, continuing the dance. The two twirled around the dance floor. Malaika, despite being a nervous wreck, was having the time of her life. Unlike being in Liam's arms, where she felt trapped and caged, in Roman's she felt free and alive. Dancing with him was the most fun she'd had in a long time.

"*Te ves bonita*," Roman whispered in a husky voice.

His eyes were clouded, dark thunderclouds rumbling dangerously. Malaika hadn't the slightest idea what he meant, but her cheeks burned and her heart raced once more. Roman spun Malaika around, pulling her close. His mouth rested by her ear. Malaika gasped as his cool breath tickled her neck.

"He's watching us, Munequita," he whispered, his voice filled with urgency.

"Who?" Malaika didn't like the dangerous tone his voice took on.

"Charles."

"We need to go."

Roman pulled away and nodded in agreement. Her body suddenly felt cold. He took her hand in his and led Malaika out of the mansion. The two froze when they made it back to the car. They were not alone. Even in the dim moonlight, Malaika could see the greed shining in Mr. Charles' dark eyes. Roman pulled Malaika behind him as Mr. Charles and his men advanced forward.

"What do you want?" Roman asked in a steely voice.

"You already know," he replied lazily.

"Fucking coward. You can't do shit yourself. You need the entire crew, don't you?" Roman spat out, angered by Charles' spineless act.

Malaika gulped as her eyes scanned the scene before her. Mr. Charles' men outnumbered them. Her hands turned clammy, a sheen of sweat formed on her forehead. Mr. Charles shrugged, unaffected by Roman's words.

"Malaika," Mr. Charles spoke directly to her. "Unless you wish for me to drain every penny from Ms. Rodriguez's pockets, I suggest you sign these." He held out a manila folder.

As soon as Mr. Charles threatened Roman's family, Malaika stepped up to the plate. "What are they?" she asked.

"Trade papers." His response was vague.

Malaika, unlike Roman, realized instantly what Mr. Charles meant. As Roman was still in the dark about her involvement with the family, he did not have the slightest idea what Malaika and Mr. Charles were referring to. By trade papers, he meant for her to give her inheritance to him rather than the O'Neals.

Roman yanked her back as she made way to sign the papers. "Munequita."

"Roman." She yanked her hand away. "I will not let your family fall apart."

Roman's eyes went wide. "Yo-You would..."

He was at a loss for words. Seeming to come back to reality, he shook his head, a hint of a smile erupting. With gentle hands, he pulled Malaika back. "If you make her sign those papers, I'll make sure the video of you screwing your secretary goes to headquarters."

Malaika, as well as Mr. Charles, could tell there was promise behind his words.

"You have a big mouth," Mr. Charles said, advancing forward.

Malaika grabbed Roman's hand, panicking. He squeezed it reassuringly.

"Maybe I should shut you up." Mr. Charles snapped his fingers.

Like a pack of ravenous hyenas, his men circled the two. Mr. Charles grinned as he saw the fear spreading across their faces. "See you at work, Malaika." Mr. Charles winked, then sped off into the night.

Roman put his fists up, ready to take on the three men.

Malaika tugged Roman's hand. "Roman, let's run, we're outnumbered."

"No, we're not," he said, then grabbed her arm.

Malaika gasped as she found herself suddenly airborne. Roman swung her with one arm, her legs slamming against the men's heads. A sharp pain shot through her legs at the impact. They fell down, temporarily dazed. Roman set her down as she fought to catch her breath. *That was fun. Terrifying, but fun.*

Malaika watched, amazed, as Roman knocked all the men unconscious before they got the chance to get back on their feet.

"Let's go home." Roman wrapped his hand around her wrist and gently pulled her along.

Malaika saw Roman's knuckles were red, the skin now ruptured, with traces of scarlet blood seeping through. The drive home was silent, both Malaika and Roman struggling to fight off the adrenaline wave. Soon enough, the house came into view. Roman pulled into the garage and killed the engine. Neither of the two made a move to get out.

"Are you all right?" Malaika asked, sneaking a glance at him.

His jaw was clenched as his eyes stared straight ahead. "I'm fine, you?"

"I'm all right."

Despite all the craziness, she felt perfectly at ease. She felt safe; she felt alive, and she could, for the first time in a long time, breathe. He stepped out of the car, opening Malaika's door for her.

"Thank you," she whispered.

As usual, Roman granted her his signature grunt. Silently, the two headed up the staircase towards their respective bedrooms.

"Good night, Roman." She paused, then let out her thoughts before she could lose her confidence. "You looked handsome tonight."

Roman froze, his eyes widening a fraction.

"S-Sorry, it just came out. I didn't mean to offend you." Malaika ducked her head, avoiding his gaze. *Stupid, stupid, stupid.*

Roman chuckled, his breaths hushed. Before she could register what was happening, rough hands cupped Malaika's face and soft lips met her forehead. "Goodnight, Munequita."

# CHAPTER ELEVEN

## Baby Steps

DESPITE LIVING IN THE same house, Malaika and Roman had two different destinations. Malaika was currently in school, taking detailed notes in history class, while Roman was nowhere to be seen.

Malaika spared a glance back at Amara. She was busy tapping away on her phone. Clearly, she was going to depend on her father's money to survive. Too bad her dream would soon shatter. Malaika and Roman were planning on draining their family of every penny.

Amara looked up, met Malaika's gaze, and gave her a tight smile. It looked as if she finally realized that while Malaika would say nothing to her, her friends would. Malaika turned away, smiling to herself as she thought of the prank Jet pulled on her. Here she sat, almost eighteen years old, being protected by a thirteen-year-old boy. Jet was just like Roman, a no filter fighter with a strong sense of justice, always protecting the ones close to him.

The class droned on, Malaika growing more and more anxious by the minute. With only a handful of seconds left in class,

Roman was still nowhere to be seen. The door flew open just as the dreaded bell rang.

Roman stood there out of breath, clothes ruffled, and knuckles bruised. His eyes searched the room. As soon as his gaze landed on Malaika, his tense posture softened, the muscles in his arms loosened, and his steel-like gaze lost their intensity.

"Mr. Rodriguez...present," Ms. Williams said as the last student left the classroom.

Roman looked at their teacher, a small smile of thanks on his lips. Malaika knew if he received another absence, his mother would have to go to court.

"Thank you." His eyes shone with gratitude.

Ms. Williams nodded in return. "First and last time, Roman."

Roman nodded. His gaze met Malaika's. "Let's go."

Malaika stood and followed his tall frame out the door, smiling at Ms. Williams in thanks. Malaika desperately wanted to ask Roman where he had been, but taking in his trembling hands and cut knuckles, she knew better than to ask.

Amara stood outside the classroom, a knowing smirk painted on her lips. Malaika froze at the hostility shining in Amara's eyes. Roman's back tensed, his hands balled into fists. He stomped towards Amara, stopping just a hair's width away.

"This isn't over," he said.

"You're right. I'm just getting started." Amara's gaze flew to Malaika. "She's next."

Roman's fist flew forward. Amara's eyes went wide with horror. Malaika felt the blood leave her face at the sight of Roman's actions. He slammed his fist into the locker, just beside Amara's face.

"I'm the one you have a problem with. Don't get Munequita involved. If you touch a hair on her head, I'll make you wish your daddy would've kept it in his pants."

"I'm not afraid of you." Though Amara's voice didn't waver, her shoulders were hunched together, her body trying to curl away from Roman's fiery gaze.

Malaika looked around. The hall was now deserted. Only the three remained. Roman noticed this too. He took advantage of the lack of eyes, pulled out a switchblade, and held it against Amara's throat. Malaika's stomach lurched at the sight before her. The silver blade gleamed under the bright light. She was rooted to the spot in fear. Malaika couldn't bring herself to move. Not to save Amara, nor to stop Roman.

"Unenroll yourself by the end of the day. You came here to hurt Munequita, but as long as I'm here, I won't let you touch her. If you don't, I'll show you what these hands can do." He slid the back of the blade against her cheek.

Amara's mouth fell open and tears welled in her eyes. She whispered a weak *okay* and took off down the hall. Roman turned around to look at Malaika. She looked up at him. Though her heart was pounding, she didn't allow her fear to dictate her.

A million thoughts were swirling around in her mind. *What was Roman talking about? What had Amara done? Why was Roman late? Where was he in the morning? Why are his knuckles bleeding?* In her confusion, she asked the least important question.

"Why did you bring a switchblade to school?"

"It's fake. I stole it from the theater department."

Malaika paused. She wanted to ask him all the questions running through her head, but judging by Roman's guarded eyes, she knew asking would be futile. If she did, she'd be met with silence. The bell rang. Malaika and Roman jumped at the sound.

"You should get to class before the late bell rings," Roman said.

Malaika nodded and headed down the hall, leaving the bleeding bad boy behind. Susan was busy writing tutoring notes when Malaika took a seat next to her. She needed a sense of normalcy, so Malaika began babbling.

"How is he doing? Is he showing any progress"? Malaika asked, reading over the notes Susan passed to her.

A faint blush crawled on Susan's cheeks "Slowly but surely, I'm really proud of him."

Malaika noticed Susan's red cheeks, though stayed silent. Susan was naturally shy and Malaika doubted she would openly tell her if she had feelings for her tutee. The bell rang, signaling that class had begun. Malaika, for the first time, fantasized rather than pay attention.

When the bell rang, releasing the class, Malaika blushed as she realized she had not taken down any notes. Rather, she had absentmindedly doodled her first name with Roman's last name. A wave of embarrassment washed over her. She felt foolish and scratched out the doodles before anyone could see. She packed up, waved goodbye to Susan, and headed to her next class.

Malaika headed inside her classroom and took a seat in the front row. She glanced around the room. Amara was nowhere in sight. It seemed Roman's threat had worked. A chill swept down Malaika's spine as Roman's fiery glare played in her mind. She had never seen him that angry. Rather than flinching away, she found herself to be entranced by his powerful emotions.

"Munequita." Roman pulled out the chair next to her and took a seat.

"Roman."

Malaika was curious why Roman sat by her today. Surely it was not because he wanted to.

"Connor has some work for us." He handed her a folder.

*Of course he does.* Malaika looked over the contents of the folder. She was both impressed and concerned by the plans Connor had concocted. Malaika read over the plans twice. She deduced there were more cons than pros.

"This doesn't look like a good idea," Malaika whispered.

Connor's plan consisted of purchasing Liam's shares. This would have been a good idea, but the price tag, unfortunately, was much too high.

"If he's going to spend this much money, wouldn't it be better for him to buy Mr. O'Neal's shares instead?" Malaika asked.

Roman stared at her, his face blank.

"Mr. O'Neal has a higher position, so buying his shares would lessen the power he has," Malaika explained.

"That's a good idea, but how do we do that? I doubt the man would willingly sell his shares."

"That's true."

"Malaika? Roman? If you two are finished conversing, I would like to start the lesson now," the teacher's voice put an end to their conversation.

Malaika looked up, her face burning in response to the open-mouthed, wide-eyed stares she and Roman were receiving from everyone. Roman leant back in his seat, smirking in response.

"S-Sorry," Malaika said.

She tried to pay attention to the lesson, but feeling Roman's arm on the back of her seat made it difficult to focus. His body heat was seeping into the back of her neck. It was as if every inch of her skin was a live wire, sparking at the smallest of touches. She exhaled sharply as the bell rang and released her to lunch. She threw her books in her backpack and ran out, avoiding Roman's questioning gaze.

"We're eating outside today," Akira said as he fell into step with Malaika.

The two made their way outside to the large oak tree. Its crimson, auburn, and golden leaves shone under the sun's warm rays. Carina, Susan, and Justin made their way over to the two. Malaika caught sight of Amara making her way towards the picnic table.

"S-Spread out guys, quickly!" she said.

In the blink of an eye, backpacks and binders were thrown on the benches, and bodies sprawled out, leaving no room for Amara. Akira's foot was wedged somewhere between Justin's butt and Malaika's elbow, but they were too focused on the task at hand to complain.

Amara sent Malaika an icy glare filled with hate and malice. Malaika gulped. Goosebumps erupted on her arms. She knew she would have to pay for this later. Her heart thundered in her chest as Amara advanced forward.

"Munequita."

In an instant, Malaika calmed down. Her hands, which had begun to shake, stilled and her racing heart slowed to a smooth, steady beat. Amara scowled as she took in Roman's towering frame. He gave her a fiery glare.

"The clock is ticking, little girl."

Amara took the hint and left. Malaika sat up, moving aside for him. Justin grinned as he took in Carina, Susan, and Akira's wide-eyed stares.

"Er, guys, this is Roman. Roman, this is Carina, Susan, Akira, and you've already met Justin," Malaika said, trying to eliminate the awkward tension surrounding the group.

Carina was the first to regain her composure. She gave him a welcoming smile. "Hello, Roman."

"What's up, man?" Akira nodded, obviously trying to seem tough.

Malaika could tell he was shitting bricks. Roman nodded back, though he stayed quiet. A heavy silence settled around the group.

"So, um, the winter dance, will you all be attending?" Susan asked, trying to break the tense atmosphere.

Carina groaned, her eyebrow twitching. "Yes, the cheerleaders have to go."

"Are you going with anyone?" Justin asked.

She shook her head.

"I'll pick you up at seven."

Malaika hid a grin. That was as bold as Justin would ever get. Akira let out a throaty chuckle and passed her a cookie. She thanked him.

"You've lost weight," he said, handing her a granola bar as well.

Susan looked at Malaika disapprovingly. "You need to eat more."

Malaika nodded in agreement. She didn't think her nod convinced them because Akira opened his mouth and said what they all hoped would be buried forever. "You better not go back to being anorexic, Malaika, or else."

Everyone at the table fell silent. Malaika froze as she felt Roman stiffen beside her. She spared a glance at him from the corner of her eye. His face was blank, his eyes giving nothing away.

With shaking fingers, she bit into her cookie, not wanting to speak. Susan cleared her throat and changed the subject.

"So, um, Malaika, are you planning to go to the dance?"

"No," Malaika said, just as Roman answered "yes."

Everyone whipped their heads to face Roman, shock etched into their features. Roman's posture was still stiff, but at least his lips were moving.

"I'm taking her."

His proclamation left Malaika stunned. Her heart skipped a beat at his sudden announcement. The bell rang, releasing everyone. Without a backward glance, Roman stood up and walked away. Though his back was to her, Malaika saw Roman run a hand across his face, almost as if he were wiping away tears.

Malaika regained her composure, stood up, and made her way towards the glass doors. Akira caught up to her.

"Malaika, I'm so sorry. Please forgive me," he begged, his voice breaking.

"It's all right, Akira," Malaika said, pulling him into a tight embrace. "Accidents happen. Everyone makes mistakes."

"Yeah. Take your parents, for example," Carina said, as she stormed towards the duo.

"Carina, chill out," Justin said, pulling her back.

"Why the hell did you say that? Especially in front of Roman?" she asked, enraged that Akira revealed one of Malaika's most sensitive secrets.

"Carina, it's all right. It was just an accident," Malaika said. Akira already felt guilty. She didn't want him to be hurt anymore.

"I'm sorry," Akira whispered, on the verge of tears.

Susan squeezed Akira's hand. Carina sighed as guilt shined in her eyes.

"I'm sorry, Akira, I shouldn't have said any of that," she said.

He nodded in thanks, though kept his gaze down. Knowing that everyone's emotions were running high, Malaika waved goodbye, assuring everyone that she was all right. But she wasn't. She was a mess. A healing mess, though a wreck, nevertheless. Now, Roman knew. The mask she so carefully wore had been removed. Roman could see for a moment the ugly truth that hid underneath. *Now that he knew, what would he do?* Malaika pushed these depressing thoughts into the deepest crevices of her mind, not allowing them to break her.

Thankfully, the rest of the day went by without incident. As she was making her way out of her last class, Malaika spared one last glance in the lab. Roman, once again, had missed class.

Upon her arrival at the parking lot, she noticed her tires were slashed. *Amara.* She eyed the mess in front of her. For a moment, Malaika felt as if she were drowning. She was losing control again. It seemed as if the light she had begun to see at the end of the tunnel was slowly starting to dim. She remembered she was alone, weak, and powerless. *Her enemies surrounded her. She could not win.*

A warm hand grasped hers. Malaika looked up and saw Roman. He pulled her towards his worn motorcycle. He got on, motioning for Malaika to sit behind him. Though nervous, Malaika knew Roman would never let her get hurt. She slid on, wrapping her arms around his waist. A swarm of butterflies flew around her stomach as her hands traced his sculpted body.

Turning around, Roman strapped the only helmet he had onto Malaika's head. Without warning, he took off. Malaika yelped, leaning into Roman's back. Roman, clearly surprised by the sudden contact, stiffened momentarily, then relaxed, his body eventually loosening in Malaika's arms.

Malaika enjoyed having her arms around Roman. She felt safe here, happy even. She couldn't be sure, but it seemed as if Roman were driving slower than usual. Malaika suspected he too enjoyed her presence, or perhaps her weight was slowing them down. Eventually, the two arrived home. Malaika reluctantly stepped off and returned Roman's helmet.

"Thank you," she said.

As usual, Roman grunted in response and made his way up the stone steps to open the door. Malaika kept her head down as the two headed to the kitchen. She was ashamed to meet his eyes. She feared what she would see in them. Mostly, she was afraid that his eyes would hold nothing but disappointment. And for some inexplicable reason, the thought of disappointing Roman hurt Malaika's heart.

"Welcome home," Candace said.

"Thank you. Will you please have my car towed?" Malaika asked. She stood on her tiptoes to whisper in Candace's ear. "I'm pretty sure Amara slashed my tires."

Candace rolled her eyes, and nodded. Malaika smiled in thanks and watched as Roman took Angel from Candace's arms. Lunch was a quiet affair. Roman ate with one hand, while the other held a bottle to Angel's lips. Though silent, Malaika could feel Roman's gaze burning into her.

She knew he was watching her to ensure she ate every bite. Not wanting to be lectured, she forced herself to finish her meal. As she took her last bite, Malaika saw Roman sigh in relief. While she was grateful for his concern, it was at the same time suffocating. Wanting a momentary escape, Malaika headed upstairs to her room.

"Meet me in the study in an hour. We have work to do," Roman said.

Shutting her bedroom door, Malaika made her way to her CD player and pressed play. Loud rock music pumped through the speakers. Laying flat in the middle of the room, she allowed the beating drums and screaming guitars to transport her to another world. Lost in the music, the melody and words stripped away her worries. She was free. She could breathe. If only for a moment.

Her thoughts flew back to lunch. Why did Akira have to reveal her secret to Roman? Her eating disorder was not something she liked to parade, and it most certainly was not a means to lose weight. Rather, it was a coping mechanism. It was a means to stay in control. Something that had been stripped away from her.

While Malaika was drowning under rules, restrictions, and regulations, her eating habits had become the only thing left she could control. She wasn't allowed to take the classes she wanted, go where she pleased, or meet who she wanted. She was nothing more than a puppet on strings, being pulled in a hundred different directions. The only thing left that was still in her control was food. She decided what went in and what came out. No one would take that from her. Not her parents, the O'Neals, or even the voice in her head.

"So you and Roman, huh?"

Malaika's eyes shot open at the sudden sound. She paused the tape and sat up. Liam stood just inside her room, peering down at her, his eyebrow raised cynically.

"It won't last, you know. You're two different breeds. You're spoon fed, he's not. He's poor, you're rich. You're a catch, he's nothing."

Malaika gritted her teeth as Liam strode forward. He kneeled down, sitting eye to eye with her.

"What's your problem?" Malaika glared at him, her fists tightening.

"You're my problem. You and Roman." His eyes glittered with malice.

Malaika flinched as he raised his hand. He traced his icy finger down the side of her face. Malaika sat frozen, too afraid to move. Her stomach lurched as he leaned forward.

"That expression she's making is one you should be familiar with." Roman walked into the room, his grey eyes gleaming dangerously. "It's disgust. I'm sure you've seen it before. Now back off before I lose my temper and break that hand of yours."

Malaika's heart jumped at Roman's words. Liam glared at him. The tension was thick in the air. The two boys stared at each other, fire practically spitting from their eyes. Liam silently challenged Roman. He reached out for Malaika again. Like a flash of lightning, Roman struck. He grabbed Liam's shoulders and slammed him into the wall. A deafening crack echoed through the room as the drywall caved in. Malaika yelped, her hands flying to her mouth.

"This is for Munequita," Roman said. He shoved his arm against Liam's throat, pinning him to the wall while his other hand wrapped around Liam's wrist. With a sneer, Roman twisted Liam's wrist. A loud pop echoed through the room. Liam's eyes went wide as his body registered what was happening. A moment of silence followed, and then Liam snapped. He let out a loud cry, his screams bounced off the walls. Roman let go of his wrist and covered Liam's mouth, silencing him.

"This time, it's just a sprain. If you ever touch her against her will again, I'll break every bone in your body." Roman said. He shoved Liam one more time, who looked on with horror in his eyes.

"Come on, Munequita."

Roman held his hand out for Malaika. She hesitated for a moment, indecision coating the knots in her stomach. One look at the venom in Liam's glare had her running. She ran forward and clung onto Roman. Blood rushed through her ears. Neither she nor Roman said a word as the two locked themselves in the study room. The minutes ticked by. Finally, Roman turned to look at her.

"Are you all right?"

His grey eyes held a multitude of emotions, stunning Malaika into silence. She nodded.

"Thank you, Roman."

He nodded back, his eyes going blank. Just like that, Roman's walls came up, keeping Malaika at arm's length once again. He let go of Malika's hand, cleared his throat, and motioned to the round table.

"This idea of yours got me thinking," Roman said, laying out some files.

"What's this?"

"It's the blueprint to the O'Neals' house. You want to buy the shares from the old geezer? This is the way to do it. He'll never sell his shares willingly, so if we go to his house and give his electronic consent through his personal computer, he wouldn't be able to build a solid enough case to win them back."

"Brilliant." Malaika was impressed. "How do we get in?"

"The front door."

*Roman would truly be the death of her.*

# CHAPTER TWELVE

## Just a Glimpse

ROMAN HAD NEVER WANTED Malaika to get a glimpse into his dark world, but the crimson blood splattered on the front of his shirt was hard to hide. It was three o'clock in the morning. He had just snuck back inside the deathly quiet house when the lights flicked on. Malaika stood at his bedroom door, a first aid kit held in her quivering hands.

Her sudden appearance surprised him. "M-Munequita, what are you doing here?"

She stayed silent, her honey eyes taking in the scarlet blood that ran down his body.

"It's not mine," he said, as she took a step forward.

"Was that supposed to make me feel better?" she asked as she took his arm and pulled him towards the bed.

Roman remained quiet and watched as she began wiping away the blood. "This is my house," Malaika started, as she dabbed at his cut and bruised knuckles. "Your enemies could have followed you here. They could very well become my enemies as well. Seeing as you thoughtlessly put not only yourself, but the members of this house in danger as well, you will tell me the truth."

Roman, though impressed by the power in her voice, stayed silent.

Malaika applied more ointment to his wounds. "Tell me the truth, Roman."

He turned his head away, keeping his lips sealed.

"NOW!"

Roman jumped, stunned by her sudden outburst. His heart pounded painfully in his chest. He took in her trembling figure with wide eyes. Munequita did not look like a little doll to him right now. Instead, she was a goddess. A bronze-haired, fuming, paradoxical goddess.

"J-Jet, it's Jet." He watched with bated breath as Malaika regained her composure. "Amara got revenge over the prank Jet pulled. She had him jumped at his school. The kids that were jumping him called their older brothers to join in. Amara promised she would pay everyone who took part in my little brother's beating."

Malaika froze, her hands flew to her mouth. Crystal tears welled in her eyes.

"That's why I was late for class. Jet called me over to help him," Roman said.

"Where were you right now?" Malaika asked.

"I would never put my hands on a child, no matter the sin. That doesn't mean I wouldn't beat his older brother." Roman's fists tightened as the bloody memories resurfaced.

"How many?"

"How many what?"

"How many people did you take on by yourself?" she asked, eyeing his swollen hands.

"I wasn't alone."

Before Malaika could comment, the door to Roman's bedroom flew open once again. Liam stood in the doorway. His cold, calculating eyes moved back and forth from Malaika's dainty figure to Roman's bloodied and sweaty body. "Some of us are trying to sleep. Can you keep it down?"

Amara joined him, a satisfied little smirk painted on her lips. Roman balled his fists, desperately trying not to lash out. Without a word, Malaika stood up and made her way to the door. Liam's eyebrows knitted together as he saw the anger coating Malaika's features. He was blissfully unaware of his sister's horrific actions.

"He can't touch you, but I can," Malaika said.

Without missing a beat, she pulled her arm back and swung, landing a hard hit on Amara's face, sending her toppling over. Liam caught her, his eyes wide with shock and confusion.

"Malaika!" he yelled, grabbing onto her outstretched fist.

Roman was on his feet in an instant. As he stormed over to the arguing trio, he struggled to control his violent tendencies. "Get your hands off of my girl."

His eyes were brewing with rage, promising that a bloodbath would soon follow if Liam failed to comply. Liam reluctantly removed his hold. His good hand wrapped around his wrist splint. Liam's gaze lingered on Malaika as Roman wrapped his muscular arms around her, pulling her back into the safety of his bedroom. Amara's enraged cries echoed around them as Roman shut the bedroom door.

Malaika stood still in Roman's hold. Roman stayed silent and held her close, knowing she was at her breaking point. Minutes passed. Both stayed still and quiet, trying to regain control of their jumbled thoughts and racing hearts. So much had happened in these past few moments, neither knew how to react.

"My hand hurts," Malaika finally said, breaking the tense silence.

Roman chuckled, leading her back to the bed. He grabbed the gel compress and applied pressure to her hand to help reduce the pain. "Nice punch."

Malaika grinned. "That was nothing."

In his eighteen years of life, never had anyone put themselves in harm's way to protect him. To protect his family. A
newfound respect formed in Roman's heart for the paradoxical girl in front of him. Once Malaika's hand stopped shaking,
Roman removed the compress. Malaika got up, thanking him.

"Where do you think you're going"? Roman asked, as
Malaika headed towards the door.

"To my bedroom."

"Do you really think I'm going to let you go out there after
what happened? You're staying with me tonight."

Malaika's cheeks flushed. She hesitated. Roman finally took
notice of Malaika's uncomfortable body language. His cheeks
burned as he realized what he was saying.

"I'll sleep on the couch. You can take the bed," he said,
grabbing the duvet.

Roman hit the lights, making his way back to the couch. As
the room was smothered in darkness, illuminated by nothing
more than starlight, Roman tensed as the static in the air
wrapped around his body. The electricity was heavy, almost
tangible. Exhaling sharply, he crossed his arms over his chest,
his fists balled. He was nervous, and it was obvious Munequita
was as well, but he wouldn't change his decision. If Amara
could harm a child over a silly prank, he could only imag-
ine the lengths Amara would go to in order to get revenge
against Munequita. Roman closed his eyes, hoping to have
a dreamless night, but to his pleasant surprise, he dreamt of
right hooks and motorcycle rides.

Malaika was making copies at the office when she heard
hushed voices speaking frantically. She poked her head into
the hall and saw Mr. Charles and Liam face to face. While
Liam was calm and composed, Mr. Charles was a mess. His

pale face was tomato red, the veins in his forehead were popping out, and his eyes were as wide as saucers.

"Trade with me!" he said.

Liam wore an amused smirk. It was clear that he found pleasure in Mr. Charles' suffering. *What were they arguing about?* Malaika quickly retreated into the copy room, when Liam's head turned in her direction.

"It's not my fault you turned down such a wonderful offer."

"You all lied to me! Give her to me and I'll give you one point five million dollars, a new car, and three percent of my shares," Mr. Charles said.

Liam chuckled in response. "The inheritance is worth more than that."

Malaika ducked behind a table as she heard his footsteps approaching. Colorful words left Mr. Charles' lips as Liam walked away. After hiding under the table for a few minutes, Malaika deemed it was safe to leave. She grabbed the copies and ran out the door, heading towards the elevators. In her nervousness, she all but fell into Connor's office. Roman glanced up at her noisy arrival. One look at Malaika's pale face sent him shooting up.

"What happened?" he asked.

"N-Nothing. I was just avoiding Mr. Charles," she said. "Sorry," she added, as she saw his shoulders sag in relief. Malaika shivered at the thought of Mr. Charles. Initially, she had been pleasantly surprised to find that Mr. Charles hadn't ratted them out. Turns out he only kept her identity a secret because he wanted to win her over, as this was the only place he had access to her. Connor and Roman had promised her they wouldn't let Mr. Charles anywhere near her.

Connor walked an elderly couple out the office. "It was nice seeing you, Mr. and Mrs. Chesterfield. Take care."

The couple smiled and thanked him. As soon as they stepped through the doors, Connor dropped the act.

"Ugh, shoot me now." He jumped onto the leather couch and stretched his long limbs. "Oh yeah, I forgot to tell you guys. You may have a shot with that little plan of yours," he said, sitting up, his exhaustion forgotten. "There's a party at the O'Neals' place this weekend which we need to attend."

Malaika didn't miss the look he gave her. By *we*, he meant *her*.

"When the party is in full swing, Roman and I will make a break for it and head for the old fart's office."

Roman nodded. "It'll be a long shot."

"It's the only shot we're going to get," Connor reminded him. "Besides, we've come out on top with less than this before." He gave Roman a meaningful stare.

Roman grinned. "That's true."

"Looks like we have ourselves a plan. Let's go home," Connor said, clapping his hands.

The three headed down to the parking garage. Malaika started her now fixed car while Roman and Connor argued about what music to play. Malaika smiled as she glanced at Roman. It was nice to see him enjoying himself, rather than be his quiet, brooding self.

It was late when they pulled in. While everyone was asleep, Roman, Connor, and Malaika sat in the living room, eating their dinner in silence, watching reruns on the television. Roman was the first to finish. "Night."

Malaika watched his retreating figure in silence. She felt guilty. *Why? She didn't know.*

"Remember, Malaika, stay by Liam at the party. One wrong move and you'll go through hell," Connor said.

Malaika nodded. "I know." *The game was nearing its end, and they had yet to make a move.*

# CHAPTER THIRTEEN

## Civilized Battles

THOUGH HE WOULD NEVER admit it, Roman's mind was swirling with panicked thoughts, anxiety, and nervousness. He and Connor sat on the roof, staring up at the infinite stars splashed against the inky indigo sky.

"Rome?"

"Yeah?"

Connor scratched his neck. Roman knew that whatever he had to tell him would elicit one of two reactions. He would either take it calmly or brew up a storm.

"During the party, no matter what happens, I need you to keep your distance from Malaika. If she's in trouble, please don't help her."

"Why not?"

"I can't get into specifics, just please promise to stay away from her. This is the only shot we have. We can't afford to fail."

Roman stayed silent, mulling over Connor's orders. Sighing in defeat, he nodded.

"I got you, man." He took one last puff from his joint, then put it out. For what he hoped was the last time.

"Boys, are you ready?" Eva asked, peeking her head out the window.

"Let's go kick some ass!" Connor jumped up.

Roman shook his head, hiding a grin at his enthusiasm. The three made their way out to the driveway, where Connor's signature electric blue car awaited them.

"What about Munequita?" Roman asked, noticing her absence.

"Malaika will arrive with Liam," Eva reminded.

Roman's hands balled into fists as an unfamiliar emotion took a hold of him. It began in his stomach and bubbled up to his throat. His mouth tasted bitter as he remembered that part of the plan was for Munequita to stick to Liam like glue. He didn't know why, but the thought of her with her arms wrapped around Liam had his heart pounding.

Nerves twittering, he settled back into his seat, mentally preparing himself for tonight's job. Suddenly cop chases, street fights, and drug deals seemed like child's play. Compared to his job tonight, all the dangerous acts he used to take part in seemed minor and meaningless.

Tonight, he would embark on a mission that not only broke multiple laws, but would also endanger his friends. Something he desperately wished he could prevent, but he knew that without his friends, he would never succeed. He needed his team at his side.

Without a word, he reached over and squeezed Eva's hand, as he caught sight of her staring nervously at Connor. Roman met her striking eyes, giving her a ghost of a smile. *Everything would be all right.*

"We're here," Connor said as pulled into the driveway.

Roman's eyes widened as he took in the vast estate that lay before him. He thought Munequita was rich, but compared to the O'Neals, her family's wealth seemed pitiful. What seemed like acres of land stretched out before him. The twinkling lights that surrounded the mansion illuminated the charcoal grey stone foundation. Golden light poured out the multiple glass windows. Luxury cars sat in front of the towering mansion.

"Twelve point five," Connor said.

"¿Que?"

"What was once an Italian castle is now a twelve point five million dollar mansion," he said, getting out of the car, his hand held out for Eva.

"Damn. With everything they have, they still want more?" Roman shook his head in disbelief.

Connor shrugged. "Some people, despite having it all, think they have nothing." He handed over his invitation as they reached the top of the stone steps.

The attendant inspected the intricately detailed card for a moment too long. Connor snatched it out of his hands, throwing the young man a glare.

"S-Sir," said the man, his lip quivering.

The butler next to him chuckled, his oversized white mustache twitching. "Mr. Connor is family. No need to worry, he will not harm you." His chocolate eyes twinkled with amusement and a hint of mischief.

Connor nodded at the butler in thanks, while Eva apologized to the attendant for Connor's behavior. Roman didn't blame Connor for his short fuse. They were about to commit a crime against one of the most powerful families on the east coast; they were bound to be nervous. The three entered the mansion. Exquisite designer gowns, sleek raven suits, and hundreds of glittering diamonds stood before them. The scent of money was practically dripping from the guests.

Feeling the panic bubbling in his chest, Roman and his friends distracted themselves by going over their plans in hushed voices and eating unhealthy amounts of shrimp cocktail and crostini. Roman observed their surroundings. Dread formed in his gut.

"Connor, there are a lot of witnesses here," he whispered as he reached for a glass of champagne. Munequita's eyes flashed in his mind as his fingers traced the cool flute. He retracted his hand as the night of the house party replayed in his mind. Munequita had trembled with fright when Amara shoved the cup of beer in her face. The thought of her anxious eyes had Roman turning away from his usual coping mechanism.

"We're going to need a distraction if we want to break into his office," Connor said, running a hand through his flaming locks.

Roman closed his eyes, a million thoughts and ideas swirling through his mind. He shifted through the pros and cons of each idea, finally landing on the most flashy and dangerous one. "Call the boys."

Eva and Connor looked at him, indecision painted on their features. Roman could tell Connor was debating in his head. After a few moments of tense silence, he nodded, taking out his phone.

"Wait," Roman said, putting a hand out to stop Connor from making the call. "Tell them about the risks first. They should know what they're walking into."

Eva nodded in agreement. Connor excused himself to make the call. Roman waited anxiously for his return. He hoped his friends came through. Suddenly, the lights dimmed. Roman reached out for Eva, pulling her slender frame behind him.

"It's all right Roman, it's just the first dance," she said, pointing to the middle of the room where the spotlight hovered, illuminating a familiar bronze-haired beauty.

"Munequita," Roman said as his gaze landed on her. He found himself at a loss for words as he took in her magnificent form.

Her copper locks were braided to the side, intertwined with baby's breath flowers. Her skin was a beautiful golden complexion, wine-stained lips, shimmering chestnut lids, dark full lashes, and her signature blushing cheeks. She was beautiful.

Absolutely beautiful. The only downfall was that the beauty before him had a disgusting pig latched to her side.

Roman's smile turned to a frown as he took notice of Malaika's dancing partner. Liam held her hand in his, twirling her around the dance floor. A brilliant flash of red against the intimate golden glow of candlelight. Roman struggled to suppress his anger. He shoved his fists into his pockets, hiding them from Eva's peering eyes.

Connor rejoined the two, an excited gleam in his emerald eyes. "They said yes. We're good to go!"

Roman sighed in relief. He made a mental note to thank his friends when this was over. Eva motioned for the two to follow her to the balcony overlooking the ballroom. In silence, the trio observed the multitude of couples swaying on the dance floor. An elegant orchestral composition played in the background, captivating the guests.

"He needs to watch his hands," Eva said, watching as Liam trailed his hands down to Malaika's bare back.

Roman chuckled as he played various scenarios in his mind, all resulting in a bruised and bloody Liam. "If they go any lower, I will break them for you."

Eva laughed, knowing there was promise behind his words. Connor cursed, his hands balling fistfuls of his hair. His eyes were wide with panic as they took in the scene in front of him.

"What the hell is he doing?" Connor's eyes moved around the dance floor, assessing the guests' reactions.

Mr. Charles, obviously a little more than tipsy, strode forward, latching onto Malaika's upper arm. He pulled her out of Liam's grasp, accidentally throwing her to the floor. Roman cursed. His rage took over, and he stormed off to beat Mr. Charles to a bloody pulp.

"No, Roman!" Eva said.

She grabbed onto his shoulders. Connor wrapped his arms around Roman's body, holding him in place. Roman struggled to break free. Connor applied more pressure, making it difficult for Roman to move.

"Remember our promise, Roman. No matter what, you can't go anywhere near Malaika," he said, his tone filled with urgency.

Roman closed his eyes. Malaika's honey eyes played behind his closed lids. Taking deep breaths, he felt his racing heart slow, and his shaking fists still. Nodding, he opened his eyes, promising Connor he was in control of himself. Connor, obviously still worried, loosened his hold.

"After this is over, I'll kill him," Roman said.

Eva grinned. "I'll help hide the body."

Connor shook his head, smiling. "'Atta boy."

He clapped Roman's back. The three headed to their respective positions. It was time to launch their plan into action.

Mr. Charles turned around to face Malaika with what seemed like an apologetic expression. He helped her to her feet. Malaika thanked him in a small voice, distancing herself, when she noticed Mrs. O'Neal's venomous glare.

Mr. O'Neal strode forward, his usually composed face quivering with just a hint of nervousness. Mr. Charles stood toe to toe with Liam, the hostility practically dripping off the two men.

"Get away from my fiancée," Mr. Charles said.

Malaika froze. *Had she heard him correctly? Fiancée?*

"What are you on about, Charles?" Mr. O'Neal asked, irritation etched deep into his facial features.

Mrs. O'Neal, Malaika noticed, diverted the guests' attention, leading them to the dining area.

"Malaika belongs to me. Not Liam."

It was then Malaika caught a whiff of the alcohol on Mr. Charles' breath.

"Let us take this conversation elsewhere," Liam said, holding his arm out for Malaika.

This seemed to enrage Mr. Charles even more. Before he could pounce, Mr. O'Neal placed a hand on his shoulder. To outsiders, it would seem like a friendly gesture, but Malaika could see the whites of Mr. O'Neal's knuckles. He, too, was enraged at the spectacle taking place before him.

For a moment, Malaika was grateful for Mr. Charles' sudden appearance. Had it not been for him, she would have never seen Mr. O'Neal's mask breaking. Watching him squirm with anxiety brought a smile to her lips.

The four made their way into the study. The blazing fireplace enveloped the quaint room in an auburn glow. Mr. O'Neal motioned for Malaika to have a seat. She nodded in thanks, taking a seat on the ivory chaise.

"All right Charles, tell me what this is all about," Mr. O'Neal said, pouring himself a glass of whiskey.

Liam situated himself behind Malaika. She could feel his body heat seeping into her. Malaika felt tiny and intimidated by the men surrounding her. While all three men were vastly different, they all wanted the same thing from her. *Money.*

"Malaika might be Liam's fiancée, but she is legally mine. I may have turned her down, but I have three months to make my final decision," he said, pulling out a manila envelope from inside his suit jacket.

Liam snatched the envelope from his hands, reading the contents of the letter that lay inside. Without warning, he tore the paper into shreds. Malaika watched with wide eyes as Mr. Charles began laughing.

"You fool! Did you really think I would give you the original documents? You truly are just a boy, Liam," he said, a manic gleam in his eyes.

Liam narrowed his eyes. His good hand balled into a fist.

"I turned Malaika down because you lied to me. Now, since I have three months, I can reclaim her," Mr. Charles said, reverting to his cool, collected self.

Malaika stayed silent, not bothering to stand up for herself. She would always be an object to them. Nothing more, nothing less.

"What you say is true, my boy, but Malaika and Liam have been publicly introduced into society. Tonight's gathering was to honor them. If she is seen marrying you, many of our clients and family members will view the O'Neals as a laughingstock. We will lose not only respect, but business as well," Mr. O'Neal said as he poured himself another glass.

Malaika realized the first glass was to calm his nerves and the second to celebrate his victory. Mr. O'Neal truly was a monster. Mr. Charles froze for a moment, pondering. What his uncle said was true. He eyed the extravagant engagement ring resting on Malaika's finger, his mind swirling with ideas.

If he, instead of Liam, were to marry Malaika, both clients and family members would laugh at the O'Neals. They would lose respect, credibility, and money. Everyone would assume that the newest addition to the family was nothing more than a high-end slut and that he was a whore.

He, along with the company, would lose money. But then again, if he married Malaika, he would gain more money than he could have ever imagined. Malaika had a fortune to her name, and if he made her his wife, he would easily become one of the richest and most powerful men in the world. A few laughs at his expense seemed like a small price to pay for infinite riches.

Mr. O'Neal moved forward, squeezing Mr. Charles' shoulder with crocodile tears brimming in his eyes. "I know you care for her, son, but Malaika is engaged to Liam now. There is nothing that can be done."

Mr. Charles' cool mask wavered for a moment. He slapped his uncle's hand away. "Shall I get law enforcement involved?"

Mr. O'Neal's booming laughter echoed around them. Malaika jumped, frightened by the sudden sound. Goosebumps rose on her skin at the malice hidden in Mr. O'Neal's laughter. He wiped a tear away dramatically. A victorious grin spread across his lips. "Law enforcement? What good would that do? I have the entire police department on my payroll!"

Mr. Charles' snake-like eyes narrowed into thin slits. Before he could strike, the revving of engines caught the group's attention. The monstrous roars grew louder and louder by the second. Malaika looked up as blaring headlights streamed through the glass walls. A scream escaped her lips as the neon green car crashed through the glass. Liam shoved Malaika, sending her sprawling towards the doors, far from where the neon car came to a screeching stop.

Malaika stood up on shaking legs as a built figure emerged from the car. The driver's face was masked, a dark silhouette against the moonlight. They held out a gloved hand for Malaika. Suddenly, screams erupted throughout the mansion. It seemed as if more vehicles were terrorizing the guests outside.

Turning tail, Malaika ran out of the room, heading up the stairs to the balcony. Motorcycles were piling in through the double doors, weaving in and out of the halls. People ran left and right, trying to find shelter amid all the chaos. Puffs of white smoke filled the foyer and ballroom as the vehicles circled the grounds.

"Connor, Roman! Where are you guys?" Malaika called out, searching for her friends. She yanked off her engagement ring and hid it in her clutch, not wanting Roman to see it. *He didn't know about her engagement. She planned on keeping it that way.*

The revving of another engine caught her attention. She turned around, hastily jumping out of the way when a sleek red motorcycle charged towards her. The driver shot out a hand, grabbing Malaika into their hold.

"I'm right here, Munequita." Roman's familiar voice calmed Malaika down.

Roman slowed, making a sharp turn as guards made their way up the east stairway. He cussed as he saw guards lined the west stairway as well. The only way to get out was to make a jump for it. A loud honk made its way into their ears. Roman laughed as he looked over the balcony. A truck lay below the two, an inflatable mattress on the bed.

"Hang on tight, Munequita."

Malaika tucked her head under his chin, wrapping her arms around his body securely. Roman revved the engine and sent the motorcycle flying towards the guards. The guards cursed and jumped out of the way as the motorcycle came hurtling at them at full speed. Roman wrapped his arms around her body and leapt off the balcony.

Malaika's heart thundered in her chest as they were airborne. Screams erupted as the guests took notice of the falling duo. Broken gasps left her lips as the two landed on the inflatable mattress. Malaika's breath knocked out at the sudden impact. Her vision blurred, spots danced around her. Warm hands cupped her face.

"Are you all right, Munequita?"

Roman hovered over Malaika, his helmet gone, worry etched into his features. It took her a few moments to regain her composure, but when she did, Malaika gave Roman a beaming smile.

"Rome, are you good?" asked the driver.

Helping Malaika into an upright position, Roman gave the driver a thumbs up. Malaika noticed it was the same masked driver from earlier. The driver nodded, revved the engine, and took off.

"Munequita, we did it," Roman said, keeping his arms securely around her tiny frame as the truck caught speed.

Malaika looked up, meeting his piercing grey eyes. *He had done it!* Overcome with emotion, Malaika's eyes brimmed with tears. "Thank you." *She owed everything to him. Without him, none of this would have been possible. Roman had given her a second shot at life. The bad boy had saved her.*

Her tears spilled over as a genuine smile graced her lips. Leaning over, Roman cupped Malaika's face once more. Malaika's cheeks tingled under his touch. His striking gaze met hers. He pulled her face up to his. Roman brushed his lips against her cheeks, kissing away her tears.

"Hold on to me, Munequita."

"Always."

She closed her eyes as the moon guided them through the dark night. Exhausted by the night's events, Malaika faded away into a dreamless sleep, tucked safely in the bad boy's embrace.

# CHAPTER FOURTEEN

## *Bloody Reunion*

IT WAS DARK WHEN Malaika came to. As she took in the neon lights and pop art on the walls, she realized she was at the pit. She guessed Roman had carried her inside when she had fallen asleep in the truck bed. Turning to her side, she struggled to suppress cry of surprise. Roman lay next to her in the cube pit, his long locks sprawled out, his upper body bare and his face a peaceful painting.

Malaika watched him sleep, fascinated by the lack of lines on his face. He looked ethereal. The scowl that seemed to be permanently etched into his face disappeared. Instead, a small smile played on his lips.

His full lashes cast a dark shadow against his beautiful copper skin. His jawline was sharp and defined, as was his body. Malaika felt ashamed and intrusive as her eyes moved down to the intricately detailed tattoo that lay on his upper chest and trailed down to his arm. The organic and geometric lines intrigued her. *What did they mean?*

"Like the view?"

Malaika jumped at the sound of Roman's voice. "You scared me." She ignored his question.

He chuckled, slipped his dress shirt back on, and left the top buttons undone. Malaika sat up, touching her braid. Laying on it all night created a knot in her neck. Malaika untied her braid and ran a hand through her hair. She eyed herself in the mirror. Her bronze hair fell to her waist, romantic curls with hints of flower petals framed her face. She grimaced as she saw that her eye makeup had smeared overnight and now circled her eyes, making her look like a raccoon. Malaika caught Roman staring.

He cleared his throat and tore his gaze away. A faint blush coated the tops of his cheeks. "It's almost sunrise. We should head home soon," Roman said, as the sun's first rays of the day peeked through the windows.

Malaika nodded in agreement, taking the hand Roman held out. She hid a smile as he pulled her to her feet and led her outside, back into the truck. Malaika watched, entranced, as the sky changed from its frosty white to beautiful shades of crimson, flaming orange, and dandelion yellow. She smiled as the sun's rays warmed her face.

"It is beautiful, isn't it?" she mused.

Roman shrugged. "I've seen better."

He reached over to tuck a stray lock of hair behind her ear. Malaika's eyes widened. Her body burned at his touch. Not used to the sudden wave of emotion, she shoved herself back into the seat, attempting to hide from view.

Roman chuckled at her reaction. "We're home."

He pulled into the driveway. They headed up the stone steps. Malaika dropped the keys twice in her nervousness. She felt Roman's gaze on her, which had her hands trembling, more so than usual.

"Here, let me." He took the keys from her.

She thanked him in a small voice, too embarrassed to meet his eyes. As soon as she stepped through the doors, a hard force connected with her cheek. Stinging pain spread across her face as her head whipped to the side. Stars blurred her vision as she tried to make sense of her surroundings. Blinking, she took in the scarlet spots that were splattered against the white tiles. Something wet trailed down her nose and lips. She wiped the substance and realized the red spots were blood. *Her blood.*

"How dare you?" a familiar voice yelled.

Malaika looked up, observing the scene before her. She suppressed her groan of annoyance as her gaze landed on the enraged witch that stood in front of her. *Oh joy. Her mother had returned.* Her mother's dark eyes were blazing with fire, her hand raised as if to strike Malaika again. Malaika's gaze travelled across the foyer. Her father, though poker faced, was clearly just as angry as her mother. His tightened fists hinted so.

Connor and Eva stood by the library doors. Both looked on with wide eyes and shaking fists. Connor was much worse. His eyes were bloodshot, his hair a flaming mess, and his appearance disheveled. His knuckles were raw. Next to him, the eggshell white walls were adorned with his crimson blood.

Liam and Amara stood at the foot of the stairs. Liam's eyes were wide with shock. Amara, on the other hand, wore a satisfied grin, her beady little eyes gleaming with triumph. *She was to blame.* Liam took a step forward, his hand outstretched, as if to stop Mrs. Evans from striking Malaika again. Amara yanked him back, giving him a frosty glare. He hung his head and shoved his fists into his pocket.

Malaika looked up at the balcony as she heard soft whimpering. Meredith was crying, her eyes overflowing with tears, sobs racking through her tiny body. Jet attempted to console her, but his body was shaking with rage. His face, though streaked with tears, was contorted in fury. Malaika smiled up at the two, reassuring them that everything was okay. A second powerful hit landed on her cheek. Her head flew to the side, her ears ringing as her mother struck her once more.

"Do you think this is funny?" her mother shrieked, as she clearly misinterpreted Malaika's smile.

Malaika wiped the blood that had dribbled down her chin, turning to look at her mother. From the corner of her eye, Malaika saw Connor restraining Eva. Both wore enraged glares.

"Hit her again," a deep voice said.

Malaika looked behind her, gasping as she took in Roman's dark features. His eyes were blazing with fury, a violent thunderstorm ready to explode. His face was red with rage, his veins protruding as he fought to control himself.

"Hit her again," he said and pulled Malaika behind him.

"E-Excuse me?" Malaika's mother faltered for a moment.

Like a bolt of lightning, Roman struck. He stood toe to toe with her. With one hand wrapped around Malaika's wrist, the other reached forward to grasp her mother's collar. He pulled her towards him, showing no mercy as she gasped in pain.

"Never touch Munequita again, or there will be hell to pay."

Her eyes widened in fear, her hand clawing at Roman's grip. Malaika's father strode forward, reaching for his wife.

"Remove your hand at once, young man, or the consequences will be severe!" he said.

Connor moved forward and pulled Roman away. "Rome, back off. It ain't worth the bullshit."

Roman released Malaika's mother, her neck now raw and red. She gasped, falling back into her husband's hold. Her chest heaved with effort. Roman pulled Malaika into a hug, holding her tight. This was a dangerous move, seeing as both Liam and Mr. Evans raced forward to remove her from his hold.

"Not another step!" Eva said.

Everyone turned to look at her. Malaika gasped as she saw Eva holding a gun to Candace's head.

"One wrong move and I'll shoot her," Eva said.

Malaika froze, her eyes wide with fright. For a moment, Malaika believed that Eva had lost it, but upon closer inspection, she realized Candace was staring at her. Candace met her gaze and granted Malaika the smallest of nods. Malaika sighed in relief. Candace was safe. It was just a ruse.

Malaika's mother fainted and slumped against her husband. Liam and Mr. Evans froze, both putting their arms up in surrender. Amara stared open-mouthed at the scene before her. Malaika hid a grin at the anger on Amara's features. *Her plan had failed. Amara had lost.*

"Kids, pack your things. We're leaving," Eva said.

Jet and Meredith ran to their rooms, emerged moments later, and raced down the stairs. Connor took Angel from Jet's hold.

"Don't follow us," Eva threatened, waving the gun around.

She stepped over Malaika's mother. Mr. Evans looked torn. Malaika knew he was not used to being challenged, but she knew he had to stand down, unless he wanted another lawsuit coming his way. Roman pulled Meredith's shaking form into his arms and tucked her head safely against his chest. Jet took Malaika's hand in his, intertwining their fingers, silently letting her know he was there for her. The group of dysfunctional allies breathed a sigh of relief as they piled into the safety of the truck.

Connor spared one last glance at the house before taking off. He could see Mr. and Mrs. O'Neal running down the driveway, fury etched into their features. Sticking his middle finger out the window, he let out a stream of curses. Jet joined in on the cursing. Roman covered Meredith's ears, not bothering to scold Jet.

Malaika's heart thundered violently in her chest. She was emotionally drained, hurt, and, above all, embarrassed. It was one thing to be beaten in private, but to be publicly humiliated in front of her friends brought a wave of shame over her. She ducked her head, hiding her tears from view. Connor reached over and grabbed Malaika's hand in his.

"Where to, Eva?" he asked.

"My house," Eva said, stroking Angel's hair lovingly.

The drive was silent; the tension was thick in the air. Everyone was shaken by this morning's events. About an hour later, Connor pulled into Eva's driveway. Her grandmother stood at the door, worry shining in her eyes.

"Oh, Eva," she said, as she saw her granddaughter step out of the truck.

Eva pulled her grandmother into a hug.

"I was so worried. Is this her?" She pointed at Malaika.

Eva nodded.

"You poor child, come here," she coaxed, pulling Malaika into her arms. "Let's get you cleaned up, shall we?"

Malaika, not used to maternal care, stayed silent and followed the woman into the house. Eva's grandmother pulled her into the bathroom and began cleaning Malaika's face with a wet washcloth.

"Looks like you took quite a hit. How do you feel?" she asked.

"Fine." Physically, Malaika was okay. She was used to being beaten, but emotionally, she was angry. *What lies had Amara told her mother this time?*

"Grams, my friends will stay with us for a while. Is that all right?" Eva asked, poking her head through the doorway.

Grams smiled. "Of course it is, honey."

"Thank you, Grams. You're the best." Eva kissed her grandmother's head.

"All right, sugar, go on and take a warm shower." Grams stroked Malaika's face. Her worried eyes lingered on the red marks on Malaika's face. Malaika knew they would bruise.

With one last smile, she left the bathroom, granting Malaika some privacy. Malaika sighed in relief, thankful for the time she would get to herself. Now she could finally cry in peace. She turned the water on, stripped down, and headed inside the shower, allowing her tears to fall freely. Not wanting anyone to hear her, she suppressed her sobs. She didn't care about the blood or the pain, not even the bruising, only the shame. Now the entire world knew about her demons. She had kept them under lock and key for so long, and now, in the blink of an eye; the door came crashing down, bringing her secret life to light.

A knock on the door caught her attention, breaking her out of her self-pitying thoughts. "Y-Yes?"

"It's Eva. Can I come in?"

"Yeah." Malaika wrapped a towel around herself.

Eva stepped inside, giving Malaika a quick smile. "Here you go, they should fit."

She handed Malaika a pair of sweatpants and a long-sleeved shirt. Malaika thanked her in a small voice. Eva turned around, giving her some privacy.

"I wanted to apologize in case I frightened you with the whole Candace situation. It turns out that the O'Neals were in the library with a legal team ready to marry you off to Liam this morning," she said.

Malaika froze. "Why the sudden push?"

Eva turned around and led Malaika to the vanity stools. "Amara has convinced your parents that you and Roman are sleeping together. To save themselves from shame, they were going to marry you off. This would have worked out perfectly for the O'Neals, seeing as they now have Mr. Charles to worry about."

Malaika froze, her limbs seized as if someone had dropped a bucket of ice on her. "B-But I'm still seventeen. Legally, I can't get married until I'm eighteen. That's why the O'Neals are waiting for my birthday," Malaika said.

Eva scoffed. "You'd be surprised at how much money they spent buying off those lawyers."

Malaika stayed silent, absorbing all the information that was thrown at her. "What now?"

Eva smiled. "We get revenge."

She held out her hand for Malaika to take. The two left the bathroom just as Roman and Connor were turning the corner.

"So basically, Malaika got beat because her conservative parents thought you slept with their daughter..." Connor broke off as he took notice of Malaika and Eva.

Roman's gaze landed on Malaika. A crimson blush spread across his cheeks. His usually calm demeanor broke, allowing Malaika to see his emotions for once. The intensity in his eyes took her breath away.

*Looks like the bad boy's walls are crumbling down.*

# CHAPTER FIFTEEN

## *Midnight Rescues*

MALAIKA HAD NO INTENTION of listening in on Roman's private conversation, but seeing him storm out of the room caught her attention. His body had stiffened, his soft expression hardened, and his fists tightened as he stared down at his ringing phone. With a quick glance thrown at his mother, Roman left the room.

Carmen held onto Malaika's hands, continuing with her unnecessary heartfelt apologies. Connor, Eva, and Malaika had been working overtime to keep the truth not only from Roman, but Carmen as well.

The two thought Malaika was beaten because her parents had wrongfully assumed that she and Roman had slept together. A secret existed in this misunderstanding. This part Malaika, Eva, and Connor kept to themselves. Malaika's parents were infuriated that Malaika had *slept* with Roman despite being engaged to Liam.

Malaika hugged Carmen, promising her it was not Roman's fault she was beaten. It was all just a big misunderstanding.

Carmen stroked Malaika's face lovingly, her fingers trembling over the purple and blue bruises.

"All right, Jet, follow Malaika to your room. It's way past your bedtime, young man," Carmen said, then kissed her son's head.

He wiped away her kiss, though sported a light smile. "Good night, Ma."

Malaika and Jet walked to the other side of the house. Jet snickered, breaking the comfortable silence.

"What's so funny?" Malaika asked, hoping it was nothing inappropriate.

"I ain't finna lie, when I saw you this morning with all that makeup smeared down your face, I thought you were some crackhead Roman dragged home."

Malaika snorted, amused at his metaphor. "Good night, Jet."

Jet caught her hand, giving it a quick squeeze. "We love you, you know that, right?" He stared into her eyes. Malaika was at a loss for words. Goosebumps rose on her skin at the intensity of his stare. In his eyes, she saw Roman.

"Th-Thank you," she said, a smile spreading across her lips.

"Ew, don't get all emotional now." He grinned.

Malaika laughed, then headed back. She was outside of her room when she heard Roman's furious whispers.

"Don't worry, I'll be there, but if you come packed, I'll kill you myself."

Malaika's blood ran cold. For a second, she believed the rumors. *A worthless pothead, who regularly drank himself into oblivion. Quiet, brooding, and covered in a shroud of mystery, Roman was a bloodthirsty beast who would fight anyone, anytime. He would go to great lengths to exact revenge. Roman was a monster.*

Malaika shook her head, erasing these thoughts from her mind. Roman was not a monster. She knew this better than anyone. He was a paradox. A gentle soul with a hard demeanor, a loving heart covered in thorns, and an angel with a little red devil sitting on his shoulders.

With her eyelids drooping, Malaika entered her room and plopped down on the bed. A lot happened in the past two days. They had successfully transferred Mr. O'Neal's shares to Connor. Unfortunately, with the good came the bad.

The O'Neals were now on the hunt for Malaika, trying to marry her off to Liam as soon as possible. Mr. Charles was on the verge of a psychotic breakdown, trying to win Malaika back in order to receive her inheritance.

The pressure was on; they needed to transfer Liam's shares fast. With enemies at every corner, the group of friends were running out of both time and options. Drained and worn out, Malaika fell asleep instantly.

In her dream, she was running away from Mr. Charles and his bloodshot eyes. Adrenaline pumped through her veins as she desperately tried to find shelter in the desolate city streets. She turned the corner and ran into an empty alleyway. Walking backwards, she lost her footing and tripped over a huddled figure. With trembling hands, she reached forward, knowing deep down who the crouched stranger already was. Malaika gasped, her hand flying to her mouth, as fear crept through her body at the sight in front of her. She was terrified that the stormy eyed boy before her was dead. "ROMAN!"

She shot awake. Violent tremors shook Malaika's body. Sweat ran down her limbs. Without hesitation, Malaika jumped out of bed, slipped her glasses on, grabbed the keys to Eva's car, and went off in search of Roman. The phone call, the threats, the bruised knuckles, were all telltale signs the O'Neals were not the only enemies Roman had. *How could she have been so blind?*

With her heart hammering in her chest and her stomach a knotted mess, Malaika slammed the gas pedal, speeding around the city, without a clue of where to start her search. With shaking hands, she took out her phone and called Roman. It went straight to voicemail. She tried two more times only to be met with a monotone voice telling her to try again. She grit her teeth together, trying hard not to cry. She dialed Akira next.

"M-Malaika?" Akira said, his voice heavy with sleep.

"Akira!"

Akira cursed. Malaika heard groaning and shuffling. Akira had fallen to the floor. "Malaika! What is it? What's wrong?" His voice wavered as fear overtook him.

"I need you to track a number for me, please," Malaika said, slamming the brakes, almost hitting the drunkard dancing around on the road.

"What's the number?"

Malaika scrolled through her contacts, searching for Roman's number. She recited it, hearing Akira clicking and typing away. After a few moments of tense silence, Akira let out a celebratory laugh.

"Hunter's Point, corner of Cedar Avenue," he said.

Malaika felt as if a weight lifted off her chest. "Thank you, Akira."

"No problem. Do you need my help, Malaika?"

He probably guessed that whatever Malaika was doing right now could not be good. It was the middle of the night. To top it off, she was going to a crime plagued city, alone and unprotected.

Malaika made a sharp U-turn, knocking down a few trash cans. "No. Thanks for everything, Akira. I'll text you when I get back home."

"All right, good night, Malaika."

"Good night, Akira."

Malaika sighed as she heard Akira's heavy breathing rather than the dial tone. She knew Akira was too anxious to hang up.

"Akira, go back to sleep. I'm going to be fine, I promise." She eyed the GPS. Ten more minutes.

"Okay. Please be careful," he said one last time before hanging up.

Malaika made her way through the night, the moon guiding her through the darkness. She hoped she would find Roman...*alive*. Screeching to a stop, she parked the car and ran out, wrapping Eva's robe around her body. It was chilly, and in her rush to leave the house; she forgot to slip on some shoes. Her toes curled as the cold air bit at her bare skin.

Malaika ran to the nearest convenience store. Its neon lights lit up the darkened, empty street. Unfortunately, the cashier had seen no one that resembled Roman. The only company he had was the occasional drug dealer popping in for a quick sell and the strung-out customers that were lost enough to give in to their desires.

Malaika ran out of the store and headed down the street, popping her head into every alleyway, hoping that her nightmare was just that. A nightmare and not a premonition. Her lip quivered, tears threatening to spill as she reached the end of the road, still not having found Roman.

The sound of breaking glass echoed around her. Malaika whipped her head to the side and entered the darkened alleyway. The stench of urine and alcohol invaded her nostrils. The pungent stench was overpowering. Malaika gagged as she struggled to maintain her composure.

She plugged her nose and crept through the alleyway slowly and silently, like a lioness ready to pounce. A sigh escaped her lips as she peeked her head around the corner. Roman was alive. An eerie orange glow wrapped around him and his enemies. Three roughed up, stony-eyed figures stood across him with malice in their features. The blazing flames in the barrel danced wildly, waiting for either side to attack.

"Roman," she whispered.

Though his back was to her, Malaika could tell he was tense. His muscles were taut, his shirt was torn, hanging on by threads, and his jeans stained with crimson red. Malaika hoped the blood was not his. She moved forward, then froze as a tiny movement caught her eye.

The amber glow from the fire illuminated his tightened fists. Slowly his index finger shot out, silently ordering Malaika to stop. Malaika obeyed and crept back into the alley.

"*Vamos perros.* Show me what you got!" Roman said.

Colorful words were spoken as Romans enemies ran forward to attack. The echo of violent, bloody hits made its way into Malaika's ears. Grunting, groans of pain, and cursing rang through the air.

Malaika fought with herself. She knew she needed to help, but what could she do? Inspiration struck her as she remembered she had a car. She took off, sprinting towards Eva's car. A sharp pain shot through her foot.

"Damn it!" Malaika cried, as she fell forward.

She tripped over, groaning as her knees collided with the cold cement. She looked down at her foot, horror swimming through her when she saw scarlet blood seeping from her foot onto the sidewalk. With trembling fingers, she pulled out the glass that had stabbed the arch of her foot. She gasped. Her foot shook as the emerald glass gleamed under the city lights.

Throwing the blood-stained glass aside, Malaika forced herself to run back to the car. Roman needed her. Her pain was meaningless. She got into the driver's seat and took off, turning off the headlights. Carefully, she made her way down the alley towards Roman. She inhaled, readying herself.

*Floor it, throw the door open and drive like hell.* With that plan in mind, Malaika floored the accelerator and shot forward. The revving of the engine startled the group. Malaika flipped the headlights on, the blaring light caught everyone off guard. Roman's wide eyes stared at her in shock and admiration. With a grin, he ran forward and caught the door handle as Malaika threw the door open. Roman shot inside and slammed the door behind him. Malaika turned the wheel and took off into the field opposite them, her foot never easing off the accelerator.

Malaika's heart pounded against her ribs. Spots invaded her vision as her breathing became ragged. She was afraid she would give herself an asthma attack. She took a deep breath to calm herself down. As the adrenaline wore off, Malaika could think straight.

"A-Are you all right?" she asked.

Roman did not respond. Panic bubbled in the pit of her stomach. Looking over at him, she relaxed as she saw a small smile on his face. His skin was damp with sweat and blood. His jet black locks were matted to his skin, covered in dirt and ash. Roman's stormy eyes, at the moment, were a calm sea.

"M-Munequita."

Malaika's heart clenched at the tone of his voice. Defeat, exhaustion, and fear were clear in his slurred words.

"You c-came."

"Of course I came, you idiot!" she said. Her tears finally betrayed her and streamed down her face.

Roman's gaze softened, his hand reaching up to wipe away her tears. "It's all right, Munequita. We're safe now," he whispered, closing his eyes.

"S-Stay awake, Roman. Don't go to sleep."

She was scared that if Roman closed his eyes, she would never see his hypnotizing gaze ever again. Roman chuckled, catching Malaika off guard.

"I'm not dying, Munequita," he said with a smile in his voice. "I won't leave you." With that last promise, his head fell to her shoulder as he drifted away into his dreams.

# CHAPTER SIXTEEN

# Runaways

MALAIKA HEAVED ROMAN INTO the house, struggling under his weight when he came to. Blinking away his confusion, Roman straightened up and pulled himself out of her hold.

"I'm all right now, Munequita, thanks."

Malaika froze. A cold wave washed over her body. A flame of anger engulfed her, her eyes spitting in anger. "Don't you dare push me away!"

Roman stared at her in shock, his eyes wide with surprise. Malaika grabbed his arm and pulled him into the bedroom. He winced as her nails dug into his flesh, but stayed silent. Malaika threw him onto the bed and headed to the bathroom, digging around for the first aid kit.

She came back, grabbed Roman's bloody knuckles, and dabbed away the crimson stains. Malaika worked in silence, wiping away his blood and taping up his wounds. If Roman was in pain, he made no sign of it. With the moon shining over Roman's body, Malaika could see the extent of the damage.

Bloody cuts zig zagged across his arms and hands; dark red bruises were forming on his knuckles. His upper cheek was swollen, bruises trailed up to his eye. Malaika, despite herself, maintained her composure. She made sure not to waver. For Roman's sake, she wouldn't cry or break.

"Not so fast," Roman said and caught Malaika's arm as she made way to pack the first aid kit.

He got up and gently pushed her onto the bed. Roman bent down on one knee and grabbed her bloody foot. Embarrassed, she pulled away. He was unfazed. He cradled her scarlet stained foot in one hand and held a rag in the other. With a soft touch, Roman cleaned her wound.

His eyes flickered to Malaika's face, his gaze lingering on the nasty bruises that sat on her skin. Malaika whimpered as his hold on her foot tightened. With a hushed apology, Roman broke his gaze away and wrapped up her wound.

"Get some sleep. It's been a crazy day," he said.

He placed the first aid kit on the nightstand, then headed to the door. Malaika walked him to the hall. Abruptly, he turned around. Malaika crashed into his chest. His arms shot out to steady her.

"Thank you, Munequita."

He lowered his head, his lips meeting her forehead. Butterflies soared in Malaika's stomach, a warm blush spread across her cheeks.

"That's twice now," he said in a voice so soft it almost sounded vulnerable.

The scent of buttermilk and maple syrup made its way into Malaika's nostrils. Sniffing, she ran to the bathroom. She freshened up for the day, then sped off towards the kitchen. Jet had the same mindset as her. He was racing towards the breakfast room, with toilet paper stuck on his right foot and toothpaste smeared around his lips.

"Jesus, kid." Roman laughed.

He grabbed a napkin and wiped down his little brother's face. Meredith smiled at the two, her eyes shining with happiness. Eva cut the young girl's pancakes up for her. Malaika went to the kitchen to help Grams.

"Good morning, sugar. How are you feeling?" Grams asked.

Malaika smiled. "Much better, thank you." She was grateful for the kindness the woman had shown her. She carried the last batch of pancakes to the breakfast room, taking a seat at the crowded table. "Mmm food, how I have missed you," she said as she placed three chocolate chip pancakes onto her plate.

Jet, who sat next to her, froze. Malaika took notice. It seemed as if Roman had informed Jet of her past eating disorder. Suddenly, she did not feel as hungry anymore. She picked at her food, not having the heart to finish her meal. Roman's fork joined hers. He helped her finish her breakfast. Though hurt that he told Jet of her eating disorder, she knew his intent was not malicious. Knowing there was no harm in his thoughts, she forced herself to take the last bite. Roman gave her a small smile.

"Meet me in the backyard in ten minutes," Connor said as he took his dishes to the kitchen.

Malaika nodded. Everyone pitched in to clean up their mess. Eva, Roman, and Malaika made their way over to the patio.

"What's going on?" Roman asked, as he took a seat next to Connor.

Connor looked up and laughed. The high octaves morphed into a cry of despair. "Man, we are so fucked!"

"Language," Roman calmly chastised, motioning to the baby in his arms.

Connor mumbled an apology, the worried line in his forehead getting seemingly deeper. "Your folks have tracked down where you are."

Malaika sighed, feeling a headache coming on.

"We need to hide. All of us. The O'Neals have money, power, and connections. Unfortunately, all we have right now are Mr. O'Neal's shares. Honestly, that's not enough to kick the family off the board."

Eva shared a long look with Malaika. In seconds, Malaika grasped the severity of the situation. Connor was speaking in code because of Roman. Roman was blissfully unaware of Malaika's engagement to Liam. Connor called this meeting to warn her. It was not Roman, Eva, and Connor who needed to hide. *It was her.*

If the O'Neals caught up to her, they would force her to marry Liam. She closed her eyes as she felt panic bubbling inside of her. She had escaped the O'Neals' clutches yesterday, and now she would have to hide. *But where? Where could she go?*

"I think it would be best for Malaika to stay at the beach house. I live with Grams now. The beach house is empty. It's the best place for her to stay. It's far enough from the city and hours away from her house. The O'Neals won't look for her there," Eva said.

"I'll go with her," Roman said.

Connor, Malaika noticed, fought a smile as he saw the faint red blush coating Roman's cheeks.

"I-I mean, she can't stay all by herself unprotected. With people as powerful as the O'Neals on the hunt for us, it's best to stick together," Roman said, avoiding Malaika's gaze.

"So it's settled. Eva and I will hide uptown. Malaika and Roman will stay at the beach house, and Roman's family will stay with Grams."

Malaika's heart hammered in her chest at the thought of living alone with Roman. She snuck a peek at him. Her eyes went wide as she saw that his piercing gaze was on her as well. She tore her gaze away. Her fists shook as she thought of the O'Neals. After just one victory, so many obstacles were blocking their way.

An hour later, Malaika stood by the door, hiding her face from view, as Meredith's sobs echoed around the house, tugging at her heartstrings. Hastily, she wiped away her tears as footsteps approached her. She turned around, staring at Roman as his siblings clung to him.

"D-don't l-leave us," Meredith cried.

Jet, though silent, was shaking as dry sobs racked through his body. His red-rimmed eyes landed on Malaika. He regained his composure and made his way forward, motioning for Malaika to crouch down. She did so, bringing her ear close to his lips.

"Take care of my brother."

Malaika nodded. "I will." She pulled Jet into a warm embrace. She could feel the guilt slowly creeping into her system.

"All right, that's enough now, Meredith," Jet said as he broke from Malaika's hold.

Malaika sniffled. The more tears Meredith shed, the harder it would be for Roman to leave. Eva moved forward, resting her hand on Meredith's head.

"Don't worry, Roman. Grams and I will take good care of them," she said.

Roman nodded at her in thanks, never taking his eyes off of his siblings. Malaika saw the sacrifice behind his eyes. The guilt came back full force. Connor grabbed Malaika's shoulder.

"Don't be too hard on yourself. Roman isn't doing this just for your sake. He's got a score to settle too."

Despite Connor's reassurance, Malaika couldn't shake off the feeling that she was ripping his family apart. *Roman had sacrificed so much. For what exactly? What was he fighting for?*

"I'll see you all soon. Jet, Meredith, watch each other's backs. Take care of Ma and Angel," Roman said, and pulled his siblings in for one last hug.

The sun reached its high point, engulfing the group in its warm hold. Roman broke away, not looking back. Malaika watched him with sad eyes. Had Roman turned around, he wouldn't have the courage to leave them.

Malaika followed him out the open door. It seemed as if hell was approaching much more quickly than expected. They were outnumbered and overpowered, but still they fought. For if they did not, what difference was there between dying and giving up?

Malaika looked up at Roman. His jaw was clenched, his striking eyes stared forward with a gaze so intense it could kill. He looked down at Malaika, as she unknowingly grabbed his hand. He squeezed it once. "We'll be okay." *A lie the two desperately wished was true.*

# CHAPTER SEVENTEEN

## Cars and Girls

"ROMAN!" MALAIKA RAN SCREAMING into the living room.

Roman shot up, raising his fists instinctively. "What? What's wrong?" He pulled Malaika into his arms.

"We don't have any money."

"Huh?" Roman stared at her, dumbfounded. Slowly, a grin spread across his lips. *"Oh Dios, me asustaste."* Roman removed his hold, sitting back on the couch. "What about the money from the company?"

Malaika shook her head. "All of that goes directly to our card. Connor cancelled them, so we can't be tracked."

"We're going to need cash if we want to remain undetected." Roman sat up as an idea struck him. "Let's go for a ride, Munequita."

"Where are we going?" Malaika had to jog to keep up with his long strides.

"You trust me?"

Roman gazed down at her as they slid into the car. Malaika gasped as his gaze held hers. There was an adventurous gleam in them she had never seen before. Seeing Roman like this, her answer was instantaneous.

"Yes."

A grin spread across Roman's lips. "Good." He revved the engine and took off.

It was late in the afternoon when Roman pulled up to the pit.

"Hey Roman," a seductive voice purred as Roman stepped out of the car.

Malaika peered around Roman to look at the source of the sound. Immediately, her self-esteem took a hit, as she took in the woman that stood before her. The long-legged lioness strode forward. Chestnut locks fell down to her waist. Full lips, almond eyes, and long lashes graced her heart-shaped face. She wrapped her slender arms around Roman's body. Malaika realized this was the girl she had seen when Roman brought her to take her ID photo. That seemed like a lifetime ago.

Roman met Malaika's eyes as the woman's hands trailed up his arms. Malaika tore her gaze away and forced her limbs to carry her to the pit, not wanting to be a third wheel. For some inexplicable reason, her heart felt rather heavy. She made her way to the pit and took a seat across from a young man. His black curls were bent over a Rubik's cube.

"Hey," he said, looking up. His dark eyes met hers.

"Hi."

"You don't recognize me, do you?"

Malaika shook her head, apologizing.

"Makes sense. My face was masked when we met."

"Oh!" Malaika exclaimed, as she realized who the stranger was. "You were the one who saved Roman and me the night of the party."

She stared at him in awe. The young man smiled in confirmation.

"Thank you," Malaika said.

Had it not been for him and his friends, they would have never gotten a hold of Mr. O'Neal's shares.

"I'm Sebastian, Seb for short," he said, holding his hand out.

"Malaika." She smiled and took his hand.

"Malaika? That's an interesting name. What does it mean, if you don't mind me asking?"

"I'm mixed. My mother is white and my father is Lebanese. My name is Arabic. It means Angel."

"Angel? That's beautiful."

Malaika thanked him, her ears burning.

"Seb," Roman said, walking into the room. The mysterious woman still clung to his arm. "I see you've met Munequita." He took a seat next to Malaika and pried the girl's hands off his arm.

Seb was busy eyeing the girl in what seemed like distaste. "Yeah, I have. What brings you guys down here?" he asked, picking up his Rubik's cube again.

"We need money," Roman said.

"Cash?"

"Yeah."

"You're lucky. We have a lineup tonight."

Roman chuckled. "Is my ride still here?" he asked and followed Seb out of the room, leaving Malaika alone with the doe-eyed temptress.

The woman typed away on her phone, leaving Malaika to stare at her surroundings in an awkward silence.

"Who are you?" the young woman asked.

"I'm Malaika—Roman's friend," she added, rather unsurely.

"I'm Natalie, Roman's girl."

Natalie stared at Malaika in a calculating manner. With a sneer on her lips and malice in her eyes, Natalie caught Malaika off guard with her next question.

"You like him, don't you?"

Malaika's cheeks burned in response, her eyes going wide with shock. "N-N-No."

Natalie scoffed, rolling her eyes. "Oh please, it's written all over your pathetic little face. Every girl wants a bad boy. Not that you're any actual competition, but keep your hands off my man."

Though no threat was given, Malaika could tell that Natalie could cause some serious damage. Roman walked into the room, not giving Malaika a chance to respond.

"Munequita."

Malaika spared one last glance at Natalie, then followed Roman's towering frame out the door. He led her through the garage, to the back of the pit. Malaika smiled, surprised to find that the land behind the pit did not consist of rusted railroad tracks or burnt fields. Instead, she was greeted by a lush green field that stretched out for miles.

The wind caressed the thin blades of grass, tickling the white daisies that were scattered around the field. Aged willow trees sat across the ends of the field, creating a protective barrier around the white gazebo that sat in the center. Malaika, entranced, moved forward to make her way to the field, but stopped when the roaring of an engine caught her attention.

She turned around, staring at the royal blue car in awe. Seb shut the hood, wiping his greased hands on a rag. Roman peeked his head out the driver's window. Seb nodded at him. Roman put his hands on the wheel, taking the car for a test run. Malaika watched, captivated, her own hands itching to get behind the wheel.

"Come on, let's get you geared up," Seb said.

Malaika trailed after him, sparing one last glance at the gazebo. Seb led Malaika into the building, up the steps, heading towards a room at the end of the hall.

"Hey Ginger. Mind gearing Malaika up for me?"

A tall girl with flaming red hair and coffee brown eyes stepped out. Though the girl herself was striking in appearance, it was not her beauty that had Malaika frozen to the spot.

It was her lack of clothing. Dressed in only her undergarments, Ginger chirped a bright "okay," and pulled Malaika into the room.

Seb, with blazing cheeks, muttered a small thanks and ducked out of the room, after reassuring Malaika that Ginger was harmless. And so Malaika was left alone to face the mystical creature that was Ginger.

"So you're Malaika," Ginger said, looking Malaika up and down, but her gaze was warm, welcoming even, unlike Natalie, whose gaze was cold and calculating.

"Y-Yes."

"Take a seat while I find something in your size."

Ginger rummaged around in the closet for a few minutes, then emerged with an armful of clothes and a bathrobe secured around her waist. Malaika was secretly grateful. Her confidence took a hit every time she saw Ginger's slim waist.

"Here you go."

Ginger handed Malaika the clothes. She turned around, giving Malaika some privacy. Malaika thanked her and slipped on the clothes, trying not to grimace. The clothes Ginger had given her were out of her comfort zone, but she was not in her world right now. She was in Roman's, so she needed to play by their rules.

Jet black leather tights embraced her legs, a maroon lace bralette enveloped her rather small chest, and an oversized denim jacket covered her shoulders. Malaika inspected herself in the mirror, her confidence wavering every second. The tights highlighted her bones that still stuck out; the bralette did nothing for her flat chest, and her ribs were peeking through.

"Shut up!"

Malaika jumped at Ginger's sudden exclamation.

"You're perfect just the way you are. Don't let the voice in your head say otherwise." Ginger threw her a wink.

Malaika's heart swelled. Ginger was the mother she always wanted.

"Let's do your makeup. Nothing too crazy, just a little to piss off Natalie," Ginger said and grabbed a wine-stained lipstick.

Malaika's mouth fell open at her words. Ginger laughed as she took in Malaika's wide eyes.

"Yeah, I hate her too." Ginger shrugged as she revealed this to Malaika. "If we all weren't friends when we were younger, she would've been kicked out long ago. Connor's best trait is his loyalty. Unfortunately, it's also his worst. It's hard for him to cut people out of his life. It was a miracle he was able to break off his engagement to Brittany. Now if he could only kick Natalie to the curb."

Ginger worked on Malaika's face quickly, keeping her makeup minimal. There was never a dull moment with Ginger. She filled the silence with jokes, gossip, and pep talks.

"Oh, heads up, don't take the jacket off. It's padded," Ginger said as she helped Malaika tie up her combat boots.

"P-Padded?" Malaika's stomach flipped.

Ginger laughed, her eyes shining with amusement. "Don't worry, with Roman by your side, you won't even need it."

Malaika, though wary, waved goodbye, and headed down the hall to venture off a little further into Roman's world. She reached the top of the stairs, sparing a glance at the mirror. Ginger had done a phenomenal job.

Behind her glasses, dark, full lashes framed her eyes, and a fierce cat eye sat on her eyelids. Wine stain gloss covered her full lips, and her cheeks were a roaring flame, though she wasn't wearing any blush. Her excitement had her face blazing.

Her abdomen was on display, the lace fabric kissed her skin. Her legs seemed to stretch on for miles as the dark leather sat in all the right places. The combat heels Ginger had lent her added a few more inches to Malaika's petite frame. Malaika hadn't realized that Roman was standing at the foot of the stairs until Seb's voice rang out.

"Are you going to keep staring at her or what?" Seb chuck-led.

Malaika snapped her gaze to Roman, meeting his wide eyes and pink cheeks. He cleared his throat and tore his gaze away. "Let's ride, Munequita," he said, heading out the door.

Seb threw her a wink, a wide grin on his face. Malaika shook her head, laughing. She slid into the car and looked up at Roman. His usually gloomy eyes were shining at the moment. *The sun peeking behind the thunderclouds.*

"Ready?" he asked.

Malaika hadn't the slightest idea what was coming, but she trusted Roman and that's all that mattered. "Ready." With her heart racing, the two took off, riding into the sunset.

As the night sky emerged, Roman pulled into an alley-way, skillfully maneuvering the car. Malaika could hear music pumping, people cheering, and engines revving on the other side. "No way," she said, sitting up.

Sports cars lined the streets, shirtless guys ran around, bundles of money flew through the air, and cans of beer were being tossed around. Malaika's heart raced as the adrenaline pumped through her veins.

"Street racing?" she asked, a wide smile spreading across her lips.

Roman chuckled at her reaction. "I hope you like to go fast, Munequita."

Malaika grinned. "You have no idea."

*Malaika loved driving fast. It was one of her secret hobbies.* The two stepped out of the car. Malaika, too excited to stay put, ventured off on her own. Roman pulled her back.

"Stay close," he said.

Malaika nodded, inching towards him, as she saw handguns strapped to the men, who waited at the starting line. "What's with the guns?" she asked, her hands shaking.

"Insurance," Roman said, peeking down at her. "Don't worry, I won't let anything happen to you."

"I know."

The two made their way to the starting line, approaching the man who stood in the middle, counting the wads of cash that lay on the table.

"Hey Roman, it's been a minute. Are you racing tonight?" he asked, shaking Roman's hand.

Roman nodded in confirmation, handing the man a wad of cash.

"Is that your girl"? the man asked, nodding towards Malaika.

Roman froze, looking down at Malaika. Malaika looked away, fiddling with her fingers.

"She's family," Roman finally said.

"Nice to meet you, short stuff," the man said and gave her a friendly smile.

Malaika smiled back tightly. She was trying to figure out whether Roman's use of the word *family* should offend her. Roman led her back to the car, helping her buckle in.

"Hold on tight, Munequita," he said, as he slid into the driver's seat and made his way towards the starting line.

Malaika grabbed onto her harness as the excitement began bubbling inside of her stomach. Ginger made her way to the starting line, holding a flag.

"Are you guys ready?" she asked, a broad grin on her lips.

The crowd roared. Adrenaline coursed through Malaika's veins. Goosebumps erupted across her skin as the hum of the crowd rang in her ears. Engines revved loudly, gears shifted, and the scent of smoke invaded her nostrils. Malaika's grip on the harness tightened, as an excited grin spread across her lips.

"Ready, set, go!"

The car lurched forward, catching speed quickly. Malaika yelped as her back slammed against the seat. Roman chuckled, his eyes bright. Malaika watched, amazed, as cars zoomed by. Some raced forward, while others got lost in the dust.

"Hold on," Roman said, as he took a wide turn.

Malaika gritted her teeth together and pressed her feet against the floor to hold herself in place. Roman gripped the wheel tightly, squeezing the car in between the two cars that tried to run him off course.

"Put your feet against the dashboard," Roman said, slamming the accelerator.

Malaika did as she was told. She screamed as a car cut them off, but Roman swerved, dodging the car as it attempted to hit them. Malaika glanced at the speedometer. Roman was going a hundred miles per hour, inching towards one hundred five. Malaika had never driven over ninety before.

"Brace yourself," he said and glanced at her harness.

Malaika tightened the buckles once more. Roman skillfully made his way through the winding roads, dodging the cars that attempted to run them off the street.

"There's only two more cars ahead of us," Malaika said.

"Not for long."

The car raced forward, easily overtaking one racer. Roman leaned over, peeking at the driver of the last car. Malaika laughed as she saw Seb's curly locks. Roman chuckled.

"Sorry, man, I can't let you win today," he said and overtook Seb.

Suddenly, Seb's car shot forward, leaving Malaika and Roman behind. Malaika stared wide-eyed as Roman started laughing. "Way too soon, buddy."

His hand hovered over the Nos valve. Malaika counted down to the finish line, calculating when Roman should use the boost.

"Now," she said.

Roman turned the valve, flooring the accelerator. Malaika fell back against her seat, her body vibrating as the car rumbled dangerously. Roman shot an arm out just as he overtook Seb. He pushed his arm against Malaika's torso, holding her in place as he came to a screeching stop. Malaika gasped while Roman cursed.

"T-That was i-intense," Malaika said, fighting to catch her breath.

Her heart was racing as the adrenaline flowed through her body. Roman nodded, a smile breaking across his usually stony face. Before he could say anything, the cheering spectators pulled him out of the car.

The crowd yelled and shouted loudly in excitement. Malaika was pulled out as well. Drunk faces danced in her vision, bright eyes, excited grins, and gleeful laughter echoed in her ears. Roman's world was fascinating.

Roman caught her eye through the crowd. He flashed her a wad of cash, throwing her a wink. Malaika smiled and made her way over to him, to give him a proper congratulatory hug. She fought her way through the crowd, finally making it to Roman. He reached an arm out. Malaika leaned forward but was shoved to the ground before she could reach him.

A stinging pain spread across her palms. Picking herself up, she inspected her hands, her palms were cut, bleeding openly. Wiping away the blood, she turned back to Roman and froze at the scene in front of her.

Natalie had her lips latched onto Roman's, her red nails digging into his arms. A wave of pain washed over Malaika. Shock coursed through her veins, and tears welled in her eyes as her heart clenched. Turning away, she shoved through the crowd, wanting to get away from the unfamiliar ache building in her chest.

Slim hands grabbed Malaika's shoulders, pulling her into their embrace.

"Relax, girl," a familiar voice whispered.

Malaika turned around. Ginger stared down at her, with worry swimming in her eyes. "Don't run too far. There's a lot of heat here," she said.

Seb caught up to the two, tucking away the gun he held. "I thought you guys were in trouble," he said, as he saw Ginger's questioning gaze.

Ginger led Malaika to Seb's car. She sat Malaika on the hood while she and Seb sat on the roof. The trio watched as the line up cleared, making room for the next set of racers. Natalie strutted forward. Malaika's nostrils flared as Natalie stopped in front of her.

"Do you enjoy sexually harassing people?" Malaika asked, feeling rather brave.

Natalie scoffed. "Oh please, I'm his girlfriend."

Ginger coughed. "Ex-girlfriend," she said, with a grin on her lips.

"For your information, he kissed me back. Besides, why does it matter to you, anyway?" Natalie asked, eyeing Malaika with distaste.

"Why wouldn't it matter?" Malaika got up, her fists tightening on instinct. "Roman's my friend, of course I'm going to care about him."

Natalie laughed at Malaika's outburst. "Oh please. Look at you. Do you really think you matter to him? You're a nobody. You're not even one of us. Roman doesn't do weak girls like you. You're just some spoiled little brat. You won't last a day in his world," Natalie said. With that, she stormed off, leaving Malaika stunned.

Malaika froze. Natalie was right. *Who was she kidding? Malaika was nothing like Roman. The two were worlds apart.* Ginger grabbed her shoulder, awakening her from her depressive thoughts.

"Are you going to prove her wrong?" she asked.

Malaika stole a look at Roman's idle car. She grinned, a plan formulating in her mind. "Hell yeah, I am."

Ginger laughed. "Go get em', girl."

Sliding into Roman's car, Malaika waited for Ginger's signal. As the last flag fell, Ginger winked at Malaika. With an excited smile on her lips, Malaika slammed the accelerator, taking off into the night. Over the roar of the engine, Malaika could hear an enraged voice echo through the streets.

"MUNEQUITA!"

Malaika stole a glance in the rearview mirror. Roman's beautiful features contorted in fury. *He was a frightening storm on a calm night.* "I'm so dead."

# CHAPTER EIGHTEEN

## Changes

WITH HER EYES FOCUSED and body tense, Malaika swerved between the speeding cars. She kept a steady hold on the accelerator and weaved in and out of the lanes, making her way forward. "You got this," she whispered, her palms dripping with sweat. She cursed as a car attempted to throw her off the course. She swerved out of the way and floored the accelerator, speeding away. Narrowly avoiding the car in front of her, she spared a glance in the rearview mirror, a flash of brilliant orange caught her eye.

Angry flames erupted behind her, claiming the car that tried to run her off course. With her body quivering, Malaika hit a hundred miles per hour, wanting to get away from the flaming car. The auburn glare bounced off the rearview mirror, chilling her to the bone. Roman's world was intense. *Natalie was right. She wouldn't last a day.* Making a sharp turn, Malaika overtook the car ahead of her, hiding a smile as the driver of the car stared at her with wide eyes. She pressed the accelerator and squeezed the car in between the two cars in front of her as they attempted to box her in.

Counting down to the finish line, Malaika waited for the cars next to her to overtake her. As soon as they were halfway to the line, Malaika turned the valve, releasing the Nos. The car took off, easily passing the cars in front of her. With her hands gripping the wheel, Malaika came to a screaming stop, the tires smoking and engine rumbling. Her hands were shaking as the excitement vibrated through her body. A smile broke across her face as the sound of cheering reached her ears. *She had done it. She had won!*

Excited onlookers pulled Malaika out of the car. They cheered and hooted at her victory. She smiled so wide, her face hurt. Malaika searched for the stormy grey eyes she was so accustomed to. A rough hand grabbed her upper arm. She yelped as someone yanked her forward. Knocking into a hard chest, she steadied herself; her bleeding palms resting on a man's chest. She could feel his heart racing. She looked up, meeting the stranger's gaze. Malaika's smile fell as she took in the furious glare on his face. *Roman.*

Without a word, he dragged her to the car. He slammed the door shut and took off into the night, leaving the drunk spectators behind. Malaika snuck a peek at his face. *If looks could kill, she'd be dead.* Without warning, Roman pulled over and slammed the brakes. Smoke erupted around them as the tires screeched to a sudden stop. Malaika lurched forward. Roman shot his arm out to keep her in place. Malaika looked up, finally meeting his hard gaze.

"Munequita," he whispered, his arm falling into her lap.

"Roman."

Roman exhaled sharply, closing his eyes. Guilt flooded Malaika's system. "I'm sorry, Roman," she whispered, wringing her fingers together.

Roman's eyes snapped open. Like a flash of lightning, he turned towards her, grabbing her by the shoulders. "What were you thinking? You could have died!"

His eyes, usually so inviting, were hard like steel. The disappointment in them broke Malaika's heart. She looked down, too ashamed to meet his eyes. *Roman was right. What she did was stupid and reckless. She didn't belong in his world.*

Not knowing what to say, she stayed silent. Roman scoffed and let her go. He grabbed the wheel and took off. The rest of the drive was quiet. Malaika did not dare break the silence, nor did Roman. An hour later, the two arrived home.

"I'm sorry," Roman said. He killed the engine. The car's dim lights engulfed them in an intimate glow. "I shouldn't have reacted that way."

"It's okay. I shouldn't have taken off like that either," Malaika said.

Roman reached out to touch her, but let his hand fall back into his lap. Malaika was grateful he kept his distance. She knew that the moment Roman touched her, she would burst into tears.

"G-Get some sleep. We have a tough morning ahead of us."

Roman got out of the car and opened her door for her. Malaika thanked him and followed him into the house. Roman was right. Both of them sported bruises on their faces. She was sure questions and suspicions would arise. Malaika knew they would have to come up with lies to sell to everyone. She hated the idea of hiding the truth from her friends, but involving them was out of the question. She would do nothing that would put them in harm's way. Malaika prayed to fall asleep instantly, but Mr. Charles' snake-like eyes, and Amara's wicked grin, kept playing behind her closed lids.

Malaika woke up the next morning to the smell of chocolate chip pancakes. Roman stood by the stove. Fresh stacks of pancakes sat at the table. Malaika smiled. "Good morning."

"Morning."

"Thank you for breakfast."

Roman turned his head away. Malaika guessed he was trying to hide the pink spreading on his cheeks. The two ate breakfast in silence, arguing without words over the radio station. Roman wanted to listen to rap, while Malaika wanted to listen to rock. They came to a mutual agreement and stopped turning the dial on a random station. The mutual agreement, of course, followed after the two successfully broke the radio.

"Ride with me," Roman said, holding a hand out.

Malaika, hid her smile and took his hand, following him out the door. The two got onto his worn motorcycle and took off. Malaika enjoyed the cool wind kissing her skin. Her arms were wrapped tightly around Roman's waist. Not wanting anyone to follow them after school, they parked in the middle of a neighborhood and walked the rest of the way to school. They entered Ms. Williams' classroom and sat in their designated seats. Malaika was surprised when she saw Roman take out his textbook. She stared at him wide-eyed.

"Close your mouth, Munequita." Roman chuckled at her.

Malaika snapped her mouth shut. Apparently, she was not the only one who was caught by surprise. Ms. Williams stared at Roman. Behind her thick-rimmed glasses, her eyes were as wide as saucers. She cleared her throat and began the lesson, a proud smile playing on her lips. Even though Roman had taken out his textbook, it proved no use, as he fell asleep fifteen minutes into the lesson. Malaika rolled her eyes. She slapped his arm. Roman grunted in response.

"Roman, wake up, we have work to do," she said.

Roman groaned and turned his head away. "You do it."

"Unless you want another detention and a zero, I strongly suggest you wake up right now."

Roman's eyes snapped open. He glowered, though he didn't argue. "You're lucky you're you."

Malaika, not knowing what that meant, ignored his comment and explained the lesson objective to him. Roman did his best, but Malaika could tell he was still a little lost.

"Wipe your drool." Malaika handed him a tissue.

"Thanks," he said, his face tomato red.

The two continued working on their paper. The bell rang, signalling the end of class. Roman stretched out his muscles and let out a long yawn. Malaika giggled. She was sure this was the most school work Roman had done in a long time.

"Malaika, Roman, stay after class, please," Ms. Williams said.

Malaika's stomach dropped. She saw Roman's hands ball into fists. As the last student left the classroom, Ms. Williams turned to the duo. Now that the room was empty, the poker face Ms. Williams wore came crashing down. Confusion and pain swam in the depths of her eyes as she inspected them.

"Where did those injuries come from?" she asked, getting straight to the point.

"We were in the wrong place at the wrong time," Roman said.

Ms. Williams slipped off her glasses and stared at Roman with a penetrating gaze. Roman shifted under the woman's intense scrutiny. Malaika wanted to pipe in, not liking the way Roman's feet were shifting from side to side, but couldn't think of a lie that would cover both her and Roman.

"*Es culpa mía. Ella se lastimó por mi culpa. No soy ningún santo. Tengo enemigos. Desafortunadamente mis enemigos la lastimaron por mi culpa. No dejaré que vuelva a suceder.*"

Ms. Williams' mouth fell open. Her sharp gaze flew back and forth between the two. She shook her head. A small smile graced her lips. "*Amor, ¿eh?*"

Malaika looked from Ms. Williams to Roman. She didn't understand a word, but judging by Roman's shy smile and Ms. Williams' bright eyes, she assumed the two weren't in any real trouble.

"Good work, you two," Ms. Williams praised. "I like the new you, Mr. Rodriguez." She squeezed Roman's shoulder.

Roman looked away, hiding his pink ears. Malaika looked up at him, pride bubbling in her chest. Roman caught her gaze as the duo left the classroom. She wiggled her eyebrows at him, a goofy grin spreading across her lips. He rolled his eyes.

"Shut it," he said, and gave her a playful push.

Malaika yelped and slammed into the lockers. Her books fell from her hands and toppled to the floor. Roman's smile dropped, and he flew forward to grab her.

"My bad, Munequita," he said and picked up her books. "I forgot how fragile you were."

Malaika slapped his shoulder but couldn't help but smile as he carried her things for her. He walked her to her next class. Malaika's body burned at the stares she was getting. She couldn't tell if it was because of the injuries on their faces or if it was because the notorious *bad boy* was walking the *nobody* to class. Regardless, she knew there was no place she'd rather be than at Roman's side.

"Hey Akira," Malaika said, sneaking behind the raven-haired boy.

He screamed in response, gathering the hall's attention. Akira whirled around and stared at Malaika with wide eyes, which slowly softened as he took in her bruised face.

"Who?" he asked, tracing her bruises with his slim fingers.

Malaika shook her head. "Things got a little out of hand with my mother," she said, not wanting to give him the whole truth.

She knew if her friends knew the entire story, they would raise hell. Akira nodded and pulled her into a hug.

"Thank you for helping me," she said.

If Akira hadn't stepped in, Malaika would never have gotten to Roman in time. Akira gave her one last smile, then took her hand and led her to their table. Malaika was exhausted. She hadn't been able to sleep last night without waking up from violent tremors as Mr. Charles' dark eyes flashed behind her lids. She was low on sleep, which meant she was low on patience.

A student at the front of the class kept sneaking peeks at her during the lesson. Malaika stared back, unblinking. She didn't know what his problem was until they were in the hall. She heard him whispering to his friends about how Roman was beating her. Fury engulfed her, her limbs acting out. Seeing red, Malaika sprang. Akira tried to hold her back, but he was a second too slow.

"Malaika, don't!"

Malaika pulled her arm back and swung. The boy's satisfied grin turned to a horrified frown when he saw the fist flying his way. He groaned as Malaika slammed her fist into his nose. He fell back and cupped his face, whimpering. Malaika crouched down to his level and yanked him up.

"Never disrespect Roman again. He's twice the man you'll ever be," she said.

A familiar warm hand pulled her back as she stared into the boy's terrified gaze.

"Let it go, Munequita, it's not worth it," Roman said and pulled her away, before she could get caught.

Malaika blinked, trying to hide the angry tears that formed in her eyes. Roman squeezed her hand.

"Thank you, Munequita." Roman kissed the back of her hand.

Malaika blushed, a smile replacing her scowl. "Anytime," she said and wiped away the tears that fell.

The boy stood up. He raised his fists. Roman pulled Malaika behind him and stood toe to toe with the boy.

"You started it, she finished it. Don't test her again. She was nice enough to stop after that first hit, but I won't be. Now unless you want me to break your bones, I suggest you back up," Roman said.

"All right, kids, that's enough. Get to class."

Malaika turned and saw Mr. Dibb walking towards them. He was fighting back a smile. Malaika grinned as he threw her a wink. Akira gave Malaika's shoulder a squeeze before following the dispersing crowd down the hall.

"I'd like to have a word with you, Malaika. Mr. Rodriguez, will you give us a moment, please?" Mr. Dibb asked.

Roman nodded and walked down the hall to wait for her. Mr. Dibb stared at Malaika, his gaze traveled over her bruised face.

"As impressive as that punch was, fighting is prohibited. I'll let it slide this time because I know you well enough to know that you would not act unless prompted."

Malaika thanked him, her ears burning.

"Now, onto your face. Wanna tell me what happened?"

Malaika's heart skipped a beat. *Lie.* "I, er face planted while ice-skating."

She looked up to see if Mr. Dibb believed her lie. His piercing gaze travelled over her, searching for signs of deceit. Finally, he nodded. "Enjoy the rest of your day. Keep those hands to yourself before you knock someone out." He chuckled at his own joke, then left.

Malaika caught up to Roman, and the two made their way outside to the bench under the oak tree, where Akira, Justin, Carina, and Susan sat, waiting for them. Malaika saw that there were three boys standing by the tree. Upon closer inspection, she recognized Seb. Malaika waved at him. Roman nodded at his friends and grabbed one boy who tried to run away. He yanked him down, squishing him in between Susan and himself.

"Guys, these are my boys. This is Sebastian, Dominic, and Nicholas."

Seb smiled at everyone. Dominic grinned, revealing a mouthful of chips. Nicholas nodded, though he was staring at Dominic, his lip curling in disgust.

"Sup guys, I'm Dominic, Dom for short."

As he spoke, a large glob landed on Seb's chest. Seb huffed, reaching across the table to punch Dominic's arm.

"Oh shit, my bad, fam," Dom said with a grin.

"Shut your mouth," Nicholas said.

"What?" Dominic asked, as he shoved another handful of chips into his mouth.

"You're spitting on Susan."

Everyone turned to look at Susan, whose white blouse had specks of red on it.

"Oh man, my fault," Dominic apologized, his grin falling.

"For the love of God, swallow already," Seb said.

"That's what she said!" Justin screamed.

The boys roared in amusement. Dom had tears streaming down his face, while Nicholas fought to hide his grin. Malaika, despite herself, joined in. She was pleasantly surprised to find that her friends hit it off rather quickly with Roman's.

As the bell rang, Susan rushed to Malaika. "That was him," she whispered, sneaking a peek at Roman's friends, who were making their way to the double doors.

"Who?"

"Nic, er Nicholas, he's my tutee."

Malaika looked back at him, turning away when his honey eyes landed on her. She could see why Susan had a crush on him. He was very handsome, quiet, and calm, like a warm summer day. Unlike Roman, who was a thunderstorm, hiding behind the clouds, waiting to explode.

As the bell rang, Malaika and Roman took off hand in hand as they made their escape. Looking around to see if anyone was looking, the two threw themselves onto the motorcycle and sped away. They headed to the office. Connor had a plan to steal Liam's shares. Today, they would discuss details.

"Oh, shit," Roman said as he pulled into the parking lot.

Liam was stepping out of his car, his eyes lingering for a moment on the two. Even though they had their helmets on, they were exposed. Roman revved the engine and sped away from view. Malaika's heart hammered in her chest.

"Do you think he recognized us?"

"I hope not."

Malaika felt Roman's body trembling underneath her hold.

"Let's put our disguises on," he said.

Malaika nodded, exchanging her glasses for the large rimmed ones and slipped on her black wig. The two made their way up to Connor's office, stopping just outside of the door when they heard raised voices from inside. Malaika realized the arguing duo was Mr. Charles and Liam.

Liam sounded triumphant while Mr. Charles sounded desperate. Malaika's eyes widened when she saw board members heading their way. Roman nodded at her. Both moved to the side, allowing the men and women to walk into Connor's suite.

As the door was thrown open, Malaika caught a glance of the shock and horror dawning on the duo's faces. Liam and Mr. Charles both had a hold of each other's collars, their faces red with effort. Connor stood in the back, fighting off a grin. Roman tapped Malaika's shoulder. She nodded, understanding the signal he was giving her. This was another opportunity to plant doubt against the O'Neals.

"Is everything all right, gentlemen?" asked one of the board members.

Mr. Charles slid out of Liam's hold. In the blink of an eye, he fell back into character. Just like that, he had transformed into the cool, collected man he portrayed himself to be. Running a hand through his slick hair, he let out a dangerously charming laugh.

"No problem at all, just a friendly debate regarding the game tomorrow."

The board members, though wary, fell to his charm, believing his lies. Malaika noted the female board members were staring at both Liam and Mr. Charles apprehensively. The members made their way into Connor's private office for their meeting. Malaika and Roman began their tasks, conversing with each other about how to plant seeds of doubt.

"You can talk about how Mr. Charles makes you uncomfortable," Roman said.

Malaika nodded. "And you can talk about how Liam's tried to overpower you."

Roman grinned at her words. They both knew that Liam would never win in a fight against Roman. As the door opened up again, half an hour later, Malaika set her shoulders and made her way to the female members, determined to fill their heads with enough hate to turn them against the O'Neals. *It was time to break them.*

"Would you like some help with those?" Malaika asked, pointing to the stack of folders in their hands.

"Oh thank you, darling."

Malaika grabbed a stack from each of the women. She walked with them to the elevators. Thankfully, the men had gotten onto the second elevator.

"Are you all right?" Malaika asked, keeping her tone innocent. "The argument between Mr. Charles and Liam must have been frightening."

"I seriously doubt they were arguing about a game. Did you see the hatred on their faces?"

Malaika nodded as the second woman spoke up. "And that Charles, how quickly he composed himself. Something is not right with that one."

"Mr. Charles frightens me," Malaika admitted, shivering. This time, she wasn't acting. The shiver of disgust that ran down her spine was all too real.

"What do you mean? He didn't hurt you, did he?" asked one woman, her eyes filled with worry.

"Er, my boss, Connor, instructed me to go to his client's party. Mr. Charles was there. He created a scene because I refused to be his date," Malaika lied partially.

"How awful. What a demanding man he is. I heard he goes through his secretaries like its nobody's business."

"It's true. My niece lasted only a month. His advances were constant. She could only take so much."

"Why did she not press charges?" Malaika asked.

"He's an O'Neal. Who would be foolish enough to go against an O'Neal?"

"I would," Malaika said, her eyes spitting fire. "Why should I keep my mouth shut? It doesn't matter if the O'Neals have money. I'm sure if enough people spoke up, even the O'Neals' pocketbooks won't be enough to keep the truth from spreading."

The two women looked at Malaika with wide eyes. Malaika could see the indecision on their faces. Slowly, their worried frowns turned to soft smiles.

"You youngsters nowadays are much braver than we ever were."

The two women chuckled, thanking Malaika for her help, and made their way back to their offices. Though a definite answer wasn't given, Malaika had succeeded. She had left a trail of animosity in their hearts. Soon enough, she and Roman would turn every member against the O'Neals.

She made her way back to Connor's office to discuss the next part of the plan. It was time to steal Liam's shares. Mr. O'Neal's shares did not give Connor enough power to overthrow the rest of his family. In order to free her from her debt, Connor would need more money and power.

"How did it go?" Connor asked as Malaika made her way into his office.

She smiled. "Not bad."

Roman walked in, a grin on his face. He, too, succeeded. Connor motioned for the two to sit down.

"All right guys, here's the deal. Buying my uncle's shares didn't give me enough power to kick my family off the board. It looks like we'll need to get a hold of Liam's shares as well. Another problem we need to add to this is my uncle's mental state. He's flipping shit! He knows his shares are gone and that

I have them. So far, he doesn't know how we did it, but he will do anything in his power to regain them. We need to get a move on. The faster I get Liam's shares, the faster I can pull the trigger."

Malaika nodded, deep in thought. She and Connor both knew that another problem to add to this pile was her fake relationship with Roman. Her family was under the delusion that she and Roman were actually dating. Despite her engagement to Liam, Malaika was in a "relationship" with another man. This was why the O'Neals had paid off a handful of lawyers in order to marry Liam and Malaika, even though Malaika was still underage.

To make matters worse, Mr. Charles had entered the picture. Legally, he could claim Malaika, but Mr. O'Neal had more influence than he did. No matter who Mr. Charles went to, odds were that they would already be on Mr. O'Neal's payroll. Mr. Charles was desperate to marry Malaika. He, too, wanted to claim her inheritance. Connor was right. They needed to hurry. She and Roman could only hide for so long. Malaika looked at Connor. His brows were furrowed, his eyes focused.

"How do we get Liam's shares?" Roman asked.

"I have an idea, but you won't like it."

"What is it?"

Connor's blush matched his blazing locks. "S-S-Seduce him."

Malaika's cheeks burned. Roman choked on his coffee, the dark roast dripped down his chin. Malaika looked at him, her face a burning mess. He pointedly ignored her, staring at the floral painting on the wall, his ears scarlet.

"I can't do that," Malaika said once she regained her composure.

"Other than that, I've got nothing," Connor said.

"What if we drug him?" Roman offered.

He turned to face the duo. His gaze landed on Malaika for a moment. Malaika wasn't sure, but it looked as if his grey eyes were brewing with jealousy. *But it couldn't be, could it?*

"Drug him and then transfer his shares?" Connor asked.

Roman nodded.

"That's not a bad idea."

"Guys!" Malaika scolded. "This is wrong and you know it."

"Relax, Munequita, we're just going to knock him out, not kill him."

"But Roman—"

Roman's lips tilted up. "When and where should we do this?"

"There's another party, but it's extremely private. I can't even bring Eva."

Connor threw Malaika a cautious glance. She understood. Since the O'Neals had formally introduced her and Liam into society, it was time for her to meet his family.

"Is it even safe to go?" Malaika asked. *What if she entered the party single and left as a married woman?*

"It's not safe. In case the mission goes south, I'll have Roman and the boys on standby."

Malaika noticed Roman's questioning gaze but stayed silent. She knew he wanted to know what her role was. She knew he wished to know the true nature of her relationship with the O'Neals, but she couldn't bring herself to tell him the truth. Not now.

"When's the party?" Roman asked.

"January first," Connor said.

"We've got a few weeks to prepare then."

Connor nodded. "Get some rest, guys, you look like crap."

He chuckled and ruffled Malaika's hair. She slapped his hand away, though she wore a grin. Roman handed Malaika her helmet. The two went to the safe house. Neither of them said a word as they entered the house. They sat in a comfortable silence and stared at the setting sun, eating their dinner. The sky danced with orange flames and strokes of pink. Looking even higher, Malaika could see traces of indigo, with silver specks shining through.

"Munequita?"

Malaika looked over and gasped, jumping back when she saw how close Roman was. The sun danced on his face, bringing to light both his fresh injuries and old. She saw the soft scars that sat on his face. Faint freckles splattered over his nose and cheeks. His eyes shone bright, like the stars that looked down on them.

"Thank you for standing up for me."

For the first time in the months she had known him, Roman, the bad boy who fought anyone who looked at him the wrong way, who drank away his sorrows and smoked away his fears, let his guard down and gave her a smile. *A genuine smile.*

His smile was beautiful. It was intense, like the sunlight that pours in after a violent thunderstorm. It warmed her soul. Malaika knew she could no longer deny it, she could no longer fight it. As much as the truth frightened her, it exhilarated her as she accepted it. She was in love with Roman Rodriguez.

# CHAPTER NINETEEN

## Drug Runs

THE NEXT DAY AT work, Connor dragged Malaika into his private office, an excited gleam in his eyes. Roman followed the duo inside, his face wary.

"What's going on?" Malaika asked.

Connor locked the door and turned to face the two, a grin spreading across his face. "The move you guys made yesterday has got a lot of members talking. Now's the time to strike. We need to make a play that will ruin Charles' image. When one O'Neal falls, they all take the hit."

"Won't that affect you as well?" Roman asked.

Connor shrugged. "Not really. Everyone knows I don't get along with the rest of my family."

"So what's the plan?" Malaika asked.

Connor hesitated. "It's a little risky, but it'll be worth it."

Roman stared at Connor, a storm brewing in his eyes. "What is it?"

"I was thinking of drugging Charles. There's a board meeting today and Charles is presenting. If he embarrasses himself, then that's another point for us."

"Oh, that's it? I thought it was something big."

"What do you mean, *that's it*? Drugging someone is a big deal," Malaika said, a cold sweat breaking across her forehead. "This is wrong, Connor."

Roman patted her head. "Relax, Munequita. We're not trying to kill him, we're just fucking him up."

Malaika sighed, her shoulders sagging as Connor and Roman high-fived each other. "How will we do this?"

"That's where you come in." Connor pulled out a small resealable bag with two white pills inside. "Charles' secretary has the day off. I need you to deliver this folder to him. Help him with anything else he needs. When you get the chance, slip this into his drink, at least an hour before the meeting. You have three hours."

The sound of shattering glass echoed around them. Malaika looked up, her eyes going wide at the scarlet blood dripping down Roman's fist. The shattered remnants of the mug he held slipped to the floor. Connor cursed and cleaned up Roman's wound.

"You want Munequita to be alone with him for three hours?"

Connor sighed. "I know he makes you guys nervous, but he won't do anything in public."

Malaika almost believed him, but his red ears gave him away. "Keep your phones close. I'll call if something happens," she said.

Roman looked at her as she took the bag of pills. "Be careful, Munequita. If he does something, you let me know. One word from you and I'll tear him limb from limb."

Malaika's cheeks burned, her heart raced at Roman's words. She nodded and ran out of the room, his smoldering gaze engraved into her mind. Malaika made her way out of the office, clutching the folder to her chest. She caught sight of herself in the mirror as she stood outside of Mr. Charles' office. Her stomach lurched as she saw how low cut her collar was. Hints of black lace peeked through. She fluffed her wig, trying to hide her exposed skin, not wanting Charles' invading eyes to look at her. With a groan, she threw herself into Charles' office and locked the door behind her. She took a deep breath, trying to calm her racing heart.

"Hello, Malaika, what are you doing here?"

Malaika turned around and adjusted her collar. Charles' snake-like eyes trailed down to the exposed skin.

"Th-These are for you." She handed him the folder.

"Ah, yes, thank you."

Malaika eyed his cluttered desk. Files and folders were scattered everywhere. The amount of work sprawled out was chaotic and for a moment, she felt sorry for him. "Do you need any help?"

Mr. Charles stared at her. Malaika's neck burned at the intensity in his eyes.

"Yes, please. Can you address and stamp these?" He motioned towards the second desk where a pile of envelopes sat.

Malaika nodded and sat down, getting to work. A half an hour later, the mail was ready to be sent out. The drugs in her pocket were like an anchor, weighing her down, reminding her she had a job to do. "I'm finished. Would you like me to put these in the mailroom?"

"Yes, after that, will you please manage my appointments for tomorrow?"

"Yes, sir." *Time to put her plan into action.* "I'm going to grab a coffee while I'm down there. Would you like one too?"

Mr. Charles began clicking away on his computer. "Dark roast."

Malaika made her way downstairs, mail in hand. Her thigh was tingling. It was as if the drugs were burning a hole through her leg. Giggling to herself, Malaika headed down the elevator. Slowly, excitement bubbled in her chest. Never in a million years did she think she would drug someone, let alone look forward to it. *Roman and Connor were rubbing off on her.*

She set the mail in the mailroom, then made her way to one of the self-serve cafes. Thankfully for her, the room was empty. She made the drinks, her heart in her throat. The adrenaline pushed her forward, urging her to finish the job. Angling her body so the camera wouldn't catch her, she slipped the drugs into Mr. Charles' cup and stirred vigorously. Once the pills dissolved, she breathed a sigh of relief, her heart slowing to a steady beat. She placed the lids on and made her way back to Mr. Charles' office.

The excitement wore off as she stepped into his office. She hoped his serpent gaze couldn't see past her façade. She handed him the coffee, not meeting his eyes. "D-Did you need help with anything else?"

Mr. Charles' dark gaze snapped up to meet hers. Malaika licked her lips, her throat suddenly parched.

"I don't think you have the experience to help me with what I need. For now, organize the appointments."

It took Malaika a moment to decipher his words. When she finally did, it took her everything she had not to throw her steaming latte at his face. Malaika balled her fists and went back to her desk. *Don't worry, in a few hours, Mr. Charles' demise will begin.*

Fifteen minutes later, Mr. Charles shrugged out of his blazer. Thirty minutes in, he loosened his tie and ran a shaking hand through his now messy locks. Forty-five minutes later, he was teetering in his chair. Sweat dripped down his body. His head lolled back and forth as Malaika got up to inform him of his meeting.

"Mr. Charles, head up to 1505 now. The board meeting will begin shortly."

He nodded and stood up. His legs quaked with every step he took. He tripped out the door. Malaika grinned at his pathetic state. *Karma is a bitch.*

An hour later, back in her office, Malaika jumped as Connor threw open the doors and ran to her. He peppered her face with sloppy kisses. Malaika squirmed, trying to free herself. Connor loosened his hold and beamed at her. Something soft touched her face. Roman wiped away the spit with a tissue. Malaika's neck burned at his thoughtful gesture.

"Charles is screwed. He made a fool of himself in front of everyone. The board has ordered a mandatory drug test tomorrow. If you fail, you get put on suspension."

It was the morning of the drug test. Malaika was both nervous and exhilarated. She couldn't believe she had drugged someone and gotten away with it.

"First and last time, Munequita," Roman said as he revved the engine.

"Was I speaking out loud again?"

Roman chuckled and nodded. The two drove in silence. Malaika closed her eyes, enjoying the chilly wind that caressed her face. Roman's broad back was comfortable. Malaika leaned forward, resting her body against his. Unlike before, Roman no longer froze under her touch. Rather, he melted in her arms. As the sun peeked over the clouds, the duo arrived at the office.

An aged woman greeted the two as they stepped inside the building. "ID badges, please."

Malaika and Roman handed their ID badges to her. The woman stared at the two with a piercing gaze. Malaika couldn't help but run a hand through her wig, making sure it was secure. Roman grabbed her free hand as the woman's eyes trailed over his face. The woman sniffed, then continued to type away on her computer. Malaika's heart jumped as Roman's fingers intertwined with hers. She hoped she wasn't sweating.

"Follow me, please." The woman led the two down the hall.

"How do we take the test?" Malaika asked.

Roman snorted and turned his head away. His shoulders shook as he tried to suppress his laughter. Malaika yanked her hand away and slapped his arm. The woman laughed, a smile breaking across her stern face.

"Given that you're asking that, I don't think you need to be taking one."

"You pee in a cup," Roman said, finally composing himself, though he still sported a grin.

"In you go." The woman ushered the two into a small office at the end of the hall.

Malaika gasped as she bumped into something hard. "Oh, sorry." Malaika looked up. Mr. Charles stood in front of her, the same chilling look in his eyes as yesterday. "S-Sorry," Malaika said once more, retreating into her shell. She stood aside so he could leave.

Roman stared at Mr. Charles' retreating figure through narrowed eyes. "Check your pockets."

"What?"

"Check your pockets, Munequita."

Malaika dug through her pockets, her fingers traced something foil like. She took the object out, her eyes narrowed in confusion. "Ramen seasoning?"

Roman snatched the packet out of her hand and stormed out of the room, his body shaking with rage. Malaika wanted to go after him, but the woman ushered her into the bathroom, handing her the test kit.

Malaika rushed through the process, not wanting to leave Roman alone with Mr. Charles. She knew all too well what would follow if he got his hands on Mr. Charles. That look in his eyes was haunting. It was one she had seen before. One that was used when his family had been threatened. One that was used before he spilled blood.

Malaika ran out of the bathroom and found Roman standing against the wall, his arms crossed over his chest. His hands adorned with blood.

"Roman?" Malaika grabbed a tissue off the desk and reached for his hands. "Are you all right?"

Roman stayed silent. His jaw was ticking dangerously. His gaze trailed over her as she wiped the blood off his hands. "You're too innocent. That wasn't ramen seasoning, it was a condom."

Malaika's stomach lurched, her hands shook. Roman's warm hands took a hold of her trembling fingers.

"Breathe," he said and pulled her close.

Malaika shivered, disgust creeping into her veins. She wanted to vomit. *How dare he?*

"Are you all right, Munequita?"

"I-I'm fine. Are you okay?"

Roman chuckled. "I'm good."

"You didn't hurt him too bad, did you?"

"Nah, I only punched him once."

"You drew a lot of blood for one punch."

"It was a strong punch."

Malaika laughed, her nerves easing. She pulled away, giving Roman a smile. "Thank you, Roman."

Roman ruffled her hair, his eyes shining. "Anytime, Munequita."

# Chapter Twenty

# Saving the Bad Boy

MALAIKA AND ROMAN SAT in focused silence. It was past midnight. Bruise-like shadows sat under their eyes, their eyelids drooping in sleepiness, but the stubborn duo did not care. They were determined to fix the radio they broke.

"I didn't peg you as a rock girl," Roman said.

"What did you peg me as?"

Roman hesitated. Malaika shoved him playfully. "You can tell me, I won't hit you," she said, her fingers crossed behind her back.

Roman chuckled, his eyes crinkling at the sides. "Honestly, I thought you were some sheltered little rich girl who got what she wanted with the snap of her fingers. I figured your biggest worry in life was whether you had passed the pop quiz...but I was wrong."

His voice fell to a whisper. "You have so much to fear, so many reasons to run away and yet here you stand." Roman studied Malaika's face, confusion swimming in his eyes. Malaika's cheeks burned at the intensity of his stare.

"You're the reason I haven't run yet," she said. "You, Connor, Eva, and everyone else. All of you taught me how to fight. Thank you."

Roman smiled at her, ruffling her hair. "Goes both ways, Munequita."

He stared at her, his rough hand running down her wavy locks. "*¿Qué ves cuando me miras?* Good night, Munequita."

The week went by uneventfully. Amara had not shown up to any social events all week, which raised Connor's suspicion. He did some digging and found that she was rarely at home. She was always out with her new boyfriend. Roman, Malaika noticed, received calls in the middle of the night. When he was smiling, she knew he was talking to his siblings. When there was a murderous glare plastered on his face, she knew he was speaking to his enemies. *Just how many enemies did he have?*

Finally, the day she'd been waiting for had arrived. Holiday break. Two entire weeks of freedom. No homework, no droning teachers, and above all, no more looking over her shoulder. Malaika could finally relax. She woke up early the next morning, wanting to make Roman breakfast. He had cried over the phone the previous night when talking to his mother. Malaika, wanting to cheer him up, made the duo's favorite. Chocolate chip pancakes.

"Roman?" Malaika knocked on his door. "Are you awake?"

She heard no movement. Malaika opened the door, took a peek, and froze when she saw the havoc wrecked in his room. His clothes were strewn everywhere, his bed unmade, and the drawers thrown open, as if he were frantically looking for something. Malaika threw the door open, searching the room.

Roman was gone. Panic swelled inside of her chest, as a million thoughts, all plagued with blood, invaded her mind. She ran throughout the house. There was no sign of him. It was as if someone had a vise tight grip on her throat. Malaika wheezed, struggling to catch her breath.

*Breathe!*

She gasped, clutching her chest as Roman's voice played in her head. She inhaled deeply, counting down to ten. Finally regaining control, she ran back to his room, trying to figure out what was missing. After what seemed like an eternity, she figured it out. *Their money was gone.* Malaika screamed as the shrill ringing of the phone echoed across the deathly silent house. She ran for her cellphone, sliding it open.

"H-Hello?" she said, her fingers shaking.

"Bring me the money or your boyfriend here dies."

Malaika could hear Roman in the background, cursing up a storm. "Munequita, don't!"

The stranger hung up, leaving Malaika to her chaotic thoughts. *This is no time to panic. Roman needs you.* It was time to enter Roman's world again. Malaika grabbed the keys to his motorcycle and ran out of the house, hesitating as she eyed the handlebars. *No. She couldn't do this alone. She needed her friends.* Slipping out her phone, she dialed Akira's number.

"Malaika?"

"Akira, meet me at Mystic Beach. I need your help."

"On my way."

Malaika planned while she waited for Akira. She knew she needed money, but the cash she and Roman won from the race was gone. There was about one thousand dollars in there. If that much wasn't enough for these guys, how much would she need? And where would she get it from?

There was only one place Malaika knew of, where she could get five thousand dollars. The only problem was that if she went back there, she would be tied down and forced to marry Liam. As the honking of a horn echoed outside, she realized that perhaps this plan might work after all. She ran out, opening the door to the driver's side.

"I'll drive, you search," she said.

Akira slid over and grabbed her phone. While Malaika sped down the streets, he tracked the unknown number on Malaika's phone.

"Trinity Hill," Akira said.

Malaika could feel him burning a hole through her head.

"What's going on?" he asked.

"I got a call this morning. Roman's in trouble. If I don't bring an envelope full of cash, he goes six feet under."

Akira yanked the steering wheel from her. Malaika shrieked, panicking, as Akira pulled the duo over, applying the handbrake. Rage-filled voices rang out, curses in every language, and loud honks echoed around them.

"Malaika, what the hell? We need to call the cops, now!"

Akira pulled out his cellphone, Malaika reached over and snatched it out of his grip.

"We can't get the cops involved," she said. If the cops came, who was to say they weren't on Mr. O'Neal's payroll? *She and Roman were in hiding. They couldn't risk being found out.*

"Malaika..."

"I'm going to call the boys. We're going to need all the help we can get," she said, before he could argue.

Malaika scrolled through her phone. Her finger hovered over Connor's name for a moment, indecision knotting her stomach. She took a deep breath, then hit the call button. *Roman needed her. It was her turn to save him.*

"It's under your floorboards?" Akira asked for the millionth time.

Malaika nodded. She couldn't risk being seen, so Akira would go instead. He would crawl into her room, lift the floorboards, and grab her emergency envelope. She had hidden five thousand dollars in there in case she ever grew the balls to run away from home.

She watched with bated breath as Akira tiptoed across her lawn, keeping away from the windows. He crept over to the side of the house, reaching up for the vines criss-crossing along the white panels. Even from a distance, she could see his shaking limbs. He was afraid, and rightfully so. Slowly but surely, he made his way up the vines, heading up to her bedroom window.

Suddenly, the front door was thrown open. Malaika ducked down, peeking up nervously. Mrs. O'Neal made her way down the driveway. Malaika's father waved goodbye, a forced smile on his lips. She got into her car and sped off, nearly knocking Akira's side mirror off. Her father's head snapped in her direction. Malaika crouched, hiding under the steering wheel. She bit her nails, hoping her father hadn't seen her. *Hurry, Akira!*

She slowly lifted her head. Her father was gone, and so was Akira. Malaika shrieked when a sharp tap came from outside. She turned and found Akira grinning at her, his hands clutching the envelope. She unlocked the car; he hopped in, trembling as adrenaline coursed through his veins.

Malaika kissed his head. "Let's go."

The duo headed to Trinity Hill to meet up with Roman's friends. Malaika prayed they would get to Roman in time. Her eyes travelled to the digital clock. It had been over an hour since the call. *What if they got impatient and pulled the trigger?* The mental image of Roman's splattered guts and bloody face invaded her mind. Malaika gagged, heaving. Akira swore and reached over, rubbing comforting circles on her back with one hand, while the other hand took the wheel.

"It's going to be okay."

Malaika closed her eyes, focusing on her breathing. Akira was right. Roman would be okay. He had his team behind him. An entire family, who would make sure that nothing would ever happen to him. With a renewed sense of hope, she clutched the wheel, pressing down on the accelerator.

*Hold on, bad boy, I'm coming.*

Malaika shivered as the first snowfall of the season touched her skin. Seb grabbed her shoulders, pulling her into the safety of his chest. Akira and Justin stood by her side.Connor peeled into the lot in a mess of crimson red and smoky tires. He got out of the car and stormed towards Malaika. Alarmed at the wild gleam in his eyes, Malaika moved back, but Seb tightened his grip. Connor grabbed her hands. Malaika held her breath, waiting for the onslaught.

"Are you all right?" he asked.

Malaika blinked, caught off guard. "I-I'm okay. Roman will be all right. We're all here, we got this," she said, as she saw tears well in his emerald eyes.

Eva pulled Connor away, giving Malaika a warm smile. She gathered Connor into her embrace, muttering reassurances under her breath. The angry roaring of engines caught the group's attention. Dominic and Nicholas pulled into the lot, their neon green cars gleaming dangerously. The two stepped out, armed. Malaika's heart jumped at the sight of the weapons.

Seb let Malaika go, giving her one last squeeze. He, along with Dom, Nic, and Connor, conversed in low voices, hatching up a plan. More than once, she saw Connor shake his head. Malaika remembered that Connor was older than them. He was in his early twenties. Though his soul was young, she couldn't deny that at this moment he was an adult. He had the most experience and knowledge. Today, he would be the captain.

"All right guys, here's the plan. Akira traced the number to that warehouse over there." Connor pointed to a faded brown building in the distance. "Dom and Seb will head in through the back and take count. Then, Malaika will go inside and make the trade. Nic, Akira, and I will slip in through the front.

We'll stick to the shadows and jump in if things go south. Justin and Eva are our wheels."

Connor walked up to Malaika and handed her a bullet-proof vest. Malaika took it, her hands shaking. Eva pulled Malaika behind her, blocking her from view, so she could slip the vest under her shirt. Seb stood next to Eva, his back to Malaika. She slipped on the vest, thanked the duo, and stepped out from behind them. Seb nodded at her as he loaded a handgun. Malaika's stomach flipped at the sight. *Roman's world was terrifying.* Connor finished loading his gun. His breath trembled as he leaned in to kiss Eva one last time.

"That better not be our last," Eva said.

Connor chuckled, throwing her a cheeky wink. "Of course not, babe. For those lips, I'd rise from the dead for another taste."

Dominic gagged dramatically, breaking the tense atmosphere. Malaika laughed, feeling some of the tension ease off of her shoulders. Nic, Malaika saw, was staring at her, his eyes full of curiosity.

"Dom, let's go," Seb said, cocking his gun.

Malaika flinched at the sound. Justin and Akira jumped. It seemed as if they, too, were afraid. Malaika held their hands, intertwining their fingers.

"Thank you guys for everything," Malaika said, her eyes filling with grateful tears.

Akira and Justin squeezed her hand in return.

"This is going to make one hell of a college essay," Justin said.

Akira snorted, though he sported a grin. Malaika closed her eyes, praying that her friends would remain safe. These extraordinary people were risking their lives today, all for different reasons, but shared by a common thread: love.

The group waited in silence for Seb's signal. Connor checked his phone as he received a text message. His eyebrows furrowed as his eyes skimmed the words on the screen. Malaika's heart leapt.

"There are six guys inside. Most are armed. Roman's with them. He looks pretty bad." He clicked the safety off his gun. "Nic, Akira, Malaika, let's go."

Clutching the envelope in her trembling hands, she walked with Nic, Akira, and Connor to the warehouse. Slowly, she could feel the tension building inside of her. Her stomach was in knots, her heart was beating painfully fast, and her head was pounding. An aching pain spread through her temple. She took a deep breath, calming herself. She couldn't afford to break. Not right now.

"Good luck," Nic said.

Connor pecked Malaika's cheek, then he, Akira, and Nic slid into the shadows, leaving her to enter the enemy's lair. Knowing she was not alone reassured her. Malaika stepped into the warehouse, her eyes squinting as she tried to navigate her way through the darkness.

The air was thick. Dust invaded her nostrils. Malaika choked, her coughs echoing around her. Her senses were clogged. She could not see, nor hear anything. Panic welled in her chest when the warehouse got darker the further she made her way down. *Where was everyone?*

"H-Hello?"

A light flicked on. Malaika wanted to cry out at the scene in front of her, but words failed her. In the middle of the warehouse sat Roman, tied to a chair. His hair was drenched in sweat. His clothes were covered in dirt, ash, and blood. A trail of scarlet slid down his face. His eyes were bloodshot. Angry red bruises sat on his face.

"Roman—"

Roman's drooping eyelids flew open. "M-Munequita," he said. His body heaved with effort. "You sh-shouldn't have come."

"Shut up," a harsh voice rang out.

Malaika flinched, her eyes welling with tears as the armed man next to Roman backhanded him. Her fists shook with rage, her fingers crumpling the envelope in her hands. Now that the room was lit, she could see the enemy's faces. Two men and four boys around her age. Recognition dawned on her as she identified three of the boys. They were the ones who attacked Roman in the alley. The trio advanced towards her. Malaika kept an eye on the gun held in one of the boy's hands.

"Give me the money," the boy in the middle demanded.

His eyes flashed dangerously. Goosebumps rose along the back of Malaika's neck as the barrel of the gun danced in front of her face.

"H-Here." Malaika handed him the envelope.

He snatched the envelope from her, heading back to the man who hit Roman. Malaika realized he was in charge. She whimpered as the remaining two boys slid behind her. One of them shoved the gun into her back. She shivered at its touch. With just a twitch of a finger, Malaika's life could end. Her lip quivered as the boys pushed her forward, towards the leader.

The leader sifted through the contents of the envelope. His thick black eyebrows knitted together as his fingers ran over the last of the bills. Malaika gulped as his menacing gaze landed on her.

"This is it?" His jaw was twitching furiously, the veins in his forehead bulging.

"Th-That's all I had."

Malaika stepped back as the man stormed towards her. The boys behind her grabbed her arms, holding her in place. Malaika's heart thundered in her chest. Her limbs quaked as the man's flared nostrils and beady eyes invaded her personal space.

Through her peripheral vision, Malaika could see Roman struggling to stand up. Curses flew out of his mouth as the man put the gun to Malaika's head. She didn't dare close her eyes.

Instead, she looked at the man head on. She was sure he could see straight through her façade.

"There's only five grand in there, you stupid bitch."

Malaika spluttered, trying to figure out what to say. Under all the stress and panic, her brain latched onto the least of her worries. "Stupid?" Malaika, despite herself, was offended. "I have a 4.0 grade point average. I'm not stupid."

"What the fuck?" said one boy.

The one on her left snickered, but a harsh glare from the leader silenced him. The man turned his attention back to Malaika. She gulped as he stared at her, unblinking. She gasped, her hands flying to her neck as he latched his hands around her throat. Malaika wheezed. She clawed at his hands; her nails digging into his flesh.

"Five grand ain't going to cut it, woman."

Malaika struggled to speak. Splotchy tears streamed down her face as the world spun. Before everything could go black, the man let go. Malaika fell back, toppling over her captors. She wheezed, struggling to get some air through her wounded pipes. She could hear Roman yelling in the back, threatening to kill everyone in the room. Blinking away the dark spots and tears, Malaika stood up, her legs wobbling.

Malaika wasn't sure if it was the sight of Roman's bruised face that led to her outburst or if it was her period. "Well, damn, maybe if you had specified how much you wanted, we wouldn't be in this predicament, dumbass!"

Silence engulfed the room. Malaika knew by the ticking of the man's jaw, she had made a mistake. The man pulled his arm back and swung. His fist collided with Malaika's face with such force, she collapsed to the ground, her head flying back. Red hot pain spread across her face. Ears ringing, blood dripping, and adrenaline pumping, Malaika crumbled, her eyes rolling back into her head. She cupped her face, tears streamed down her cheeks, dry sobs racking through her body.

Roman's enraged roars echoed throughout the room. The man grabbed Malaika's hands, holding them in his fist, and squeezed painfully. "No one speaks to me like that." He pointed his gun at her. "Let this be a lesson to all."

Before Malaika could gather up the air to scream, shots rang out around her. She could hear shouts of pain and curses flying out. Seb and Dom stormed into the room, guns blazing. Gunshots ricocheted around the warehouse. The man turned back to face her, fury blazing in his eyes. Malaika's eyes widened when she saw the malice in his glare. He pointed the gun at her.

"No ple—"

Despite her pleas, the man shot a single bullet, silencing her. Excruciating pain spread through her. Malaika curled into a ball, her body shaking. She wrapped her arms around herself, the saltiness of her tears danced on her tongue. She could hear an ear-piercing scream splitting through the sky. When her throat burned, she realized it was her own screams. Her lungs ached as her stomach constricted painfully.

"Malaika!" Roman yelled.

Though he only spoke her name, Malaika knew by the raw pain in his voice, he would burn the world to ash just to avenge her. She desperately wanted to tell him she was wearing a vest, but her body was drained. Words failed her as her breath knocked out of her lungs.

Connor leapt over her, ordering Roman to fall back. Akira and Nic followed in his shadow. Malaika watched the scene unfold through drooping eyes. Akira ran to Roman, cutting the ropes off of him. Connor, Seb, Nic, and Dom hid behind the steel barrels and shot at the enemies, trying to drive them away. Roman fell to his knees, crawling over to Malaika. Through her tears, she could see the agony on his face.

"M-Munequita." He gathered Malaika into his shaking arms.

"I-It's okay, I have a vest on," she whispered, fighting to keep her eyes open.

He chuckled through his tears, a smile replacing the broken frown on his face. "*Dios mio*." Collapsing, he fell over, holding Malaika against his chest.

"A-Are you all right?" she asked.

She knew it was a stupid question, but she needed his reassurance all the same. She wouldn't be able to rest unless she knew he was okay. Malaika inspected his face. Now that he was close enough, she could see the severity of his wounds. His eyes were bloodshot red, with purple and blue shadows under them. His face was swollen, a nasty cut sat on his eyebrow, the crimson blood trailing down to his lips.

"Thank you, Munequita. If it weren't for you, I'd be nothing more than a pile of blood and bones."

"Thank your friends," Malaika said as Eva and Justin came crashing through the doors.

They drifted around the drained duo. Making another round, Eva drove towards Malaika. Seb threw his door open and reached out. His chilly hands wrapped around Malaika's waist and pulled her into the car. Connor and Akira pulled Roman into their car. Staring at Roman through the window, Malaika gave him one last smile as he faded off into unconsciousness.

"Thank you, guys." She closed her eyes, joining Roman in peaceful bliss.

# CHAPTER TWENTY-ONE

## Reunion

SUNLIGHT GREETED MALAIKA AS she awoke from her dreams. It was a rather odd dream. Burnt chocolate chip pancakes, shootouts, and thievery. Usually her dreams consisted of her failing her exams or forgetting to turn in her homework. Nothing too exciting. So why did she wake with a racing heart? Turning to the side, she realized why.

Roman's face was inches away. Malaika's heart raced as his cool breath blew across her cheeks. The sun bounced off his russet skin. His wet raven tresses were splashed against the pillow. It seemed as if someone had cleaned him up. Since the blood had been washed away, Malaika could see the severity of his wounds.

His cheek was swollen and bruised, a mean knot sat on his temple. Violet and indigo bruises circled his eyes, and a deep cut lay across his eyebrow. His face, just a breath away from hers, was covered in old scars. Faded and feather light, these scars showed the horrors Roman had faced in his life. These scars hinted at untold stories. It was these scars that told her how heartbreaking Roman's life truly was. The shadow his lashes cast on his face moved. His eyelids fluttered as he woke from his slumber.

Roman's eyes were like the moon on a clear night, specks of Prussian blue glimmered around his dark pupils. His gaze landed on Malaika's face and froze, drinking in her features. Though no words were spoken, Malaika could feel the electricity between the two. She, with no shame, took in every inch of him, her eyes greedily sweeping over his chiseled jaw, his muscular chest, and intricately detailed tattoo.

"You could've died today, Munequita."

"True."

"And yet, you still came?"

"Of course."

"You truly are something else." Roman reached out and tucked a stray hair behind her ear.

Malaika's heart raced as his fingers caressed her cheek and trailed down to her chin, coming to a stop on her neck. Her breathing hitched as his fingers traced the bruises that sat on her neck. Goosebumps rose where his fingers touched. She could see the guilt swimming in his eyes.

"You have some good friends, Roman," Malaika said to distract him.

His fingers stopped. "Those boys are my brothers. They're my family and I would die for them."

"And they for you."

"I hope I'm not interrupting anything," an amused voice rang out.

Roman jumped, his cheeks blazing. Malaika yelped, pushing away from Roman so quickly she toppled off the bed. A stinging pain shot through her body at the sudden contact. She groaned as her abdomen constricted in pain.

Roman cursed. His worried face hovered over the bed, inspecting Malaika. Connor shoved him back down and picked Malaika up, holding her against his body. She could feel the laughter rumbling in his chest.

"Don't move too much Rome, you're still in bad shape."

Connor carried Malaika out of the room, leaving Eva to tend to Roman's wounds. She gave Malaika a comforting smile as the door shut behind the retreating duo.

"How is everyone?" Malaika asked, as Connor set her on the couch.

"Good. No casualties, which is funny. Those guys were so careful with their shots. It was almost as if they didn't want to hurt us." Connor's brows furrowed together.

"Do you think there's something bigger at play here"? Malaika asked, noticing the edge in his voice. *Something was wrong.*

"I was at the office just now and my aunt paid me a visit. She was particularly interested in Roman."

Malaika froze. The gears in her mind turned. "I saw Mrs. O'Neal at my house today."

"Hmm. Amara missed all of our family events, gets a new boyfriend, and now my aunt has an unhealthy obsession with Roman."

"You don't think that Amara and Mrs. O'Neal planned this, do you?"

Connor looked at her, a resigned look on his face. "I'm an O'Neal. If I can break into my own uncle's house and steal his shares, I'm sure my aunt and cousin can hire people to get rid of Roman."

"Then why ransom? Why not kill him immediately?"

"Maybe the men they hired found out Roman was running with a rich girl and wanted to make some quick cash. Besides, killing someone in Trinity Hill is not the best idea."

"It sounds as if the O'Neals got played."

Connor chuckled. "Yeah, it wouldn't be the first time."

A comfortable silence engulfed the two. Malaika sunk into the couch. She held her stomach, which still stung, though it was tolerable.

"That could have ended badly," Connor said, his eyes lingering on her abdomen.

An angry trail of purple and blue spread from her ribcage to her belly button.

"Good thing you brought the vest," Malaika said and gave him a small smile.

Connor didn't smile back. "This game is getting more and more dangerous. I need to end it before someone gets hurt or worse. Just a few more weeks, Malaika, and then we'll make our move. Rest up, you're going to need it."

Malaika and Roman spent their first week of holiday break playing board games, binge watching their favorite shows, taking long motorcycle rides, and watching the sun's flames fade away into the inky indigo night. Malaika liked to sit outside and write songs under the moon's watchful eye. Roman would occasionally join her. Unlike the beginning, when Malaika could not even look at Roman in the eye, she now revelled in his company.

*"When I take my last breaths, will you tell me you love me? May it be a lie, indulge me, my love, for it is my dying right."*

Malaika yelped, hiding her papers from view. Roman looked down at her, his eyes shining in admiration.

"You have a lot to say, Munequita. Don't hide it."

Roman removed her hands and skimmed over her lines. Malaika held her breath as his brows furrowed with every new line he read. He met her gaze once more, a smile breaking across his usually stony face.

"I didn't realize the words of an angel could be so beautiful."

Malaika's body burned at the intensity of his stare. She broke her gaze away first, biting her lip, to keep from smiling. "Th-Thank you."

"Sing for me, will you?" He took a seat across from her.

Malaika was caught off guard. "How did you know I sing?"

Roman's eyes went wide. He looked away, ducking his head. "Er, your solo in the choir performance last year. I thought you were amazing. After that, I would stop by Mr. Dibbs room to listen to you record your songs."

Malaika couldn't believe what she was hearing. Roman Rodriguez went out of his way to listen to her sing. He looked up, his eyes staring straight into hers. A spark of electricity shot through Malaika, butterflies danced in her stomach. She licked her lips, her throat suddenly parched.

"Munequita, I have to tell you something."

What Roman was going to say, she never knew, because at that moment the doorbell rang.

"I'll get it," Malaika said, getting up.

The heat of Roman's gaze had her stomach doing somersaults. Another minute alone with him, and she would have puked from nervousness. Roman exhaled sharply. Malaika could hear him cursing under his breath. She made her way over to the front door, peering through the peephole. She grinned when she saw who it was.

"Quickly, come inside," she whispered as she unlocked the door.

Jet tiptoed into the house, pulling Meredith behind him. Carmen followed suit, cradling Angel in her arms.

"*Hola, mi amor.*" Carmen pecked Malaika's cheek and crept into the house.

Malaika froze. Her body went warm, a fire blazed in her stomach. Her hand touched the spot where Carmen kissed her. For a moment, Malaika was thrown back in time. Back when alcohol had not consumed her parents. Back when her mother used to brush her tangled locks, kiss her goodnight, and share midnight snacks with her.

Meredith's giggling broke Malaika out of her trance. She laughed ruefully to herself. That part of her died a long time ago, so why did Carmen make her feel like a little girl again? Shaking her head, she shoved these intrusive thoughts to the back of her mind and focused on the task at hand. Tonight was for Roman. He had been through so much these last few days;

he deserved to have a slice of happiness. Malaika was able to get Connor to agree to a brief reunion. She hoped Roman would like her surprise.

"In the closet," she said, holding the door open for the family to hide inside. They quickly shoved themselves in the closet, excited grins on their lips. Jet's eyes were shining with glee.

"Munequita?" Roman called out.

Malaika could hear shuffling in the kitchen. The clanging of pots and pans followed.

"Munequita, you good?"

Roman's shadow approached. Malaika slid into the linen closet, holding her breath. She caught Jet's eye through the crack in the door. Nodding, she mouthed 'one, two, three'. On the count of three, everyone ran out into the hall cheering "Surprise!"

Roman's body seized. A high-pitched scream erupted from his throat. The cheering died down as Roman's screams echoed throughout the house. Not a word was spoken as his eyes landed on his family members. Jet was the first to break the silence.

"Hahaha, you screamed like a little bitch." Tears streamed down his face, his eyes bright with amusement.

Carmen regained her composure and slapped Jet's back. "Language, young man!"

"Wh-What are you guys doing here?" Roman asked, dropping the skillet he wielded.

Malaika noticed that his voice was a degree deeper than usual. She snickered. It seemed as if he was trying to regain *man points*. He ran to his family, his arms outstretched. Meredith leaped into his awaiting arms. Jet punched Roman's arm, though he snuggled up against his chest.

Carmen kissed his head, tears in her eyes. Her gaze was taking in his damaged face. Malaika could tell she was furious, but she kept it together for the sake of her children. Malaika nodded at Roman, who caught her eye. They would tell Carmen the truth, partially, of course, but they would not lie. She didn't deserve to be lied to.

"Malaika invited us over for the weekend," Meredith said, holding a hand out for Malaika to take.

Malaika took her hand, gasping as Meredith yanked her towards her. Roman steadied her with his free hand.

"Dang, Mama, what are you feeding these kids?" He laughed.

"Come on in, make yourselves at home." Malaika ushered everyone to the living room.

Roman pulled her back before she could join his family.

"Roman?"

Without a word, he pulled her into a bone-crushing hug. Malaika's heart soared as his muscular arms wrapped around her waist. His hands pressed against her lower back. Heat seeped into her bones. She could feel her cheeks getting warm as he rested his chin on her head.

"Thank you, *mi amor*," he said.

Malaika felt something wet splash on her forehead. Roman was crying. She wrapped her arms around him, rubbing comforting circles on his back. He pulled away and gazed into her eyes. Malaika felt a spark of electricity rush through her as he leaned his head down. He kissed her forehead, threw her a wink, then headed to join his family. Malaika stood transfixed, rooted to the spot. Her shaking fingers traced the spot his lips had been just a moment ago. She giggled to herself, then trailed after him.

"Have you slipped back into your old habits?" Carmen asked, her tone critical.

Roman shook his head. "No, ma'am."

"Then why the bruises?"

Malaika raised her hand. "Roman didn't go looking for trouble, I promise. This is all my fault."

Roman grabbed her hand, silencing her. "It's not your fault. Ma, I swear, this time, I'm innocent."

Malaika's hand trembled under Roman's touch. Carmen looked back and forth between the two, her eyes trailing over the black and blue bruise that was splashed against Malaika's nose and cheeks.

"Why is Malaika hurt as well?"

Before Roman could stop her, Malaika blurted out the truth. She wasn't sure why. Maybe she was tired of lying, or maybe it was the way Carmen looked at her with a gaze as warm as a summer's day, that made her want to tell the truth.

"Certain people are not happy with our relationship, so they hired help to get rid of Roman."

Carmen was at a loss for words. Her eyes searched Roman's. The minutes ticked by. Silence fell over the trio. After an eternity, Carmen sighed, pinching the bridge of her nose.

*"Debes amarla de verdad, si decides quedarte con ella a pesar de todo lo que ha pasado."*

*"Es ella. Siempre ha sido ella,"* Roman said, his grip on Malaika tightening.

"Can I expect any more surprises?" Carmen asked.

"I can't promise you anything," Roman said.

"Take care of each other." Carmen kissed Malaika's head, then Roman's. She waved goodnight, then headed into the spare bedroom where Meredith and Angel were.

Malaika got up to go to bed, but Roman stopped her. "Why did you tell her the truth?"

"Your mother doesn't deserve to be lied to."

Roman chuckled, his eyes trailing over her. "You really are something else. Goodnight, Munequita."

"You've changed him."

Malaika shook her head, smiling. "No, he's changed me."

She looked up, sparing a glance at Roman, who was fast asleep on the couch with Angel tucked safely under his chin.

"Have you made any progress with your family?" Carmen asked.

Malaika shook her head. "Not yet. Hopefully, we can come to terms soon."

Jet walked into the kitchen, wiping the sleep from his eyes. "Something smells good. What are you making?" He peeked under Malaika's arm at the various pots and pans on the stove.

"Oatmeal," Malaika said, holding a spoon out for him to taste.

He made a face. "Ugh, you eat that *gringo* shit?"

Malaika gasped, at a loss for words. Carmen reached over, grabbed Jet's ear, and twisted it. Jet groaned, muttering hasty apologies. Carmen let go, leaving Jet to massage his ear.

"It was just a joke," he said.

Roman yawned loudly, waking up. He placed Angel down on the couch, surrounded her with pillows, then made his way to the kitchen.

"You should have woken me up, Munequita." He frowned as he took in the scene in front of him. He grabbed the griddle and began on the pancakes.

Jet stole a handful of chocolate chips and hopped onto the counter. "Since you two are so into each other, when are you getting married?"

Carmen reached for his ear again, but he was too quick. He leapt off the counter and ran, evading Carmen and the wooden spoon she held. Roman, though blank-faced, sported pink ears. He looked up, catching Malaika's eye. She turned away. Her body temperature rose at the depth of his stare. She could feel Roman burning a hole through her back.

Carmen came back with a satisfied grin on her lips. It looked like she had won. Malaika grabbed a stack of bowls and headed to the dining area to set up the table for breakfast.

"I wouldn't mind having her as a daughter-in-law," Carmen said in a low voice.

Malaika froze. Her heart leapt at Carmen's words.

"M-Ma," Roman stuttered. His voice fell to a whisper, "It's not like that."

"Really? Because from where I stand, I can see that she's in love with you."

"R-Really?"

Carmen laughed. "Roman, my boy, are you that blind?"

Malaika snuck back to her room and shut the door. She couldn't believe her ears. *Were her feelings towards Roman that obvious?* Her cheeks burned and tears sprang to her eyes as a wave of humiliation washed over her. Rooted to the spot, she reminded herself that it was not all bad news. Carmen had said she approved of Malaika. With that positive thought in her head, she skipped to the bathroom to freshen up.

Taking a quick shower, she laughed at herself. Here she was, all giddy and excited because Carmen simply approved of her. It's not like Roman had said he liked her. She was surprised that Jet caught on to her feelings so quickly.

Running a hand through her tangled locks, she reached for the doorknob. Something heavy collided with her. Her breath was knocked out of her, leaving her stunned. She fell back, groaning as a heavy weight pushed her to the ground. She felt as if a boulder was sitting on her chest. Wheezing, she opened her eyes and found that Roman was pinning her to the ground, rubbing his chin, which had knocked into her head.

"S-Sorry, Munequita." He groaned. "You good?"

He looked down, finally meeting her eyes. Malaika's breath hitched when she realized just how close he was. Their noses almost touching, his lips just an inch from hers. She could hear his sharp intake of breath as his gaze trailed down from her eyes to her lips. His eyes snapped back to meet hers.

Malaika's body felt as if it was on fire. The intensity of his gaze made her aware of just how entangled their bodies were. Roman's chest was pressed against hers, holding her down. His heartbeat matched hers, a violent stream of thunder. Her legs were trapped between his, Roman's body heat seeped into her.

"Oooh, Mommy! Roman is trying to make babies with Malaika," Meredith said.

Her outburst broke Malaika from her trance. Malaika's face heated in embarrassment, while Roman froze, his eyes going wide. Malaika was the first to break away. She shoved Roman with as much force as she could muster, squeezed out from under him, and escaped to the dining room. Jet's laughter echoed through the house.

"Hahaha! Ma told you to get Malaika for breakfast, but you tried to get a little more, didn't you? Hey Malaika, if you ever need a real man to practice with, call me, not my brother. Judging by his face, he probably wouldn't get past first base."

Roman was lying face down in her room, unmoving. "Shut up," he yelled with a mouthful of carpet. He sat up and stormed into the dining room, his arms outstretched for Jet. Jet tried to make his escape, but Roman was quicker. He grabbed Jet into a chokehold.

"I-I was just caught off guard."

"S-Sure you w-were," Jet choked out, though he wore a wide grin.

Roman let go, ruffling Jet's hair. Malaika's cheeks burned when Roman met her gaze. He looked away, his ears turning pink again. Carmen cleared her throat.

"Let's eat, kids."

Thankful for the diversion, Malaika took a seat next to Meredith and began eating. A comfortable silence fell over the group as they ate their breakfast. Malaika noticed that with Roman's family, she could eat in peace. Unlike at home, where she felt like she was choking every time her parents looked at her.

"Meredith, how do you know how babies are made?" Roman asked, wiping his mouth.

"Oh, one time I walked in on mommy—"

"Why don't we see what's on the news this morning?" Carmen cut her off and ran to the living room, tripping over the rug in her haste to grab the remote.

Roman and Jet stared at each other wide-eyed. The two shoveled food into their mouths, wanting to escape the suddenly awkward atmosphere. Malaika blushed as she realized how Meredith found out how babies were made.

The rest of the day, Roman spent with his family. Malaika's heart soared every time he laughed or rolled over, trying to hide his smile. He was happy. Truly happy. They watched movies, played board games, and cracked jokes at each other's expenses. As night fell, tears welled in Carmen's eyes.

"Thank you for arranging this, Malaika. I wish you all the best. Stay safe and take care of each other." She kissed Malaika's head, then stepped out with Jet trailing after her.

"Yeah, *take care of each other*, as if Roman knows how to do that," he said, then ran off before Roman could understand what he was implying.

Roman waved goodbye, watching as his family faded away into the distance. He turned to face Malaika. He said nothing, he just stared at her. Though no words were said, she could tell by the tears in his eyes what he wanted to say. The intensity in his charcoal eyes took her breath away.

He reached a hand out, tracing her cheek. His eyes smoldered darkly in the moonlight. His hand shook as he caressed her face. Malaika's body trembled under his touch, her skin tingled. His eyes trailed over her bruises, taking in the nasty shades of purple and blue.

*"Sé que no soy bueno para ti, pero maldita sea, no puedo vivir sin ti."*

# CHAPTER TWENTY-TWO

## Checkmate

CONNOR STARED AT MALAIKA as Eva worked on her face. Malaika saw his brows were furrowed with a small $v$ between them. His eyes were swimming with worry. She couldn't blame him, she was afraid as well. It was finally time to steal Liam's shares. It was time for them to make their move. Her fingers trembled as she thought of stepping into her house. It had been almost a month since she had seen her parents. She was terrified to see what emotions their cold, blank eyes would hold for her today.

"All right, let's get you into your dress," Eva said.

Connor turned away. Eva removed the dress from the bag. Malaika's heart raced as she eyed the ivory fabric.

"Connor, what is this?" she asked. Her body betrayed her and shook uncontrollably. Her lungs constricted as her breath left her. Eva grabbed Malaika's shaking form into her arms.

"Breathe for me, doll, breathe," she said.

"It's okay, Malaika. It's just a dress. You're going to be all right, I promise. We won't let anything happen to you," Connor said.

Malaika's ears were ringing. Pins and needles enveloped her body, entrapping her in a suffocating hold. She closed her eyes, holding onto Eva for support.

*Breathe. In and out, in and out.*

Malaika exhaled shakily and opened her eyes. Slowly the world stopped spinning, the rushing in her ears silenced, and her heart slowed to a peaceful beat. By no means was everything all right but for now she was okay. She was alive. Eva squeezed her shoulders, gave her a loving smile, and helped her slip the dress on.

"It's not a wedding dress," Connor said, turning back around. "Liam made a last-minute change to the dress. I'm assuming he's pulling an alpha male card and wants to claim his territory," he said, disgust swimming in the depths of his eyes.

"What do you mean?" Malaika asked.

Eva cringed. "Honey, you look beautiful, and Liam is going to want to showcase what he thinks belongs to him."

Malaika scoffed as she eyed herself in the mirror. The dress was form fitting, sleeveless with a little exposure at her lower back, and a high slit sat on her leg. In short, it left nothing to the imagination. She did not feel confident in this dress, instead; she felt like an object.

"There's no other way?" Malaika asked, turning to look at Connor.

He shook his head. "This party is our only ticket to get those shares. We couldn't steal them at the company. It was too risky, and we couldn't afford to send you to meet Liam in private. As soon as you come out of hiding, my folks would tie you down and force you to marry him."

Connor was right. This was their only chance. She couldn't afford to make any mistakes.

"How do we know they won't force her to marry Liam at the party?" Eva asked.

"We don't. That's why Roman and the boys will be on standby in case things go south."

Malaika gulped. Eva had sent Roman to the pit in the early hours of the morning so he wouldn't figure out the true nature of this party. It was her and Liam's formal introduction to the family. She looked down at her engagement ring. The sunlight bounced off the delicate emerald cut. Anyone else would kill to get their hands on a ring like this, but for Malaika, the gleaming diamond represented her captivity.

"We're so close, Malaika. Let's finish this, yeah?" Connor took her hand in his. Malaika nodded.

"Good luck," Eva said.

She kissed Malaika's head, then gave Connor a quick peck. Connor led Malaika to his car. Do or die. He revved the engine and took off, leaving Malaika to her thoughts. She was terrified, not only because of the mission, but its outcome. Once the shares were transferred and her parents' debt re-paid, would she remain friends with Connor? Eva? Roman? *Would they stay in her life, or would they part ways now that the job was done?*

The trees passed by in a blur, slowly morphing to beautiful skyscrapers, to familiar shrubbery as they entered her neighborhood. Connor dug around in his backpack and produced a small resealable plastic bag filled with white powder.

"Tape this to your thigh. When you get the chance, mix it into Liam's drink. It should take about ten minutes for the effects to kick in and then it's show time. Are you ready?"

"Absolutely not."

"That's the spirit!"

Malaika taped the bag to her thigh, using her dress to hide it from view. She looked out the window, her fists clenched as she eyed the many luxury cars piled in her driveway. Rage bubbled in the pit of her stomach. Despite having it all, they still wanted more. She would take everything from them, just as they had done with her. With a newfound resolve, she stepped out to face her enemies.

"Straight upstairs," Connor said, pushing her towards the staircase.

She looked back at him as her anxiety crept up to her again. He nodded at her, giving her a reassuring smile. She ran up the stairs before the guests could see her. Malaika stepped into her room and collapsed on the bed.

"Malaika."

Malaika screamed, jumping up.

"Sorry. I didn't mean to scare you."

Malaika looked to the side. Liam sat at her desk, skimming through her journal.

"How are you? It's been a while since we last saw each other," he said, his emerald eyes blank as usual.

"I-I'm well, thank you. Why are you going through my things?"

"You're an admirable writer," he praised, ignoring her questions.

"Th-Thank you," Malaika stuttered, knowing he was just like his father. He would ignore any question or problem he didn't want to deal with.

"You look beautiful. I see you got the dress I ordered."

"Why the sudden change?"

Liam shrugged, though his eyes flashed dangerously. For a moment, Malaika was reminded of Mr. Charles.

"You'll be eighteen next month. It would be in our best interest if we moved the wedding up to spring break rather than wait for summer," he said.

"Why? Afraid of a little competition?"

Liam scoffed and placed her journal down. "There is no competition. Your relationship with Roman was momentary. Our marriage will last forever."

"H-How are you okay with this? You're getting married against your will! You're literally a game piece."

Liam fell silent, his eyes trailing over Malaika. Malaika recognized that dark gaze. It was the same way Mr. Charles looked at the female population.

"I wouldn't say *against my will...*"

Malaika froze. Liam couldn't possibly mean what she was thinking. There was no way he actually *liked her*. They had barely spoken to each other during their year-long engagement.

"It's time." Amara poked her head into the room.

Liam stood up, holding his arm out for Malaika to take. She grimaced, though she took it, knowing it was time to make her move. The two headed out of the room, waiting for their cue.

"Introducing Liam O'Neal and his fiancée Malaika Evans."

Polite applause greeted their ears as the two descended the staircase. Malaika's grip on Liam tightened as she saw just how many people were watching her. Their eyes were all the same. Cold, judgmental, and filled with greed. For a moment, she was sure she imagined it. Liam squeezed her hand. She looked up at him, but his eyes were blank as usual, giving nothing away. She tore her gaze away and looked straight into her mother's eyes as she descended the staircase.

"Malaika," she greeted, a furious glare plastered on her face.

Malaika huffed, turned her nose up, and walked away, dragging Liam with her. She was no longer afraid of her mother. She was stronger now. Braver. She would not allow herself to be abused anymore.

"Hello Liam, Malaika. Congratulations."

Malaika stared at the goddess in front of her. Judging by her fake smile and icy stare, Malaika guessed she was Liam's ex.

"Malaika, this is Nina, my ex," Liam introduced.

Malaika hid a grin. She was right. "Nice to meet you," Malaika said, lying through her teeth.

She didn't hold out her hand, and neither did Nina. Liam cleared his throat and steered her towards his other family members.

"Why invite your ex?" Malaika asked.

Liam shrugged. "She comes from a wealthy family. It would have been rude not to."

Malaika almost believed him, but the red coating of his ears informed her of his lie. She took another look at the blonde beauty. Malaika realized why Liam had invited her. Nina's long legs and goddess-like figure could make any woman jealous. Even her. Malaika rolled her eyes and bit her lip to hide her grin.

"Don't you look ravishing, darling?"

The hairs on the back of Malaika's neck rose as Mr. Charles slithered behind her. She whirled around to face him, her grip on Liam tightening once more. Liam pulled Malaika behind him. Mr. Charles' eyes were glittering with malice. His smile, while charming as usual, was oozing with anger.

"Charles," Liam said.

"Liam."

The atmosphere was swimming with hostility. Liam's eyes narrowed into thin slits. Mr. Charles' jaw was twitching furiously as he eyed the engagement ring that sat on Malaika's finger. Before either of the men could swing, Connor walked over, a glass of champagne in his hand.

"Now, now, cousins, let's keep the testosterone in check. There's a lot of eyes in here," he said, motioning towards the bystanders who were eagerly watching the drama unfold.

Liam pulled Malaika away, taking her a safe distance away from Mr. Charles and his intrusive eyes.

"Th-Thank you," she said, leaning into his side. This time, she wasn't acting. Mr. Charles frightened her, and right now, regardless of whether she liked it, Liam was her only means of protection. Liam nodded, sparing her a quick glance.

Malaika gasped when she stepped through the glass doors and into the backyard. Twinkling lights, white roses, baby's breath, and pink daisies danced in front of her eyes. Sheets of chiffon and tulle lay across long rectangular tables. Delicate silverware and magnificent china graced the tables where waiters were serving lunch. Liam led Malaika to the two seats in the middle.

Malaika picked at her food, too nervous to eat. Her eyes kept darting between her thigh and Liam. She knew she had to drug him, but when? And where? There were too many eyes here. She caught Connor's line of vision. He nodded at her and gave her a smile.

"*Breathe,*" he mouthed.

Malaika exhaled and took a sip of water to calm her twittering nerves.

"Are you not hungry?" Liam asked.

"Huh? Oh, I'm sorry, I must have zoned out," Malaika said and stabbed her filet with a little more force than necessary.

Feedback from the mic caught Malaika's attention. Her father stood by the DJ, a mic in hand and a fake smile plastered on his lips. "Ladies and gentlemen, please help me in welcoming Liam and Malaika to the dance floor."

Malaika choked on her filet as all eyes turned to look at her and Liam. Polite applause broke out while she expelled her filet into the napkin Liam held up for her. She gasped for air and blinked away tears.

"Th-Thank you," she said.

Getting up, she took Liam's outstretched hand. He led her to the dance floor. A beautiful melody played as Liam trailed his hand down to her waist while the other intertwined their hands. Malaika stared into his jade eyes, trying to read him. Like Roman, his eyes were blank, giving nothing away. But while staring into Roman's eyes felt warm and safe; staring into Liam's eyes frightened her.

A cold shiver shot up her spine when Liam leaned close to her. Twirling herself out of Liam's hold, Malaika spun into the arms of various family members who were dying to meet her. She was dancing with Liam's cousin when a familiar voice spoke up.

"Mind if I cut in?"

"Mr. Charles," Malaika said as he took her into his arms.

"Malaika." His lip curled into a frosty smile. "I see the wedding is still on. It would be in your best interest to reconsider. I assure you, compared to my aunt and uncle, I am a saint."

Malaika scoffed. "I would never marry someone like you."

"Someone like me?" He pulled her close, his fingernails digging into her back. "Please enlighten me."

Malaika winced. "Cold, calculating, and money-hungry."

"Hmm, those are quite a few adjectives. It seems you spend a lot of time thinking about me."

He grinned and yanked her flush against him. Malaika could feel the hard planes of his chest. His glacier-like eyes stared down at her. Malaika shivered as his eyes trailed over her. She pulled back, but Mr. Charles tightened his hold. Malaika's heart raced as he squeezed her hand. Her knuckles collided, cutting into each other. Pain shot through her fingers as he held her captive in his hold. Before the tears could form, Connor squeezed himself between the two, taking Mr. Charles' hand in his.

"Hello, cousin, shall we dance?" Connor gave Mr. Charles a cheeky smile.

Malaika used this opportunity to escape. She inhaled deeply as she made it to the safety of the refreshments table. With her hand over her racing heart, she counted to ten and exhaled. Connor locked gazes with her. He threw her a wink. *It was time.* Mr. Charles' enraged features were quite the sight, but she didn't have time to amuse herself. It was time to execute the last play of the game. Making sure no one was looking, she poured the contents of the plastic baggie into a flute of pink lemonade. She stirred it, then made her way inside the house, searching for Liam.

Her stomach was in knots as she walked through the halls, looking for him. Her hands turned clammy as thoughts of failure and loss plagued her mind. *What if she failed? What if they lost?* If she was forced to become Liam's wife or Mr. Charles', she would have no choice but to put a gun to her head and pull the trigger. She refused to live in a world where she was just a puppet, a game piece, a toy with no meaning or value. Just a tool for amusement to be thrown away once its purpose was served.

She peeked her head inside her bedroom. Liam sat on her bed, flipping through her journal once more. Shutting the door, she handed him the flute of lemonade. Luckily, he was so preoccupied with invading her privacy, he didn't think twice about taking a sip. Malaika watched in amazement as he downed the entire contents.

*"Your grey eyes tell no lies. The horrors they hold are too much to bear alone. Take my hand and scream and cry, for I am here. You are no longer a single soul."*

Liam's hand traced the pages of her journal. "Interesting word choice. Was this inspired by Roman?"

Malaika stayed silent, licking away the blood that erupted from her ruptured lip. As Liam read the lines of her song, she bit her lip to keep from cursing. It annoyed her that Liam was going through her belongings, but she needed to stay calm if she wanted to complete the mission.

"Are any inspired by me?" Liam asked, turning the pages of her journal. *"As you stare into my soul, what do you see? A caged bird yearning to be set free? Blank jaded eyes surround me, choking me, as I battle to breathe. Your greedy soul has accomplished its goal, so please throw me away, now that I am no longer of service."*

Liam looked up, his eyes shining with an emotion Malaika had never seen before. Pain.

"Do you h-hate me that much?" Liam asked, his words slurring.

*The drug was working!*

"I don't hate you," Malaika said, honestly. "I pity you."

Liam's eyes narrowed. He walked towards Malaika and took a seat across from her. "Elaborate."

"You're just like me. You're nothing but a puppet."

Liam blinked. "N-No, I'm not. Roman is though."

Panic shot through Malaika's spine. Her hands turned clammy, her blood ran cold. "W-What do you mean?"

Liam laughed as his eyes drooped. "Y-You two aren't dating. You never were. I figured it out the day your parents came back. If he really loved you, he wouldn't have held himself back. He would've beaten your father to death, but he didn't."

Malaika yelped as Liam grabbed her wrists and pulled her onto his lap.

"L-Let me go," she said, her limbs seizing up in fear.

"Why should I?" Liam challenged. "W-We are getting married soon. O-On the contrary, I think we should close the d-distance between u-us."

Tears sprung to Malaika's eyes as Liam skimmed his nose down her cheek. Her body shook, her breath trembled, and her heart raced. The fear she felt when facing off with Mr. Charles was nothing compared to the fear she felt right now, captive in Liam's hold.

"L-Liam, please," she said, her voice cracking as his stiff fingers traced the skin on her exposed back.

Liam pulled away, a glazed shadow over his eyes.

"Liam?"

His eyes rolled back, and he fell forward, collapsing on top of Malaika, pinning her to the floor. Malaika yelped as his elbow knocked into her head. Pain spread through her cranium as Liam's chin slammed into her forehead. His body held her to the ground, taking her breath away.

Malaika groaned. "Are you all right?"

Liam muttered unintelligible words. His cool breath tickled her skin. *This is it. Time to make the last move.*

"L-Liam?"

"Hmm?"

"If there was no money to be gained by marrying me, would you still marry me?"

Liam stayed silent. Malaika wasn't sure if he had fallen asleep or if the drug had slowed down his thought process.

"N-No," he said, then yawned.

"So money must truly mean a lot to you."

Liam groaned in response. "N-No. F-Father and Mother want money. They want it s-so much." His icy fingers pressed into Malaika's side, raising goosebumps on her skin.

"And you? Do you want money as well?"

"I h-have money. I d-don't need anymore."

"Then why not sell your shares and take a stand?"

Liam froze. Malaika cursed. *Has the drug stopped working?*

"S-Stand?" Liam said, propping himself on his elbows to stare at Malaika.

"Sell your shares. Free yourself. You are already so rich. Do you really need more money?"

Liam's eyes searched hers. His gaze skimmed over her eyes, to her nose, to her blazing cheeks, down to her blood-stained lips. He lowered his head. Malaika panicked and began to sing. Liam froze, clearly entranced.

*"Trapped your whole life. Without a hand to hold, with no one to call your own. Take a stand, light the fuse, and burn it all. Don't think twice. Wield the knife and claim the throne. Go ahead, now that you are free, dance away as the night falls and sing for all eternity."*

"S-Sell shares?"

Malaika nodded.

"Be free?"

"Mm-hmm."

Liam stared at her, unblinking. Slowly, a smile spread across his lips, lighting up his usually dull eyes.

"O-Okay, I will," he said, then collapsed on Malaika once more.

His head rested on her chest. The door was thrown open and Connor walked in, a laptop in hand, and a proud smile on his face. Locking the door, he yanked Liam off her and got to work. It took him quite a while to persuade Liam to log into his account and sell his shares. The entire ordeal had Malaika swearing and sweating. She was sure that Jet would have been proud of the classless, obnoxious, and harsh language pouring out of her mouth.

The clock ticked by slowly. With every passing minute, Malaika chewed off more and more bits of her nail. Connor's tresses were now a flaming, jumbled mess. His hands were running through his locks repeatedly. Malaika had to stop him from ripping tufts of his hair out. As the clock struck six, a ding from Liam's laptop alerted the trembling duo of their victory.

*They did it. They won. She was free.*

It was as if someone had lifted a weight off her chest. For the first time in a long time, Malaika could breathe. She inhaled, enjoying the crisp air that flowed through her lungs. She didn't shake, she didn't tremble, nor cry. "We won."

"Damn right we did," Connor said, and pulled her into a hug.

Malaika clung onto him, smiling. She was finally free. She was no longer an object. Instead, she was Malaika Evans, a human being. A human whose life held worth and meaning.

"Sorry about this, doll, but I need to make it believable."

"Make what believable?" Malaika asked, pulling away.

She never got an answer. Connor tightened his hold, clasping his fingers on the back of her neck. Her body froze and darkness danced in her vision, dragging her deep into the depths of unconsciousness.

# CHAPTER TWENTY-THREE

## Bittersweet Endings

MALAIKA YAWNED, WIPING THE sleep from her eyes as she woke up. *Woke up? When had she fallen asleep?* She sat up and looked around the room, trying to make sense of her surroundings. Her gaze flew to Liam, who lay on the bed, his head on her lap. His copper locks stuck up in random directions. The suit jacket he wore earlier lay abandoned on the floor. His dress shirt was open and untucked, his shoes thrown off.

Malaika gasped as she observed her reflection in the mirror. Her lipstick was smeared, the dusty rose color trailed off her lips. She looked down, the same color sat on Liam's lips. With trembling hands, she threw Liam off of her and wrapped her arms around herself as panic swelled in her chest.

"W-Wake up, Liam." Tears welled in her eyes. *Why couldn't she remember anything? What had she done with Liam?* The sheets were rumpled; the blankets thrown to the ground. "L-Liam!"

Liam groaned, rubbing his eyes. "Malaika?" He sat up, his eyes widening as he took in the room. "What's going on?"

The clattering of a bottle caught their attention. Liam reached for the fallen bottle. *Alcohol.* Liam took a whiff from the bottle and winced. He exhaled into his hand and sniffed his breath.

"I must have drunk too much," he said. He turned to Malaika. "Are you all right?"

Malaika looked away, her cheeks burning. "I-I'm fine."

"We should tidy ourselves up and head back down. The guests will leave soon."

Malaika stood up on trembling limbs. Wiping all the makeup off her face, she took deep breaths, not wanting to cry in front of Liam. She refused to break in front of her enemy. Malaika rubbed the last of the eyeshadow off her face, and blinked, trying to refocus her dried contact lenses. Sniffling, she fixed her hair, tucking away the flyaway strands. Her eyes trailed down to her lips once more, her fists balled as she realized Liam got what he always wanted.

The door flew open, rebounding off the wall. Malaika jumped as Amara's face poked into the room. She took in Malaika's and Liam's disheveled appearances, a grin spreading across her lips.

"Ooh, Mr. and Mrs. Evans, come up here," she said.

Thundering footsteps rang in Malaika's ears. She stood frozen, her eyes glued to Amara's gleaming ones.

"Malaika!" her mother yelled, as she stood in the doorway.

Her bulging eyes trailed from Liam to her. Malaika's father gaped at her. His usual poker face was gone. Instead, it was replaced by wide eyes and a grim frown.

"Malaika, you are to be wed soon. We expected better behavior from you."

Mrs. O'Neal stormed into the room, shoving Malaika's mother out of the way. She stomped towards Malaika, a sneer on her lip. Her wicked eyes trailed over Malaika, disgust in her gaze.

"We will need to move the wedding up in case she is pregnant. We cannot have people talking. It would ruin the O'Neal name."

"Couldn't keep your hands to yourself, could you, Malaika?" Amara said with a sinister smile.

Malaika's fist balled, her fingernails digging painfully into her palms. "I am fully clothed, Amara! Nothing has happened," she said, her chest heaving. "Besides, you can't do anything clothed anyway," Malaika said to herself.

Mr. Charles, who was close enough, grinned. "My innocent little Malaika, a lot can be done whilst clothed," he whispered, his cool breath touching Malaika's neck.

Malaika shivered, taking a step back from his slimy presence. Mr. O'Neal walked over to Liam, his face grave. He grabbed Liam's shoulder. "My boy, did anything happen between the two of you?"

Liam looked at Malaika, his face blank. He shook his head. "Unlike some, Father, I can control myself when drunk."

Malaika was not sure if it was a trick of the light, but it seemed as if a flicker of fear crossed Mr. O'Neal's usual stony face. His grip on Liam's shoulder had tightened, revealing the whites of his knuckles.

A familiar laugh echoed through the room. Connor wiped away his tears with a wide smile. "As amusing as all of this has been, we really should get going."

He walked over to Malaika and pulled her close. Malaika grabbed his arm, just as Malaika's mother grabbed hers. Malaika's heart froze as she gazed into her mother's cold, calculating eyes.

"Malaika is my child. She will not leave this house until she is married."

Connor scoffed. "Yeah? Try putting your money where your mouth is." He snatched Malaika into his arms and took off, bounding down the steps two at a time. Malaika's heart hammered as the O'Neals and her parents chased after Connor. Their eyes shone with greed and rage.

Malaika gasped as Connor jumped through the main doors. Excitement flooded her system, her toes curled as she took in the scene in front of her. Outside, she was greeted by racing cars parked all over the driveway and up and down the street. Engines roared loudly as Connor began calling out instructions. He placed Malaika in a car and ran off to Eva, who sat behind the wheel of a yellow cab.

"Don't let her get away! Follow every car!" Malaika's mother said. She stood at the door, spitting out orders, her arms waving wildly, a crazy gleam in her eyes.

"Good luck keeping up with us," a familiar voice said.

Malaika looked up and smiled as she saw Roman behind the wheel. He slammed the accelerator and took off, freeing Malaika from her chains. The adrenaline slowly left Malaika's system, allowing her to catch her breath. She sat up, fixing her appearance. Roman chuckled as she gave up trying to salvage her hair. Instead, she tied it into a messy bun.

"You look beautiful, Munequita."

Malaika's face burned. "Th-Thank you."

Roman held an arm out. Though embarrassed, Malaika crawled over to him and sat awkwardly at his side. She refrained from putting all her weight on him, afraid that it would be too much. Roman, probably noticing the odd angle she was sitting at, grabbed her waist with his free hand, pulled her close, and tucked her head under his chin. She sighed and melted into his hold. Malaika's skin burned under Roman's touch. Hints of savoury wood and musk trailed up to her nose, intoxicating her. The electricity between the two was palpable. Malaika could taste it on the tip of her tongue.

"Congratulations." He kissed her head.

Malaika froze. *Had he found out about the engagement?* She looked down at her ring finger and realized her ring was missing. "C-Congratulations?"

"We won. We got Liam's shares, now Connor can take everyone down."

Memories rushed back, flooding Malaika's mind. *Drugging Liam. Stealing his shares.* Malaika stiffened as she thought of what happened during her blackout. Her rumpled dress and smeared makeup were enough to tell her what had taken place.

It seemed Roman had noticed her attitude change. "What's wrong?"

Malaika shook her head. She was too humiliated to tell him the truth. It was embarrassing enough that she had her first kiss at seventeen, that too, with her enemy. To make matters worse, she couldn't even remember it.

"Er nothing, I'm just relieved. Where are we going?" she asked, trying to divert his attention.

"Home."

Roman pulled up to the safe house and killed the engine. Malaika saw that three neon cars were already in the driveway. The smell of steak and fries reached her nose. Sniffing appreciatively, she followed the scent into the house.

"Hey guys," Nic said.

Malaika smiled at him. Eva and Connor rushed through the doors, out of breath. Connor held the stitch in his side. Eva slumped over the counter, wheezing. Her silky locks clung to her sweaty skin.

"What the hell happened to you two?" Dominic asked, shoving a handful of fries in his mouth.

"M-My folks's guards tailed us for at least five miles. We finally shook them off a little ways back," Connor said, taking the glass of water Roman held out.

"Man, they really gave you a lot of trouble," Seb said, and wiped the sweat off Eva's face.

Dom shrugged. "Or maybe you just suck at driving?"

Eva was up in an instant, her exhaustion forgotten. "Want to test that theory?"

Dominic grinned and hopped off the counter. "Let's go."

"Eat first," Nic said from the kitchen.

Malaika helped Connor to his feet and led him to the dining room. "So, does this mean we can come out of hiding?" she asked.

Connor shook his head, an apologetic smile on his lips. "I have control of their shares now, but I don't have enough money accumulated to pay back the debt yet. You and Roman may have to hide for about a month. That should be enough time to save up the money."

Malaika nodded. Now that the target was removed from her head, the thought of living with Roman didn't seem like a burden. "Can his family stay with Roman and I at the beach house?"

"Yeah."

"Grubs up," Ginger said and passed out the plates.

Malaika sat with the girls in the backyard, enjoying the oceanfront. The cold wind caressed Malaika's skin, leaving a trail of goosebumps in its wake. Though they had won, Malaika couldn't shake the feeling of guilt away. She felt bad for not having told Roman the truth about her involvement with the O'Neals. She had kept him in the dark. He didn't know the truth about her, her parents, or the O'Neals.

This wouldn't have bothered her if it wasn't for the fact that Roman had saved her repeatedly from her enemies. He deserved to know the true reason he was constantly risking his life to save hers. It was only fair. She glanced back at him, gnawing at her lip as she saw him laughing at the disgust on Nic's face as Dom ate two chops at once. One in each hand.

"Something the matter?"

Malaika jumped. Connor smiled down at her, his eyes an inviting pool of emerald green. "Walk with me," he said and held out his hand.

The two made their way down the steps, heading out to the edge of the ocean, right where the tide met the land. The sun was setting, illuminating the indigo waves in a mess of crimson, orange, and yellow flames.

"Talk to me," Connor said.

Malaika hesitated. Connor squeezed her hand, silently urging her to go on.

"I feel guilty," she said.

"Guilty?"

"Roman still doesn't know the truth about me. He's risked his life for me, time and time again. And what have I done in return? I've lied again and again."

"I see. Now that fight is over, you can tell him."

"I can?"

Connor nodded, smiling.

"What if he gets mad?" Malaika's heart lurched at the thought.

"He'll get over it."

Malaika picked at her nails, her nerves jittering. If she was in Roman's shoes, she would be upset. She glanced back at Roman. He had a bright smile on his face as Nic chased Dom with a baseball bat.

"I hope so," she said.

"Oh! I almost forgot to tell you. That little scene of you and Liam, I orchestrated it."

Malaika froze. She whirled around, her eyebrows raised. "What do you mean you *orchestrated it*?"

"I didn't want Liam to question why his memory was foggy or why he was knocked out, so I added some razzle dazzle to make him think he was just drunk and got a little frisky with you."

Malaika couldn't believe her ears. It was all a lie. A façade. An act. She hadn't done anything. *Liam hadn't touched her.* Relief flooded her system. She threw her head back and took a deep breath. "Oh, thank goodness."

Connor chuckled. "All right, we'll head out now. It's getting late. You and Roman should rest. It was one hell of a day."

Malaika gave him a quick hug, then headed inside to help with cleaning up. As the last of the guests left, the stars appeared, lighting up the night sky. Malaika snuck a peek at Roman. He looked happy. At peace. She was afraid that after revealing the truth to him, that peace would be shattered, but it was a risk she had to take.

"Come on, Munequita, let's do *gringo* people shit and drink cocoa and watch the stars."

Despite herself, Malaika laughed. Her shoulders relaxed, the tension in her forehead disappeared as she took a seat next to Roman on the patio. Roman threw a blanket over their shoulders. Malaika tensed as Roman's bare arm rubbed against hers. Her heart raced as the butterflies in her stomach made a guest appearance. Malaika could feel the heat between the two as Roman gazed down at her. His gaze never wavered. His eyes trailed over to Malaika's lips. Malaika blushed as his eyes met hers once more.

"I have to tell you something," she said.

Roman nodded at her, urging her to continue.

"I've been lying to you."

Roman tensed, his eyes narrowing. "Wh-What do you mean?"

For a moment, it seemed as if his charcoal eyes were swimming with vulnerability. In an instant, they were blank again, leaving Malaika to her wonderings.

"I haven't been honest with you about my involvement with the O'Neals. Nor have I been honest with you about my mother's behavior that day," Malaika said, recalling the beating she had publicly received.

Her grip on her mug tightened as the stings from the slap resurfaced on her skin. Roman grabbed the mug from her hands and placed it down. He took a hold of her hand and intertwined their fingers. Giving Malaika a comforting smile, he encouraged her to go on.

Malaika exhaled sharply. "Last year, my parents made a business deal with Mr. Charles and the O'Neals. Unfortunately, the deal was not profitable, which led my parents to be indebted to the O'Neals and Mr. Charles. In order to pay back the debt, my parents were going to use me."

Roman's grip on her hand tightened. Malaika ignored the painful throbbing and continued, not meeting his eyes. "My grandfather left me an inheritance, which I could only gain access to once I was married. To pay back the debt, my parents offered me and my inheritance to the O'Neals. Originally, I was to be married to Mr. Charles, but the O'Neals lied to him about my inheritance amount, so they then offered me to Liam. Since then, I have been engaged to Liam."

Roman froze, his grip loosening. Malaika stole a glance at him. His eyes were blank, carefully guarded. *His walls were back up.* Like before, he wore a mask over his emotions.

Malaika continued, sweat forming on her brow. "My mother beat me that day because she was upset that despite being engaged to Liam, I *slept* with you."

At this, Roman shot up, his eyes wild. Malaika gasped as he grabbed her shoulders.

"You've been engaged for over a year?"

He held her gaze. A multitude of emotions swam in the depths of his eyes. Rage, hurt, and betrayal.

"Y-Yes," Malaika whispered, tearing her gaze away. She was afraid her tears would spill over.

"And you tell me now? After everything we've been through, you tell me once the storm has settled?"

Malaika spared a glance at his eyes and was shocked to find tears swimming in them. "I had to tell you," she said.

"At the end? You told me after it was all over." He scoffed and backed away from her, his fists shook at his sides. "Just admit it, Munequita."

"Admit what?"

Roman leaned over her, his nose touching hers. "You didn't tell me because you didn't trust me."

"N-No!"

Roman stared at her, his eyes a violent storm. Pulling away, he took off, leaving Malaika behind, and taking the heart he had stolen with him.

# CHAPTER TWENTY-FOUR

## Goodbyes Suck

MALAIKA WRAPPED HER ARMS around herself and kept her head down, trying to make it through the halls without being spotted. She wasn't in the mood to talk to anyone. After Roman had walked out, Malaika had gone everywhere looking for him. She drove around Trinity Hill, the pit, Eva's house, but he and his family were gone. She hadn't the slightest idea where they were.

Malaika wanted to apologize. She needed to make things right. The way he looked at her broke her heart. She hurt him. She did this to him. And she was going to be the one to make it right. If he wanted no part of her life, that was fine, but she needed to apologize. She had to make amends. After that, Roman would be free to go his way.

Malaika dragged her feet to class, sludging into Ms. Williams' classroom. The bell rang, signaling the start of the lesson. Malaika looked around the room. Roman was nowhere in sight. Malaika gnawed her lip, worried that if Roman missed class again, his mother would have to go to court. Ms. Williams tapped Malaika's shoulder, breaking her out of her trance.

"Here is today's assignment. Mr. Rodriguez has already completed his part."

Malaika took the paper Ms. Williams held out and looked it over. She was impressed. Roman had outdone himself. This meant he was at school. He just didn't want to be in the same room as her. Guilt consumed her. Tears welled in her eyes as she began working on her assignment. She pulled her hood up and hid her face from view, crying silently as she wrote about the major accomplishments of the civil rights movement.

The rest of the day went by in the same manner. Malaika hid herself from view and kept an eye out for Roman. The classes she shared with him, he was not present, though the teachers did not mark him absent. When lunchtime rolled around, Malaika's eyes were puffy and red from crying. She hid in the nurse's office, applying an ice compress to her eyelids, trying to hide the damage. If her friends saw her like this, questions would arise. Questions she didn't have answers to.

When the bell sounded, signaling that there were thirty minutes remaining for lunch, Malaika headed down the hall towards the cafeteria.

"Hello, Malaika."

Malaika turned around. "Hi, Nic."

"Are you all right? Connor told us what happened."

*So they know.* "Er, I'm fine. H-Have you seen Roman anywhere?"

Nic scoffed. "No. He's running like he usually does."

"Who's running?" Another voice chimed in, rage hidden under his words.

Malaika whirled around. Roman stood in the hall, a storm brewing in his eyes. His posture was tense, his hands balled into fists. A crumpled envelope in his left hand. Roman noticed her staring and shoved the envelope in his pocket.

"You, of course. Just like you always do. Whenever a problem arises, you either break someone's bones or you take off," Nic said.

Roman's jaw was ticking angrily. "I'm not running."

Nic ignored him and continued. "I have to say, this girl right here has done more for you than any of us combined. She has risked her life more than once to save yours. I would assume that you'd be human enough to forgive her for hiding the truth, but I was wrong. You're a monster. You always have been and always will be."

That seemed to be the last straw. Roman charged forward, his fists raised. Nic pulled Malaika behind him, just as Roman threw the first hit. Nic dodged and speared Roman to the floor. Malaika was rooted to the spot, fear claiming her mind and body. Curses flew out of the boys' mouths. Malaika watched, horrified, as the two friends attacked each other mercilessly. Neither one was letting up. They threw brutal punches left and right. When drops of blood splattered Malaika's face, she woke up from her trance. Forcing her limbs to move, she ran to the cafeteria.

Terror laced her chest as she ran towards her friends. "S-Seb! Come quick, Nic and R-Roman, they're going to k-kill each other," she gasped out, clinging onto the table for support.

Seb and Dom shot up, taking off through the double doors. Justin and Akira got up, following Malaika. Susan and Carina jogged after them. They ran through the halls, towards the fighting duo. Seb and Dom were restraining Nic. Akira and Justin ran forward, tackling Roman to the ground.

"Enough! I don't care what happened. You're going to talk it out and get over it," Seb said, his nostrils flaring.

"All right, break it up, boys." Security guards grabbed both Roman and Nic, taking them away.

Roman turned back to look at Malaika one last time. His charcoal eyes were swimming with guilt. Malaika looked away, wiping away the tears that fell. *This was all her fault. She was to blame.*

Seb grabbed her shoulder. "Go home, you deserve a day off."

Malaika nodded, sniffling. Carina and Susan ushered Malaika out the door. Both made offers to join her, but Malaika declined. She didn't want anyone to watch her break down. She snuck out through the back doors and headed to her car. Slipping inside, she took off, sobbing all the way home. Nic was wrong. Roman wasn't the monster. *She was.*

The mission was complete. There was no reason for Malaika to go to the office, but she was lonely. The house seemed too big and empty without Roman in it. At the office, she would at least have Connor. Slipping on her disguise, Malaika stepped out of the car and headed inside to Connor's suite.

"What the hell?" Malaika stopped short and stared wide-eyed at the scene in front of her.

Liam and Mr. O'Neal were attacking Connor. Board members struggled to pull the men apart. Connor lay on the ground, his eyes swollen. His lip was cut and bleeding, the buttons of his shirt were scattered on the floor. Liam threw another punch at Connor. Fiery rage engulfed Malaika. She ran forward and tackled Liam, throwing him to the ground. She sat on him and kept a tight grip on his neck.

"Don't you dare touch him," she said. Her chest heaved as she struggled to control her breathing. Malaika looked back at Connor. He threw her a secretive wink. Her eyes narrowed in confusion. *What was going on?*

"Sir, you need to calm down, or we will be forced to alert the authorities," said one of the board members, his eyes wide with panic.

"Now, now, uncle, let's play nice, shall we?" Mr. Charles said as he stepped forward from the crowd of spectators.

As usual, he was calm and collected. *A little too collected*, Malaika thought as she eyed him. There seemed to be a pep in his step that wasn't there before. Malaika got off Liam when she saw his face turning blue. She ran to Connor and pulled him into her arms.

Mr. O'Neal huffed, straightening up his suit. "I don't know how you gained control over mine and Liam's shares, but trust me when I say there will be hell to pay, boy."

Connor smirked. "I don't know what you mean, uncle. You and Liam sold me your shares. Since you two are no longer shareholders of this company, you are currently trespassing, isn't that right, Chairman?"

Malaika looked up at the chairman. His beard was twitching, a twinkle in his eye. "What the boy says is true, Mr. O'Neal. You have to leave."

"Why I ought to—"

"Mr. O'Neal, I strongly suggest you and Liam leave the premises before a band of employees file complaints of harassment and mistreatment against you and your family."

Malaika recognized the speaker. It was the woman she had previously spoken to. Mr. O'Neal's eyes narrowed as he took in the room. The members of the board were glaring at the duo. Hatred was seeping from their eyes. *The O'Neals were no longer in control.* Muttering under his breath, he yanked Liam up and stormed out of the office. Roman stood in the doorway, his eyes glued to Connor and Malaika. Another battle was beginning, but judging by Roman's retreating figure, he wouldn't play a part in this game. *Goodbye Roman.*

"I don't understand." Malaika was confused why Connor was grinning. The members had left, leaving Malaika to tend to Connor's wounds.

"I needed insurance in case the plan failed. That's why I had you and Roman spread stories about the O'Neals. Now that I have control of their shares, they're angry. They want revenge, which they'll never get since you and Roman helped me gather enough complaints and accounts against the O'Neals. Now the company and board members have turned against them as well, leaving them absolutely powerless."

"So, that's why you wanted Roman and I to work at the company."

"Precisely. Now enough about me. What about you? Any luck with Roman?"

Malaika's gut clenched. "No."

"A little birdie told me he's staying at the pit tonight."

"Would that little birdie be Nic?"

Connor chuckled. "Don't underestimate him. Nic knows what he's doing. I'm sure he planned that fight out carefully."

Malaika froze. "You mean he orchestrated the whole thing?"

"Nic may not be a people person, but he's got a talent for reading them. Go get your man." Connor pushed Malaika towards the door.

She grinned at him. "Thank you, Connor, for everything." She rushed out the door, clutching her keys. *Hold on, Roman, I'm on my way.*

Night had fallen by the time Malaika arrived at the pit. The stars accompanied her as she headed inside to Roman.

"Roman?" She ran through the halls, trying to find him.

"Look who's back," a familiar voice sneered.

Natalie stood at the counter, an angry arch in her eyebrow. Without hesitation, Malaika strode forward and swung, knocking Natalie backwards into the wall.

"Munequita!"

Malaika turned her head. Roman stood there, his eyes wide. He grabbed her arms before she could strike again. Natalie stood up and stormed forward. Her claw-like nails reached for Malaika's face.

"Back off, Natalie," Roman said.

Natalie hesitated. She threw a murderous glare at Malaika, then backed away and stood at the end of the room.

"I need to talk to you," Malaika said to Roman.

"Go home, Munequita."

Malaika stomped on his foot. Cursing, Roman released her. Whirling around, Malaika pulled her arm back and swung at Roman. He dodged it easily and grabbed her arms, pinning her against the wall.

"Go home, Munequita, the job's done, there's nothing more to be said," Roman said, then released her.

His eyes were hard, like steel. Malaika's heart thundered violently. Her stomach knotted and her chest puffed as she battled to regulate her breathing. She knew she was going to let Roman go once she apologized, but she didn't think it was going to hurt. *Not this much.* Her eyes burned as the tears welled. She shook her head.

"N-No, you have to listen to me first, then I'll go."

Natalie strode forward, sliding her arms around Roman. Malaika froze as she took in Roman's appearance. His chest was bare, water dripped down his body, his hair unruly. Malaika's eyes flew to Natalie, who wore a smug smile. Her eyes were shining with triumph. Roman's hand shot out for a moment, though it quickly dropped. Malaika, not wanting to further embarrass herself, turned on her heel and left, sobbing as she made her escape.

The job was done. It was over. They had won. Roman had no reason to stay in Malaika's life. She understood the logic behind her thoughts, and yet it still hurt. She took off into the night, leaving Roman behind. The two would go their separate ways. *She would become another face in the crowd, hiding behind Roman's shadow.*

It was close to midnight. Malaika lay awake, her pain refusing to let her sleep. Knowing there was no way she would sleep tonight, she stripped out of her clothes and plunged into the pool. The warm water engulfed her, taking away her worries for a moment.

She closed her eyes, held her breath, and sunk to the bottom of the pool, wanting a moment to think. Connor had successfully gotten a hold of Liam's and Mr. O'Neal's shares, got them kicked off the board, and turned the members against them. Now the only enemy that remained was time.

Malaika's marriage contract was still valid. She still needed to pay back the debt in order to free herself. Connor was doing his best to use his newly acclaimed power and shares to collect more money, but his efforts were cutting it close. Next month would be the deadline. If she had not paid the debt back by then, she would have to marry Liam, whether she liked it or not.

Malaika inhaled, forgetting for a moment that she was underwater. The water flooded her mouth, blocking her airway. Malaika struggled under the water, flailing her arms as she fought to break free. Rough hands wrapped around her, pulling her up from the abyss she was trapped in.

"Breathe."

Malaika gagged, the water expelling from her lips, as a warm hand slapped her back. Shivering, she looked up and met her savior's gaze. *Roman.* His grey eyes looked down at her, worry engraved in his features. He pulled her close, her head against his bare chest. Malaika could hear his heart. It was racing. Roman rubbed a hand up and down her back.

"W-Why are you here?" Malaika asked, not meeting his eyes.

"I didn't want our ending to be like that."

"Ending?"

Roman sighed, resting his chin on Malaika's head. "This is it, Munequita. The job is done. You go your way and I'll go my way."

Malaika's heart sank. She was grateful her face was buried against Roman's chest. This way, he couldn't see her quivering lip or teary eyes.

"It's better this way, Munequita. It's nothing personal. I hope you can forgive me for my behavior earlier. I shouldn't have treated you like that." His arms wrapped around her, clinging on tightly.

Malaika inhaled deeply, memorizing his signature scent, the planes of his chest, the beat of his heart, and the beautiful shapes racing across his arm. This was the last time she would ever be in Roman's arms. Roman lifted her head, forcing her to look at him. Malaika was shocked to find tears swimming in the depths of his stormy eyes.

"Goodbye, Malaika." He kissed her head, then left, slipping away into the starry night.

"Goodbye, Roman."

*Dear Munequita,*

*There's a lot I need to say to you. I wish I could say all of this to you in person, but I know if I do, it'll make leaving that much harder. To start off, I'm sorry. For everything. I shouldn't have pushed you away. It was wrong of me to run out on you like that. I have no right to be mad at you for keeping secrets when I've been doing the same thing.*

*Please don't hate me for what I'm about to say. I've given this a lot of thought. Since the job is finished, it's time for us to part ways. Ever since you walked into my life, I've changed. I hate to admit it, but you made me...soft. Yeah, yeah, wipe that smile off your face. But with the good comes the bad. I'm not right for you. When I'm with you, your life is in danger.*

*I can't count how many times you've risked your neck for me. How many times you've run into the line of fire to save me. I can't have you dying, not for me. That's why I've decided to say goodbye. Our lives can't be intertwined. It won't end well. Forgive me, mi amor, I know I'm breaking your heart. It was one hell of a ride, Munequita. Thanks for taking it with me.*

*Yours forever,*

*Roman Rodriguez.*

# CHAPTER TWENTY-FIVE

## Late Night Breakdowns

ROMAN SAT ON THE roof of the pit, staring up at the ultramarine night, taking in the silver stars before him, wishing that Munequita was at his side. Despair filled him as he thought of Munequita. He missed her honey eyes, her oversized glasses, and paradoxical personality. She was a soft-spoken person with an explosive soul. Malaika was a nervous little wreck who'd run into the middle of a gang fight without a second thought. She was like the sun, warming the souls of those who met her, but she'd burn anyone who wronged the ones she loved.

He laughed aloud as he recalled her outburst when she had saved him. She had been so offended when his captor called her stupid. He shook his head, running a hand through his wet locks. *Little doll was crazy.*

"You look miserable," Nic said as crawled out of the window and took a seat next to him.

He held out a beer. Roman put his hand up, turning the drink down. It had been months since he had drunk or smoked. He didn't plan on breaking that streak.

"I'm not sorry for beating your ass," Nic said, then downed his beer.

Roman scoffed. "I won that fight."

"Sure, but you lost the girl."

Roman fell silent, pondering. "You were right, you know. About everything. I am a monster."

Nic cringed, his head turned downwards. "Sorry about that, I needed to land all those low blows to knock some sense into you."

Roman shook his head. "Don't be. It was all true. You should've seen the way she looked at me," Roman paused, blinking away the pooling tears, as Malaika's tear-streaked face flashed in his head. "I broke her heart."

"She broke yours too."

Roman chuckled ruefully. "I met up with her. I apologized for everything. It was a douche move for me to leave her like that. I was so pissed that she lied to me, and then it hit me. She wasn't the only one who lied. I did too. I never told her my deal with the O'Neals. What right did I have to go off on her when I hid the truth from her too?"

Roman's fists tightened, his nails dug painfully into his palms, as he recalled the way Munequita looked at him before she left the pit. The pain her eyes held had chilled him to the bone. Knowing he was the reason behind her tears left an aching pain in his chest. He choked, trying to suppress his sobs. Nic rubbed his shoulder, saying nothing, allowing Roman to break in peace.

"You've apologized, and she forgave you. Now tell her you love her."

Roman's heart skipped a beat at Nic's words. He opened his mouth to argue, but Nic cut him off.

"Don't bother denying it. You love her and you know it."

Roman rubbed the back of his neck, his ears burned at Nic's words. Nic was right.

"How'd you figure it out?"

Nic smiled. "You'd always leave breakfast early. Eventually I realized it was so you could listen to her sing."

Roman laughed and wiped his tears.

Nic shoved him. "Go."

Roman's smile fell. "I can't. I said goodbye."

Nic's grin turned into a frown. "What do you mean by *goodbye*?"

"I'm no good for her. Don't argue with me, you know it's true. Ever since I walked into her life, how many times has she saved me? How many times has she risked her life for mine? I can't have her dying. Not for me. I need to stay away from her. It's better this way."

Nic's eyes shone in the moonlight, his gaze was tainted with dread. "Is that why you look so sad?"

Roman nodded. "I don't want to leave her, but I can't be with her either. Her life has been in danger ever since I came into the picture. She's been hurt, beaten, and shot at all because of me. I'm not right for her. Never have been, never will be."

Roman was thankful that the moon's rays did not illuminate his face. He had, for the first time in a long time, broken. Silent tears streamed down his face as the reality of the situation hit him. He had walked out of Munequita's life. It was over. She was gone.

# CHAPTER TWENTY-SIX

# Hello Stranger

THE WEEKS PASSED. WINTER'S harsh winds blew across the city, freezing over the lakes and leaving crystal-like icicles in its wake. Life was normal. Boring, even. Malaika had turned into another face in the crowd. Her worries had disappeared. Connor had saved enough money to pay back her debt. In a few days, the transfer would be complete. She would be free.

"Good morning, Mr. Dibb."

Mr. Dibb beamed at her. "It's been a while. How have you been, Malaika?"

Malaika smiled, feeling the corners of her mouth ache. All the fake smiles she had been handing out were taking a toll on her facial muscles. "I'm fine, thank you. I was wondering if you could read over my composition, if you had the time?"

Mr. Dibb held his hand out, an excited gleam in his eyes. "You know I always look forward to reading your work." He took the paper from her hands, his eyes flew over the lines, a smile spread across his face.

*Your grey eyes I used to fear, I now look to.*
*A storm cloud that entrapped me now captivates me.*

*You are a thundercloud, hiding in the atmosphere, waiting to explode.*

*When you do, I'll stand below, waiting at the end of the rainbow.*

*My love, how do you do?*

*It's been a while, there are cracks in my heart, can you see?*

*These starry nights watch me scream and cry, by the load.*

*Do not worry, despite my broken heart, I do not consider you a foe.*

*At the end of it all, I still love you.*

*Forever and more.*

"Only you can make a broken heart sound so beautiful," he said.

"It's still a work in progress."

"I think it's wonderful so far. Great work, kiddo."

"Thank you." As Malaika headed to the door, the shadow that peeked through the cracks disappeared. *Roman.*

"Roman, will you come up to the front, please? You need to work with Malaika on your new project."

Malaika winced as the sound of Roman's chair, slamming back to the ground, echoed across the room. Roman sat down next to Malaika. Like always, Malaika's heart raced whenever he came near. A warm blush spread across her face.

"Wh-Which option should we choose for the project?" She snuck a peek up at him.

He was looking down at her, his eyes forlorn. Roman cleared his throat and looked away when Malaika locked gazes with him.

"Doesn't matter, I'll do whatever you want."

Malaika nodded and began organizing their notes. And just like that, silence engulfed them. The only time the two conversed was in Ms. Williams' class. After a few sentences, they would remain silent. Not a word spoken, nor a move made. It was how it used to be. Roman lived in his world and Malaika in hers. But no matter how hard Malaika tried to ignore Roman, she couldn't fight away the butterflies in her stomach nor the sparks of electricity that flowed through the two at the slightest touch.

Even lunchtime had changed. Roman and his friends no longer sat with Malaika and her friends. The temporary crossover had ended. Malaika and her friends lived their mundane lives, while Roman and his friends lived theirs. Though Malaika was sad, she was grateful for the time she had with them. They were a dream she clung on to in the nightmare she called-life.

"So, what are you wearing to the winter dance?" Carina asked, poking Malaika's arm, breaking her out of her depressive thoughts.

"You should wear a paper bag over your head. Those dark circles are doing nothing for you," Justin said, then snickered at his own joke.

Malaika kicked him under the table. Justin howled, cradling his ankle. Carina slapped the back of his head. Susan and Akira laughed at Justin, their faces pink.

"Justin, if I were you, I wouldn't be talking, what with that prepubescent mustache you're sporting," Akira said with a grin.

Malaika and Susan guffawed at this. Malaika noticed Roman and Nic's heads turn their way. A small smile graced Roman's lips when his eyes landed on her. Malaika ducked her head, fighting down her laughter. Susan snorted, a snot bubble dripping down her nose. Yelping, she grabbed a tissue and wiped it away. Malaika noticed that Nic suddenly seemed to be mesmerized by the dull white walls of the cafeteria.

"Come to the dance, Malaika," Carina said.

"With what date?"

"I'll take you and Susan," Akira said. "It'll be pathetic if we all went by ourselves. It's our senior year, we can't embarrass ourselves four times in a row."

Malaika nodded. Going with a group was better than going alone. "Fine, I'll go." The bell rang, continuing her monotonous cycle.

Finally, the day Malaika had been looking forward to for months arrived. Connor grinned, waving a transfer receipt in her face. Malaika gasped. Her eyes zoomed in on the number of zeroes on the receipt. Taking the paper, she examined it, not believing her eyes.

"Th-That's how much money my parents owed?" she asked.

Connor nodded.

"Holy shit!"

"And there she is. I knew Roman rubbed off on you," Connor said, and pinched Malaika's cheeks.

She slapped his hand away. "Stop, you'll pop my pimple," Malaika said.

"Oh, I have a little something for you."

Malaika's interest piqued at the tone Connor's voice took on. It was unnaturally warm. Her eyes widened at the white box in his hands.

"This is from Roman. He bought it for you a while ago. Happy birthday, doll."

Malaika's breath left her lungs as she took the box. *Roman bought this for her?* With shaking fingers, she removed the cover. Wrapped in white tissue paper was a dress. Malaika pulled the dress out, admiring its beauty. Delicate folds of pink chiffon and tulle flowed through her fingers. Sparkling silver stars were splattered against the fabric, glittering in the light.

Malaika swallowed the lump in her throat, trying very hard not to cry. Tears blurred her vision. Malaika wiped them away. She was touched. Roman did this for her. Even though they cut ties, he still remembered her birthday.

"It's beautiful."

Connor smiled down at her. "Wear it to the dance."

Malaika nodded. She hadn't been looking forward to the dance at all, but this dress changed everything. Inside the box was a birthday card. Malaika tucked it into her purse, wanting to read it in the privacy of her room.

"All right kid, it's late, we should take off."

"Can I go back to my house?"

"Yup, want me to escort you?"

Malaika pondered a moment, then shook her head. She was brave enough to face her parents on her own now. "We have repaid the debt. They can't hurt me anymore."

Connor patted her head, then left. Malaika gathered her belongings, headed to her car, and took off. Her nerves were jittering, but not with anxiety. Even though she was going to face her parents alone, she was no longer afraid. She was stronger now. Fearless. The last few months of her life changed her. She would no longer be silenced. She was Malaika Evans, and she was worthy of a voice.

It was dark when she pulled into the driveway. Her eyes narrowed when she saw there were sleek black cars parked across the street. *The O'Neals were here.* She hesitated for a moment, then set her shoulders. *No. This was her house. No one would drive her away.*

She threw off her disguise and stepped out of the car. With her head held high, Malaika made her way through the front doors. "I'm back."

Malaika's parents ran into the foyer at the sound of the creaking door. Their eyes went wide as they saw who was at the door. "Malaika?"

"Hmm?"

"What are you doing here?"

"I live here, remember?" Malaika kicked off her shoes and headed up the stairs. A cold hand wrapped around her wrist, stopping her. Malaika turned back and saw Mrs. O'Neal glaring hatefully at her.

"Did you really think you could waltz back here after publicly embarrassing my son? Despite being engaged to Liam, you dare parade around with that dog?"

Red hot rage flowed through Malaika's veins. She yanked her hand back and strode down the steps to stand toe to toe with Mrs. O'Neal. "Roman is not a dog. Rather, you and your family are. Now, if you don't mind, please leave my house as we don't allow animals inside."

"Why you insolent little girl," Mrs. O'Neal said and raised her hand to strike Malaika.

Not flinching back, Malaika grabbed Mrs.O'Neal's hand, stopping her. Mrs.O'Neal stared at Malaika, her face going bright pink.

"Remove your hand at once!" Her voice reverberated around the room.

Malaika threw Mrs. O'Neal's hand to the side and shoved her shoulder, sending her toppling down the remaining steps. Gasps echoed around the room as Amara and Liam flew forward to catch their mother.

"Malaika!" Amara shrieked, her eyes wild.

"Yes, Amara?"

"Y-Y-You—"

"M-M-Me?" Malaika mocked.

"Malaika! What has gotten into you? How dare you put your hands on your mother-in-law?" Liam asked and strode up the steps, towering over Malaika.

"Mother-in-law? Oh, that's right, you probably haven't checked your bank statements, but the debt has been repaid. I am no longer your fiancée," Malaika said and threw a sharp glance at Mr. O'Neal, whose wide eyes and gaping mouth were advancing towards her.

"Yes, Mr. O'Neal, you heard me correctly. Now if you'll excuse me." Malaika whirled around and ran up the steps, grinning at the stupefied looks on their faces.

As she made it to the safety of her bedroom, someone tackled her from behind. Malaika groaned as she lost her footing and slammed onto the floor. Her breath was knocked out as Liam landed on top of her. Liam was holding onto her, desperation painted on his features.

"N-No, you were too late. The deadline was February, it's February fourteenth, you repaid your debt too late. W-We're still engaged."

Malaika fought to remove herself from Liam's hold. His fingernails were digging painfully into her arms.

"Let go of me!" She kicked his foot, slid out of his loosened hold, and straightened up her ruffled clothes.

Liam groaned, holding his foot. He looked up at her, betrayal shining in his eyes.

"The contract states the deadline is February. You all failed to mention a date. It doesn't matter if I repaid the debt on the first or the fourteenth. I am free. Now get out of my room," Malaika seethed, her chest heaving as anger coursed through her limbs. *She would no longer be controlled.*

"M-Malaika, please," Liam begged, his eyes glistening with tears.

"I believe she said to leave her room."

Malaika's heart jumped as a deep voice spoke up behind her. She turned around, already knowing who it was by the instant calm that came over her. Illuminated by just the moonlight, Roman sat on Malaika's windowsill, his right leg hanging out the open window. His eyes were glittering with unspoken threats.

"Roman," Liam said and straightened up, his back tense.

Roman, on the other hand, lounged peacefully on her windowsill. "Are you going to get out on your own or do I need to toss you out myself?"

"Liam, my boy, it's over. Let's go home," Mr. O'Neal said, peering into the bedroom.

His usual eyes, which always shone with triumph and greed, were dimmed down to a pitiful loss.

"What? You can't be serious! Just force her to marry him right now! Who's going to stop us?" Amara cried, her eyes wide with disbelief.

Malaika jumped as something clicked behind her. Being in Roman's world for as long as she had, she instantly recognized the source of the sound. Turning back to Roman, she watched with bated breath as he toyed with the gun in his hand.

"You got thirty seconds to leave, *chica*. It's been a while since I've pulled this trigger. My hands are itching to kill someone," Roman said.

Malaika froze. The hairs on the back of her neck stood up at Roman's words. The threat was real. He wasn't joking. Not this time. He looked up, his grey eyes locking onto Malaika. A violent storm of lightning shone in his eyes.

"You all are ruining my girl's birthday."

"Amara, let's go, we lost," Liam said.

Malaika turned back to face them and watched Mr. O'Neal and Liam drag Amara away as she kicked and screamed.

"No! We were so close! All that money was supposed to be ours!"

Malaika winced as Mr. Charles slammed the door shut. He had been so silent, Malaika failed to notice his presence.

"Happy birthday, Malaika," he said from the other side of the door, then his shadow disappeared from view as the O'Neals finally left her life.

Malaika sighed, her tense shoulders relaxing. "Thank you, Roman." Malaika sat on her bed, facing him.

"Anytime. Happy birthday, Munequita." With a small smile, he slid out the window, walking out of her life once again.

Malaika fell flat onto her bed, stretching out her sore limbs. *Most exciting birthday ever!* She grabbed her purse and dug through it, looking for Roman's birthday card. Her toes curled in excitement as she opened the card, her eyes skimming over the lines.

*Happy Birthday Munequita!*

*You made it to eighteen. You may not speak of it, but I can tell by the pain in your eyes, it was hell making it this far. Thank you for hanging on, thank you for fighting. Because of your perseverance, I was able to meet you. If you had never walked into my life, I don't know what I would have done.*

*Thank you, Munequita, for breathing, living, and dreaming. I may not show it, but I need you. I refuse to live in a world where you don't exist. As selfish as it may seem, I need you to look forward to your birthdays. Not only for your sake, but mine as well. You're my saving angel. I am alive because of you. You saved me. Thank you. Happy birthday, mi amor. Though the future is always changing, one thing will always remain, my love for you.*

*Yours forever and always,*
*Roman Rodriguez.*

# CHAPTER TWENTY-SEVEN

## Closure is Overrated

MALAIKA THOUGHT BY REPAYING her debt, her life would return to normal. Oh, how wrong she was. She thought the abuse would stop, but to her horror, it only got worse. Her parents drowned themselves in alcohol every night. Minutes after midnight, her mother would barrel into her room and attack her.

Her alcohol-infused body would throw out sloppy punches and misaimed kicks. Malaika, for once, was grateful for her mother's drunken state. It made it easier to dodge the attacks. She could absorb the hits to her body. The gruesome bruises were easier to hide when they were on her body rather than her face.

Candace, having overheard Malaika's parents' conversation, relayed to Malaika that her parents were furious that she had repaid the debt. Apparently, her marriage to Liam would have been their ticket to enter high society and now their chances of entering the world of the elite were shattered. Tears welled in Malaika's eyes as her legs dangled off the edge of the roof. *She just wanted to be loved. She wanted to make her parents proud. Was that too much to ask?*

"There you are."

Malaika jumped. Her heart lurched as her body slid down the shingles. Cold hands wrapped around her arms and pulled her back to safety. She lay flat on the roof, taking in deep breaths as spots appeared in her vision. A brilliant flash of white played behind Malaika's closed lids as she was thrown back in time. Her mind replayed memories she wished to bury.

*Pain. Malaika was in constant pain. Physically, her body was destroyed, bruised and swollen beyond recognition. Mentally, she was drained, her fight was gone. Emotionally, there was nothing left. So many tears had been shed that she no longer had the energy to feel sad. Instead, she was a numb, lifeless shell.*

*Not having the will to live any longer, she jumped off her roof and into the pool. As the water ploughed through her mouth and nostrils, Malaika couldn't help but revel in the pain. The water burned her throat and clogged her senses, but she was happy. She was happy because it was all ending. It was finally ending. Darkness overtook her, dragging her into an infinite limbo.*

*Hours later, Malaika awoke. Disappointment flooded her system when she realized where she was. She was not in heaven. Damn it, she wasn't even in hell. She was in a hospital room, her hand cuffed to the bed. An aching pain spread through her head, a pounding sensation in her chest, and her throat burned every time she took a breath.*

*"Have you lost your mind?"*

*Malaika looked up. Her mother sat in the corner of the room. Her eyes were furious, her lips pressed together. Next to her stood Malaika's father. His eyes were filled with rage, the whites of his knuckles were prominent under his shaking fists.*

*"You could have cost us a fortune! Do you realize what would have happened had you died? The O'Neals would have taken everything! Our home, cars, property, all of it, just because you were having a 'mental breakdown.'"*

*Malaika winced at her mother's words. Usually she could hide her emotions well, but the heart monitor gave her away. Its rapid beeping alerted the nurse outside, who ran in with wide eyes.*

*"Mr. and Mrs. Evans, may I have a moment alone with Malaika, please?"*

*Malaika's parents left the room, giving Malaika a warning stare, just as they stepped through the doors. The nurse turned to look at Malaika, a smile on her face.*

*"Your heart rate took off. Is everything all right?"*

*Malaika stayed silent, her lip quivering. She didn't want to break. Not in front of a stranger. "Urid 'an 'akun mahbub."*

"How did you know I would be here?" Malaika asked and sat up, shoving her haunting memories into the deepest corners of her mind.

Carina and Susan sat on either side of her. Justin and Akira situated themselves behind the trio.

"Your eyes," Carina said.

"What do you mean?"

"Last year, when you attempted, you had that same look in your eyes. Lost, empty, soulless eyes," Akira whispered, his voice tinged with fear.

Malaika stayed silent. It surprised her to hear that her mask wasn't as poker faced as she thought.

"Do you want to talk about it?" Susan asked.

"There's nothing to be said. Not anymore at least."

"Meaning?" Susan prodded.

"I've given up. I've given up on my parents. They'll never love me, and as much as I hate it, I've accepted it."

"You look pretty broken for someone who's given up on giving a damn," Justin said.

A lump formed in Malaika's throat at Justin's words. "Why don't they love me?"

Carina pulled Malaika into her arms. "You don't need their love. You have ours. That's all you need."

Malaika sobbed into Carina's arms as the stars shined down on her. The silver specks provided her comfort as she broke into her best friend's arms, finally taking off her mask.

Days passed. The old bruises that had collected on Malaika's body had faded. Unfortunately, her mother had given her some fresh marks last night. This wouldn't have bothered her if it weren't for the dance. She was determined to wear the dress Roman had gotten her.

Eva locked eyes with Malaika in the mirror. "Would you like to cover them?"

Malaika thought for a moment, then shook her head. These bruises were nothing to be ashamed of. Rather, they were something to be proud of. They marked her strength, her resilience, her will to live. They were not meant to be hidden. Eva smiled and put the makeup brush down, instead working on Malaika's hair.

Connor lounged on her bed, flipping through her journal. Malaika didn't mind. Connor, unlike Liam, was not an intruder. He was a friend. Someone she loved. Her heart clenched. Connor wasn't the only one she loved. Unfortunately, the one she loved had left her. She knew it was for the best, but yet it still stung. Roman had left a gaping hole in her chest, a wound she feared was too great to heal.

*"Meet me in the lily field.*
*Dance with me amongst the daisies.*
*Let the wind caress our limbs and kiss our skin.*
*My feelings have been revealed.*
*Though the journey was hazy,*
*We have lasted through thick and thin*
*So take my hand, my love, and step into eternity."*

Connor looked up from the pages, a smile spreading across his lips. "Can I take a picture of this?"

Malaika nodded.

Akira barrelled into the room. "I've been watching dancing tutorials all day. I can guarantee that I won't step on anyone's feet today."

Malaika and Eva laughed at the goofy grin on Akira's lips.

Connor hopped up. "Show me what you got."

Akira and Connor took a hold of each other's hands. As they moved, a worried line appeared between Connor's brows.

"Uh, Akira? I don't mean to freak you out, but I think you taught yourself the follower's steps, instead of the leader's."

Akira's eyes went wide, his shoulders slumping in disappointment. "Aw man! I practiced all day."

Akira's pout tugged at Malaika's heartstrings. "It's okay, Akira, I'm sure your devilishly handsome good looks will distract everyone from your dance moves."

Akira was up in an instant, a smug smile on his lips. "Well, I don't want to brag, but I am pretty damn handsome." He slicked his hair back, winking at an imaginary audience.

"All right, doll, you're all done," Eva said, helping Malaika up.

She led Malaika to the floor-length mirror. Malaika gasped as she took herself in. Layers of delicate pink tulle and chiffon slid down her body. The silver stars splattered against the dress, sparkling under the light. Eva twirled her bronze tresses into romantic curls. Baby's breath blossoms were braided into the pinned hair, while the rest of her hair flowed down to her waist. Full dark lashes framed her amber eyes. Glittering, neutral tones rested on her eyelids, bringing her face to life. Raspberry gloss was slicked across her lips. Her golden complexion shined as hints of highlighter gleamed under the light.

Malaika's breath caught in her throat. "Th-Thank you, Eva."

"Anytime, doll."

Connor took her hand and led her down the stairs. Akira and Malaika followed him into the car.

"All right, kids, no funny business, and I want you home by midnight sharp," he said.

Malaika laughed. Akira rolled his eyes, though he wore a grin. Malaika's heart leaped in excitement as Connor took off. She was happy. Happier than she had been in a long time. And she owed it all to her friends. Connor, Eva, Akira, Justin, Susan, Carina, and Roman. Though that chapter had closed, the words were still being written. Roman had left his mark in her life. It would take a while to erase. The thought of killing him from her memories brought a wave of sadness over Malaika. It's not that she couldn't get over him, it's that she didn't want to. Roman was everything she had dreamed of and more.

As the magnificent mansion came into view, Malaika buried all thoughts of Roman to the back of her mind. Tonight was about her and her friends. It was time to be a normal teenager. She stepped out of the car and hooked her arm through Akira's. Susan joined the duo, taking Akira's other arm. The trio headed up the steps. Excitement bubbled in Malaika's chest as the bass vibrated through her body. A smile erupted across her face when she stepped through the mahogany doors. Her eyes trailed over the room, taking in the twinkling lights, delicate decor, candles, and snow-kissed evergreens.

When her gaze drifted to the dance floor, her smile fell. Dread filled her heart when she saw who was waiting for her. His emerald eyes were cold, guarded. His posture was tense and demanding. *Liam*. With a sigh, she waved for Susan and Akira to enjoy themselves. She had to play one last game.

She strode over to him with her head held high. "Liam."

"Malaika. May I have this dance?"

"Like I have a choice."

Liam shook his head, a sick look in his eyes, and took her hand in his. He pulled her close and moved along the dancefloor. Malaika looked into his eyes. Like hers, they were hard and unforgiving.

"What do you want, Liam?"

"Nothing, just checking in on my fiancée."

Malaika scoffed. "In case you forgot, I have paid off my parents' debt. I'm free."

Liam smiled, though nothing about it was warm. He yanked her close. Malaika cringed as he skimmed the tip of his nose against her cheek, down to the hollow of her neck.

"Your debt has indeed been repaid, but you are forgetting who my father is."

Malaika gulped, her stomach lurching at the malice in Liam's voice. He straightened up and met her gaze. His jade eyes stared into hers, cold and calculating. The hairs on the back of Malaika's neck rose. In this moment, she could see the family resemblance between Liam and Mr. Charles.

He twirled Malaika around the dance floor. Malaika hadn't realized that they had stopped moving. She cleared her throat, hoping her nerves weren't showing. "What have you done?"

"You will marry me, Malaika, unless you want Roman to die."

Malaika froze. Without hesitation, she yanked Liam's collar, pulling him down to meet her eyes. Her free hand clamped around his neck. "What did you say?"

Liam's face turned red as Malaika's nails dug into his flesh. Malaika loosened her hold so he could speak.

"My father has given his men orders to dispose of Roman if you do not leave with me tonight."

Malaika's head spun. It felt as if someone had thrown a bucket of ice cold water on her. Her blood rushed through her ears, panic bubbled in her chest.

"I'm going to kill you."

"Is that any way to talk to your future husband?"

Malaika shoved him away and stormed off. Her fists shook as she tried to suppress her rage.

"Woah there. What's wrong?" Akira caught her elbow as she ran towards the doors.

"I need to talk to Connor now. We've got trouble." She motioned towards Liam, who was rubbing his neck.

"Who's that?" Susan asked.

"Liam, my ex-fiancé."

Akira choked on his cake. Susan slapped his chest.

"Should I get Justin and Carina?" Susan asked, as Akira hacked out the cake.

Malaika looked at the dance floor. Justin and Carina were locked in each other's embrace. Justin was a nervous wreck, tripping over his own two feet.

Malaika smiled. "Leave them be for now."

Susan and Akira followed Malaika out into the hall. She led them to a secluded corner. Her nerves were jittering. She was terrified of what they would say when they found out the truth. Taking a deep breath, she began her tale.

"Before I begin, I want to start by apologizing. I kept a lot of secrets from you all this past year. I know it was wrong for me to hide everything that I'm about to tell you, but there was no other way. By keeping you in the dark, I was keeping you safe."

Akira and Susan looked on with worry in their eyes but urged her to go on.

"Last year, my parents made a business deal with some people called the O'Neals. Unfortunately, it went bad and my parents ended up with an enormous debt. In order to save themselves, they offered my inheritance. In order to access that inheritance, I needed to be married."

Susan grabbed Akira's hand in a tight hold. His fingers turned blue, but he stayed silent.

"And so I was engaged to Liam. There's another man involved, but he's out of the picture now. The O'Neals controlled me. I wasn't allowed to take the classes I enjoyed, I wasn't allowed to hang out with my friends anymore. My mother became more abusive than usual. Not seeing a way out, I drowned in my sorrows and attempted suicide."

Malaika stopped speaking as the painful memories resurfaced. *The feeling of the water invading her lungs and ploughing through her mouth and nostrils played in her mind. Her body screamed as her breath was stolen from her. Dark spots blurred her vision as her life was being taken from her. Then warmth. Bright white warmth as her friends' faces danced in her head. Their worried eyes and sad smiles as they saved her from herself.*

Malaika shook her head, blinking to keep the tears at bay. Akira and Susan pulled Malaika into a hug. Their faces were devastated.

"And then I met Connor. He, Roman, and his friends helped to free me from my debt. But it's not over. Liam's father has ordered his men to kill Roman if I don't leave with Liam tonight."

Susan and Akira stepped back, fiery determination in their eyes.

"What do we do?" Susan asked.

"We call Connor and his friends. If a fight's what the O'Neals want, then a fight's what they'll get."

Akira handed her his phone, Connor's name already on the screen.

"Connor?"

"Malaika?"

"Connor, get down to the hall now. There's trouble."

Connor was instantly alert. His tone was authoritative. "What kind of trouble?"

"Mr. O'Neal will order an attack on Roman unless I leave with Liam tonight. Please get Roman somewhere safe, then get down here, so we can take care of this mess."

Connor was silent for a moment. "You want to protect Roman?"

"Of course. Just because he's not a part of my life anymore doesn't mean I'm going to love him any less."

There was a sharp intake of breath on the line, followed by muffled curses.

"I'm coming, don't worry. We're going to handle this."

"Thank you, Connor." Malaika hung up and waited with her heart in her hands.

*Another battle was beginning. One where bloodshed was inevitable.*

# CHAPTER TWENTY-EIGHT

## Fuck It

ROMAN'S HEART THUNDERED IN his chest as Munequita's words echoed across the room. *"Just because he's not a part of my life anymore doesn't mean I'm going to love him any less."*

Connor stared at Roman, his eyebrows raised. "You heard that? Just because you cut her out of your life doesn't mean the violence will stop. Just because you left her, doesn't ensure her safety. By leaving her, you left her vulnerable."

Connor's words pierced Roman's soul. It was as if someone had wrapped an ice cold hand around his heart. His chest squeezed painfully. Despite everything he put her through, Munequita was still willing to risk it all for him. Roman shook his head. His heart swelled at Munequita's words. "Screw it, I'm getting my girl back." He grabbed the keys and ran out the door.

Connor whooped loudly. "Now that's what I'm talking about."

Roman threw himself into the car and took off into the night, hoping he wasn't too late. Now it was his turn to save Munequita. Just as she had saved him.

"If that poem wasn't proof enough that she loves you, was her confession enough?" Connor asked.

Roman chuckled. His heart soared as Munequita's words played in his mind. She loved him! He couldn't believe it. Munequita loved him, flaws, scars, and all. A smile broke across his face. Tears blurred his vision as the words of her poem flashed in his head. After a lifetime of pain, he had finally found his reason to live.

Furtive whispers echoed around Malaika as the light bounced off her skin. She knew her bruises were the topic of conversation. Though hurt by the stares, she didn't look down. Instead, she held her head high. She was no longer weak and spineless. If someone wanted to say something, they could say it to her face.

The clock struck eleven. The deep chords were like a sentencing for Malaika. Only an hour until the night was up. Only an hour to find out whether Roman would live or die. Roman's lifeless grey eyes flashed in her mind. Malaika's heart lurched at the thought of losing him. She wrung her hands together as Akira and Susan filled Justin and Carina in on the situation.

She looked around the room. Liam was gone. Panic shot through her at his absence. If he was gone, did that mean he would execute the attack soon? She hoped Connor had driven Roman far away. Goosebumps erupted across her skin as she felt a pair of eyes on her back.

She whirled around, her gaze landing on Roman. He stood by the doors, indecision painted on his features. A raging storm brewed in his eyes. He rocked on his heels as the two locked gazes. His eyes flashed as he fought with himself.

"Fuck it," he mouthed.

He strode forward. Malaika stood transfixed as his warm hands cradled her cheeks. He lifted her head to meet his. Roman stared into Malaika's eyes for a brief moment. But that moment was everything. She knew Roman wasn't going anywhere. Not this time. He was here to stay, forever and always. Closing her eyes, Malaika surrendered to the truth she tried so hard to bury. *She loved Roman. No matter how hard she tried to fight it, the bad boy had hypnotized her, heart and soul.*

"I love you, Malaika." He crashed his lips onto hers.

Malaika's heart soared, her eyes brimmed with tears. Her hands reached up of their own accord and tangled themselves into his raven tresses. Roman pulled her close and kissed her as if his life depended on it. Butterflies danced in Malaika's stomach as her body molded against his.

Despite the danger that lurked in the corner, in this moment, she was happy. In this moment, she was complete. Roman's hands trailed down to her waist. His warm hands left a trail of sizzling electricity as they caressed her skin. Finally, the lack of oxygen became too much, and she broke away.

"Damn," Roman said.

A fiery blush coated Malaika's cheeks as everything came rushing back to her. *She just had her first kiss. That too, with Roman! She hoped she did it right.* Judging by his pink cheeks and goofy smile, Malaika assumed she had to have done something right.

"I've been wanting to do that for a while now," Roman admitted with a sheepish grin.

Without warning, Roman scooped Malaika into his arms and carried her out to the balcony, away from prying eyes and ears. He placed her down, his gaze trailed over her. His eyes softened as he took in her bruises. He pulled her close, his lips just a hair's width away. Turning her around, he traced the bruises that sat on the back of her neck with trembling fingers. With a feather-light touch, his fingers skimmed down to her shoulders, hesitating for just a moment, then his warm lips met her bare skin. He kissed the gruesome bruises that coated her shoulder blades. Malaika gasped as he made his way down to the violet bruise that sat on her back. His cool breath tickled her skin.

"You're beautiful, Malaika," he said. He turned her around to face him. "Don't let anyone tell you otherwise."

Malaika didn't fight the tears this time. She let them fall as he pulled her into his arms. The two were silent as they basked in each other's embrace. Malaika inhaled deeply, finding comfort in his familiar scent. Intoxicating musk with hints of savoury wood. Roman's warm fingers traced patterns on her lower back, raising goosebumps across her skin.

"Say something, Munequita."

"There aren't words."

"Do you really love me?" Roman asked, meeting her eyes. Malaika was surprised to see they were swimming with vulnerability.

Malaika shook her head.

Roman froze, his face falling.

"Love isn't a strong enough word to describe how I feel about you."

A brilliant smile painted his lips. "I'm sorry!" he blurted suddenly.

"Sorry?"

"I'm sorry for being angry when you told me the truth. I'm sorry for pushing you away, and most importantly, I'm sorry for breaking your heart," he rushed out, his hands trembling as they clutched at her waist.

"I was a hypocrite. I walked out of your life when you told me the truth and yet I never told you mine. I never told you why I was after Liam's family," he said.

Malaika grabbed his face, forcing him to look at her. "You don't have to tell me anything."

He shook his head, taking her hand and bringing it to his lips. He kissed her palm. "You deserve to know the truth."

Malaika's brain felt fuzzy, and butterflies soared in her stomach as his lips brushed against her skin.

"My dad's a deadbeat," he began.

Malaika squeezed his hand, tracing circles on the back of his hand.

"He'd only show up to give my mom more children and steal her money. My mom tries to fight him off, but he's a big guy. She's terrified of him. Hell, so am I. Last year, my mom started to date this guy. I never questioned her new relationship because, for the first time in a long time, she was happy. I hadn't seen her eyes shine like that in a long time."

He paused, taking a deep breath. Malaika rubbed his arms, comforting him.

"Only now, I wish I had. Turns out he was just another big shot cheating on his wife."

Malaika's heart dropped at this revelation. *Poor Carmen.*

"The wife found out and threatened my mom. That didn't go over too well with Jet. He landed a nice hit on her cheek."

Malaika laughed. Roman joined in, after trying to fight it.

"I don't think we should laugh at this," Malaika said, wiping away her tears.

Roman nodded, his eyes turned serious as he continued his tale. "My mom left him and never looked back. There was only one problem." Roman's hands balled into fists. "She was pregnant. Jet and I told her that if she wanted an abortion, we'd support her, but she couldn't bring herself to do so. Even though the bastard was just using her, she loved him. She really loved him. And she wanted to hold on to him. Her unborn child was the only reminder she had that he existed."

Malaika wiped away his tears, her heart breaking for him.

"I wasn't about to let my little sister grow up without a father, so I did what anyone would do. I confronted the bastard and demanded he be a part of her life. Want to know what the douche did?"

Malaika looked into his bloodshot eyes, afraid of what he was going to tell her. She didn't think her heart could take anymore.

"He threw money at my face and said *'your mom charges hourly, right?'*" Roman's tall frame shook in anger as he had to relive his darkest days.

Malaika ran her hands through his hair, cradling his head to her chest. "Breathe, Roman."

He inhaled, clenching his fists. After a few moments, his body stilled, his rage leaving his body. "I wanted to hurt him, hell, if I'm being honest, I wanted to put a bullet through his head. But I couldn't, I wouldn't. I refused to act on the instincts handed to me by my sperm donor of a dad. So instead, I decided to ruin him. Your plan for revenge worked out perfectly for me because my sister's father is Mr. O'Neal."

Malaika's world stopped. She couldn't believe her ears. She hadn't realized the intensity of Roman's pain. Malaika had no clue that Roman's demons outnumbered hers. He had bottled up a lifetime of pain, hurt, and betrayal for the sake of his family. Malaika kissed his tears away.

"Let's go get that son of a bitch," she said.

Roman grinned. Akira and Justin poked their heads through the doorway.

"Roman, we've evacuated everyone," Justin said.

Roman nodded at them, a smile on his face. "Thanks for everything, guys. Take Susan and Carina far away from here. I'll see you at sunrise."

The two nodded and left, giving Malaika a fleeting smile. The sound of screeching tires and roaring engines reached Malaika's ears. She peered over the banister. Neon racing cars pulled into the driveway. A handful of black trucks were parked across from them. *Us against them.*

"One last ride," Roman muttered.

Roman reached into his pocket and pulled out a gun. Malaika froze as Roman handed her the weapon. It was cold and heavy. Its black metal grip glinted in the moonlight. As Malaika's fingers wrapped around the butt of the gun, her heart drummed against her chest. Fear crept through her veins at the thought of what would soon unfold.

"Don't do anything crazy." Roman kissed Malaika's forehead. "Wait for me."

Malaika nodded. Her eyes filled with tears as Roman made his way toward the battlefield. "Be careful, Roman," she called.

Roman stopped, turned to her, and smiled. Then he disappeared into the night.

Something hard struck the side of Malaika's head, and spots invaded her vision. Darkness threatened to overtake her. She raised the gun and tried to aim it at her assailant but missed. The sound of the gun firing echoed through the night, a desperate cry for help. Another hit to her head, and she was drowning under waves of unconsciousness.

*Come on, bad boy. Come and save me.*

# CHAPTER TWENTY-NINE

## One Last Fight

ROMAN'S HEART THUNDERED IN his chest as he left Munequita. *One last ride. One last fight.* He stepped through the doors and joined his brothers on the battlefield. His eyes trailed over the other side. He recognized some of the men Mr. O'Neal hired to kill him. Most of them were rivals that had been itching for years to take his life.

The man in the back stood out. His beefy arms and beady eyes looked awfully familiar. Roman recognized him as the bastard who had shot Munequita. Roman's body burned, his arms shook with rage, as Munequita's bruised and battered face flashed in his mind. The man smirked as he saw Roman's flared nostrils and narrowed eyebrows.

"The big one's mine," Roman said, throwing off his suit jacket.

"They've got body bags ready to go," Seb said, cracking his knuckles.

Dominic scoffed. "They plan on beating us to death with those scrawny ass limbs?"

Nic disguised his laugh as a cough. "Don't underestimate them, Dom. They may just be your downfall."

Connor cracked his neck. "We can't lose, boys. Not this time."

Both sides stood still, awaiting orders. *Which side would make the first move?* Roman's fists were balled, ready to go. Their fates were determined when a shot echoed through the night. His eyes went wide as he realized the shot had not been fired down here. It had gone off from above. *Munequita!*

Roman took off. His body moving on its own accord. His blood rushed through his ears at the thought of losing Munequita. He knew she needed him, but his friends needed him as well. *Hold on, Munequita, I'm coming.*

With an enraged cry, Roman charged forward. Pulling his arm back, he swung. The man easily dodged his attack and threw his own fist forward. Roman caught it and twisted his arm, throwing the man over his shoulder. Roman pinned him down and threw out merciless punches left and right. His fists were shaking as they connected with the man's face over and over again.

The shining excitement left the man's eyes as Roman's fists collided with his flesh. His lip split open, his eyes were swelling up, and knots appeared in his temple. Scarlet blood streaked down his face, drenching the snow-kissed ground beneath him.

"You shouldn't have touched Munequita," Roman seethed, then slammed his fist against the man's temple, knocking him unconscious.

Cold hands grabbed Roman's neck from behind. Roman whirled around, pushing his assailant back. He scoffed when he saw who it was. "Go home, Liam. This is way out of your league."

Liam smirked and pulled out a switchblade. The silver blade gleamed in the moonlight. Roman's heart lurched, though he kept a blank face. He tore off the bottom of his dress shirt and wrapped it around his hand. "Let's go."

Liam ran forward and swung the blade around. Roman stepped back as Liam swung the blade at his face. He shot his hand out, trying to knock the knife out of Liam's hand. Liam swung again. Roman leaned back, threw a right hook, and faked left. His fist collided with Liam's face. Liam's eyes rolled back, a guttural groan escaped his lips. Roman caught him before his head hit the cold cement. He dragged his body away from the fight, then went back to join his brothers.

Roman inhaled and blinked away the spots that appeared in his vision. He struggled to catch his breath as he engaged in another bloody battle. Roman recognized the duo before him. They were members of his old gang who took part in his initiation and his exit.

"It's been a while, boys."

They ran for Roman, their knuckles shining. *Knuckle knives.* Roman's stomach flipped as the first attacker swung. He stepped back, dodging the attack. His attacker was relentless. He swung repeatedly. Roman tried to knock the weapon out of his grip, but couldn't, not without facing the risk of being cut.

A stinging pain spread through his back. Roman fell to his knees, groaning as the cold cement grazed his skin. Another sharp pain shot in his side. He collapsed against the cold ivory flakes. Hot blood escaped his wounds. The second attacker stood before him, a wicked grin on his lips. "You survived one jump out, can you survive another?"

Roman cursed as the boys swung down on him. Death was inevitable. *Forgive me, Munequita.* A familiar mess of blazing red flew past him. Connor tackled one attacker, swiped the blade away from him, and knocked him out. Roman jumped up as the second attacker froze. He grabbed the hand that wielded the blade and twisted it, hearing a loud crunch echo across the night as he broke the boy's hand. Releasing him, Roman kicked the boy in his head, putting him to sleep.

Connor ran to him and inspected his wounds. "Flesh wounds, you're good."

Roman ran towards Nic, who was too busy engaged in a fist fight to notice the figure creeping up behind him. With a roar, Roman speared the man to the ground. He wrestled the crowbar out of his arms and viciously attacked the man's body. The man cried out as Roman slammed the steel bar into his body again and again, destroying his flesh and bone. With one last hit, Roman sent the man into a deep slumber.

Back to back, Nic and Roman fought their next set of opponents. Roman protected Nic, while Nic protected Roman. Roman's body was shaking. Tears and snot ran down his face as the gruesome battle continued. The intensity of the battle was breaking down his will to fight. Nic laughed as Roman threw a punch and missed.

"With hits like that, you still have the audacity to say you won our fight?"

Roman rolled his eyes, though he wore a grin. "Screw you, man."

He threw his leg up, slamming his knee into his attacker's head. The crunching sound of his nose raised goosebumps on his arms. Dominic's cursing rang through the night as the sound of sirens reached their ears. The attackers froze, horror painted on their features.

"O'Neal lied to us. He promised no cops would show. It's a setup, run!" one attacker cried.

The ones who were still conscious dragged their unconscious members into their trucks and took off in a mess of smoke and oil. Panic swelled in Roman's chest. His heart sprinted as he took in the scene before him. Scarlet blood kissed the ivory snow, hinting at the horrors that had just taken place. *They were going to be arrested.* Seb limped over to him, his eyes flashed dangerously.

"We need to go now," he said.

Roman nodded, but stopped when Connor started laughing.

"It's all good, boys. It's just Eva and Ginger," he said.

Connor's signature electric blue car pulled into the driveway. Eva and Ginger stepped out, killing the engine and sound.

"If you all look this bad, I wonder what the other guys look like," Ginger said and grinned, her fingers tracing Seb's bloody nose.

"Go get your girl," Eva said, and threw Roman a wink.

Roman ran into the venue and headed up to the balcony. His blood ran cold at the sight before him. Munequita was gone. The gun he had given her lay on the ground, a single bullet at its side. Her heel lay abandoned by the messy 'C' that was traced in the snow. Roman's body trembled as rage ran through his veins. His fists balled, his nails biting into his skin as he intercepted the code she had left for him.

"Charles."

Connor squeezed Roman's shoulder. "Let's go get our girl back."

*Don't worry, Munequita, I'm coming.*

It was the thick scent of blood which woke Malaika. Its salty scent swam around her, invading her nostrils. Traces of sulfur and hints of salt trailed up her nose. Her heart hammered painfully in her chest as a million thoughts swirled around in her mind. She was wide awake, but kept her eyes screwed shut. With each breath she took, a sharp pain shot through her lungs. As the sleepiness wore off, Malaika became more aware of the bindings that were holding her in place. Coarse rope bit into her skin, stinging her wrists.

Peeking one eye open, she looked at her surroundings. Darkness. Complete and utter darkness. She hadn't a clue where she was. The only hints given to her were the pungent scents entering her nostrils.

"You're awake."

Malaika gasped and jumped at the sudden sound. She blinked as a bright light spilled across the darkened room. Before her stood Mr. Charles. His snake-like eyes were gleaming dangerously. Triumph and greed swam in the depths of his jade eyes. A cold sweat broke across Malaika's forehead at the sight in front of her. Her body seized as he strode forward, his lips just an inch away from hers.

"Though I would have preferred you in white, you still look beautiful."

Malaika blinked, confused. She looked around the room, her gaze landing on Amara. Her eyes were glittering with malice and her grin seeped with bloodlust. Malaika turned back to look at Mr. Charles. She understood how she got here, though she didn't understand why. The last thing she remembered was Roman's retreating frame as he headed off for one last battle with the O'Neals. After that, a sharp pain rang through her head and she had drowned in a sea of darkness. It seemed that Mr. Charles and Amara were to blame.

"Why am I here?" Malaika was thankful that her voice didn't waver.

"That should be fairly obvious, darling. You are here to marry me. You are here to grant me your inheritance."

Malaika's heart sank, her stomach rolled. She fought to control the waves of nausea that overtook her. "My d-debt has been repaid. You can no longer control me."

"True, but we can hurt you." Amara walked forward, toying with the knife in her hand. The bright light bounced off the blade, its shadow resting along Malaika's neck.

"Did you really think I was going to let you get away after everything you've done? You ruined the O'Neal name," Amara said. Her eyes trailed over Malaika, her lips pulled down into a sneer. Her voice held a chilling note of menace. "You took everything from my family. Now I'm going to take everything away from you."

Malaika gulped. Her fingers shook. "I hate to burst your bubble, but I can take a hit. It'll take a lot to break me."

Amara paused. "Oh, I know. That's why I brought in reinforcements."

The doors were thrown open. A gust of cold wind flew in. A darkened silhouette moved forward into the light. Malaika fought off a cry of despair. The familiar long legged, doe-eyed temptress walked forward. Her crimson lips turned up into a smile, though, like always, it was cold and hateful. *Natalie.*

"Now, ladies, let's not be hasty. Malaika, sign these papers, so this can end before it begins," Mr. Charles said as he stepped in front of Malaika.

A short man with oversized glasses and thick brows waddled over to Mr. Charles. He pulled out various files from his briefcase. "She needs to sign the first three pages, then both she and the inheritance are yours."

Malaika's fear was replaced with anger. Her fists balled as she spat at Mr. Charles. "You can't make me sign anything."

Mr. Charles' eyebrows narrowed. "Malaika, save yourself the trouble and sign the documents. You won't even have to remain my wife. I'll let you go once I have the inheritance."

Malaika couldn't believe what she was hearing. She knew the O'Neals were monsters, but she didn't think they would stoop this low. A broken laugh escaped her lips as she tried to wrap her head around their horrendous thoughts.

"You people disgust me. Despite having it all, you still want more. I'm sorry, but I'm going to have to cut your daydream short, Mr. Charles. I don't plan on signing anything, so get to it already," she said.

Mr. Charles stared at her, his eyes flashing. "Have it your way."

He moved aside, making room for Natalie. She reached into her purse and drew out a pair of pliers. Malaika's heart jumped. The taste of blood sat on the tip of her tongue. Though she wore a brave face, she couldn't fight off the waves of fear that slid down her back. Sweat ran down her limbs, her body quaked as she fought to escape the bindings.

Natalie glared at Malaika through narrowed eyes. "Why did he choose you? What does he see in you?" she asked, her voice low, almost a whisper.

For a moment, Malaika was sure she imagined it. A flash of despair sparked in Natalie's eyes. And just like that, it was gone, replaced by a fiery vengeance.

Malaika tried to pull her fingers away from Natalie's advancing hand. Natalie stopped, her lips curled. "I'm from the streets. You all didn't think I was actually going to do this, did you?"

Malaika froze, her heart skipped a beat. *Was Natalie going to save her?* As Natalie's fist flew forward, Malaika was given her answer. *No, she wasn't.* Red hot pain spread through her face as Natalie's fist collided with her skull. Malaika's head flew back, the familiar feeling of blood dripping down her nose greeted her. Her ears rang and her head pounded as Natalie's attacks continued.

Malaika clenched her jaw as Natalie threw out punch after punch. A hard kick aimed at her ribs threw Malaika to the ground. She choked, fighting back tears as the relentless attacks continued. Screaming pain rushed through her limbs as Natalie unleashed her fury. Malaika's body shook as the pain spread from her head, down to her chest, and trailed to her ribs. There was no escape. She was vulnerable. She was exposed. Tears escaped her eyes as she realized she may die today. Malaika kept her eyes shut, finding comfort in Roman's smile as it played in her head.

Shooting pain rocked through her limbs as attack after attack followed. Malaika gasped, choking as she struggled to breathe. Crimson blood spilled from her lips. In the back of her mind, she registered that she was being sat up.

"Enough!" Mr. Charles said.

The attacks stopped. Malaika inhaled. Her body trembled as tears ran down her face.

"Malaika?" he whispered.

Malaika peeked her eyes open. Mr. Charles stood before her, his face inches from hers. "Marry me, Malaika, and it will all end."

Malaika shook her head. "I'd rather die."

Mr. Charles clenched his jaw, his eyebrow twitched angrily. "She will break you," he said.

"I'm already broken." Malaika's mask cracked, sobs racked through her chest, as she lost control of her façade. Her heart screamed, allowing her soul to mourn for the first time in her life.

"It's not in my nature to put my hands on a woman, but damn, Natalie, you're tempting me."

Malaika froze. Her sobs came to a stop and her body relaxed as a familiar voice rang out. A warm voice filled with promise. A voice that she knew would always be there to whisper sweet nothings into her ear when she lost control. *Roman.*

Roman's fiery gaze landed on Malaika. His face softened as he saw the damage that had been done to her. Ginger and Eva stormed into the room, with Carina and Susan behind them, fury etched into their features.

Ginger let out a stream of curses and ran at Natalie. Carina followed her lead and took off her heels, using them as a weapon. The confidence that had been oozing from Natalie disappeared. The cockiness in her features melted away, her face morphed into one of shock and fear. With wide eyes and an open mouth, she turned tail and ran. Ginger and Carina closed in on her, releasing their rage.

Eva stormed towards Amara, her fists raised. Nic toppled into the warehouse, a crowbar in hand. Susan yanked the crowbar away from him and ran to Amara as Eva pulled her to the ground.

Malaika turned to Roman. He didn't attack Mr. Charles. Instead, he made his way to Malaika and untied her.

"I'm sorry I'm late."

"That's all right. You're here now, that's all that matters," she whispered, her eyes drooping.

Mr. Charles' furious screams echoed across the room. Malaika jumped, her eyes landing on Mr. Charles. Connor, Seb, Nic, and Dom were beating him to a pulp. Mr. Charles' long limbs struggled to escape, but Connor kept a firm hold on him as the group of friends beat him unconscious.

Justin and Akira were close by and kept a tight grip on Mr. Charles' assistant. His pitiful whimpers and cries bounced around the warehouse. Heavy, splotchy tears fell from his eyes. A large stain appeared just below his crotch and trailed down to the floor. Akira winced, leaping away from the urine, while Justin cursed up a storm.

Roman pulled Malaika into his arms and tucked her head under his chin. Malaika melted into his hold. The relief she felt now that she was in his arms was immeasurable.

"You're safe now," Roman said, and kissed the top of her head.

"H-How did you find me?"

"The code you left was pretty damn clear. Akira traced your cell here. Hmm, Trinity Hill, pretty fitting, if you ask me."

"Why's that?" Malaika struggled to stay conscious when sleep was tugging at her, urging her to join it.

"It was here where our relationship was supposed to end and yet here is where it really began."

Malaika smiled, snuggled into Roman's chest, and inhaled his familiar scent. Entangled with his intoxicating scent were traces of blood and metal. The sound of cop sirens invaded her ears. Malaika yelped, and she grabbed a fistful of Roman's shirt.

"Don't worry," Roman said, rubbing her back. "This time, they're on our side."

"How'd you accomplish that?"

"Connor had all of his harassment claims on standby and I threatened O'Neal to go to the papers about his illegitimate daughter."

The cops barrelled into the room, breaking up the various fights.

"Fall back, guys," Roman ordered.

In an instant, the boys had let go of Mr. Charles. Ginger slapped Natalie one last time, then threw her to the ground. Carina dragged her heels across Natalie's face, then slipped them back on. Eva punched Amara in the face, flipped her hair, and threw herself into Connor's awaiting arms. Susan gave Amara a kick to her ankles, the crowbar still clasped in her hands. She couldn't bring herself to use the weapon. Nic pried it out of her hands and gave her a small smile.

"Let's go home, Munequita," Roman said.

He gazed down at her, a bittersweet smile on his lips. As she stared into his hypnotizing eyes, Malaika could see the love he had for her. So pure and honest, she wanted to drown in its depths.

Malaika smiled, her heart overflowing with joy. "I'm already home." She faded off into unconsciousness, comforted by the thought that her home was in the arms of the bad boy. *To love is to live and die in your arms.*

# CHAPTER THIRTY

# Unstable Happily Ever Afters

PAIN DOES NOT HEAL overnight. Trauma is not magically erased after a session of therapy. Happiness cannot be delivered by one pill. Malaika was well aware of this, which made the path to healing much more tolerable. Years of abuse and trauma would be hard to erase, but Malaika was not looking to eradicate these things. Rather, she was looking for a way to cope and live with these hardships.

She wanted to be able to look past the bruises and see the beautiful girl Roman saw. Malaika wanted to look at her body and see the goddess Ginger saw. She wanted to look into her eyes and see the fight Connor saw. Malaika wanted to feel her soul and embrace the good her friends told her about. In time she would, but for now, she would relish in the arms of the bad boy as they entered the next chapter in their book.

The months flew by. Malaika no longer feared the night. She no longer dreaded when the moon was at its highest.

Rather than readying her body for attacks, she readied herself for Carmen's loving embraces. Rather than hiding her compositions under the floorboards, they were pinned to the wall, proudly shown off by Roman. She no longer cried herself to sleep, instead she laughed with Jet and Meredith until she floated off into her dreams. For the first time in her life, Malaika knew what it was like to have a family.

"Roman? Malaika? Please wait a moment."

Malaika froze. She licked her lips, her throat suddenly parched. Roman nodded at her.

"Breathe."

She inhaled deeply and counted to ten. Roman rubbed comforting circles on the small of her back. Ms. Williams shut the door as the last student left the classroom. She turned around and faced the duo. Her eyes gleamed with excitement and what seemed like a hint of pride.

"Congratulations, Mr. Rodriguez."

"Huh?" Roman said.

Malaika looked up at Roman. Judging by his knitted eyebrows, he, too, did not understand. Ms. Williams laughed, her eyes lingering on Roman's hand, which still sat on Malaika's back. Malaika's neck burned at the intensity in Ms. Williams's eyes.

"Congratulations, Mr. Rodriguez. Your hard work has paid off. You have gone from the verge of failing to ranking in the top thirty percent."

Malaika's eyes went wide. She choked, gasping for air. "T-Top thirty percent!" She beamed at Roman, her eyes brimming with tears.

Roman stood frozen, his eyes wide in disbelief. "Don't mess with me, *mujer.*"

Ms. Williams laughed. "First, don't call me *mujer*. And second, it's true. I'm proud of you, Roman. Congratulations to you as well, Malaika."

Malaika's smile fell. "Congratulations? What for?"

Ms. William's eyes softened behind her thick-rimmed glasses. "You seem to be smiling a lot more."

Malaika's body burned, her heart pounded at Ms. Williams's words. "Th-Thank you."

Roman grabbed her hand. He thanked Ms. Williams and led Malaika out of the room. "I owe it all to you, Munequita."

"And I, to you."

Roman leaned down and kissed Malaika's head. His warm lips lingered there for a moment, causing butterflies to erupt in Malaika's stomach.

"Ew! Please, not in front of my innocent eyes," Dom said.

Malaika laughed at Dominic's outburst. Roman pulled away and chased after Dominic, who took off, screaming down the hall.

Finally, the day Malaika had been waiting for arrived. Graduation. Roman wiped away her tears, while she scanned the crowd looking for Carmen.

"Over there," Roman said, pointing to a figure in the distance. He grabbed Malaika in his arms and took off. "Be strong, Munequita."

Malaika tucked her head into Roman's chest, finding comfort in the beat of his heart. Her parents' piercing gaze settled on her as they stood in the throng of families, waiting for her. Her stomach lurched as her mother's frosty glare landed on her. Despite the glacier front she wore, Malaika could tell her mother was no longer the monster she used to be. She didn't know if the beast had been murdered or if her fight had died. Regardless, she didn't want her mother's broken remains.

"Congratulations, baby," Carmen said, as Roman placed her down.

Malaika's heart soared at the pride in Carmen's voice. Throwing her arms around Carmen, Malaika sobbed her heart out. "W-We did it," she said.

"Yes, baby, you did. I'm so proud of you. Both of you."

Malaika broke away. Her gaze landed on her parents. Rage and betrayal shone in their eyes. Malaika's father's fists were balled, his lips pulled down in a frown. Her mother's body shook with anger.

Jet's cackling broke Malaika out of her trance. "Haha, later, assholes!" He threw his middle fingers up and smirked at her parents.

Malaika choked back a laugh at her parents' twisted features. Her mother's eyes were practically spitting fire. Roman and Carmen scolded Jet in Spanish, both landing slaps to the back of Jet's head. Jet's grin turned to a frown. He ran a hand through his dark tresses.

"Hey now, watch the hair. There are a lot of pretty ladies here."

Roman rolled his eyes, though he wore a grin.

"My apologies," Carmen said.

Malaika did not look back as the bad boy led her away. She wanted no part of her past. Not now, at least. She was looking forward to the future and to what it had to offer. She was excited about the happiness, hardships, and adventures that were sure to come her way. For when she was in the arms of the bad boy, life wouldn't ever be mundane.

*The End*

## TRANSLATIONS

- **Munequita:** Little doll.
- **Mujer:** Woman.
- **Te ves bonita:** You look beautiful.
- **¿Que?:** What?
- **Vamos perros:** Let's go, dogs.
- **Oh dios, me asustaste:** Oh God. You scared me.
- **Es culpa mía. Ella se lastimó por mi culpa. No soy ningún santo. Tengo enemigos. Desafortunadamente mis enemigos la lastimaron por mi culpa. No dejaré que vuelva a suceder:** It's my fault. She got hurt because of me. I am no saint. I have enemies. Unfortunately my enemies hurt her because of me. I won't let it happen again.
- **Amor, ¿eh?:** Love, huh?
- **¿Qué ves cuando me miras?:** What do you see when you look at me?
- **Dios mío:** My God.
- **Hola, mi amor:** Hello, my love.
- **Mi amor:** My love.
- **Debes amarla de verdad, si decides quedarte con ella a pesar de todo lo que ha pasado:** You must truly love her, if you decide to stay with her despite everything that has happened.
- **Es ella. Siempre ha sido ella:** It's her. It's always been her.
- **Gringo:** Non native person.
- **Sé que no soy bueno para ti, pero maldita sea, no puedo vivir sin ti:** I know I'm not good for you, but damn, I can't live without you.
- **Chica:** Girl.
- **Urid 'an 'akun mahbub:** I want to be loved.

Printed in Great Britain
by Amazon

81953579R00169